M000187640

DARK CURE

CAMERON K. MOORE

1st Edition 2018, paperback.
ISBN: 978-1-925764-78-9
Publishing services by: PublishMyBook.Online

PROLOGUE

JACQUES BENOIT AVERTED his gaze from the needle gleaming in the harsh halogen light. Over his many years as a soldier, he had developed a high threshold for pain. Needles, however, had always made him feel queasy.

An electrocardiogram machine monitoring the electrical activity of his heart beeped steadily. The room he was in was fifty feet square, with no windows to relieve the starkness of its dull white walls and ceiling. It felt sterile, a sensation reinforced by a faint, acrid smell of disinfectant.

It was a laboratory, deep within the bowels of a biotech research organization, and he was in the hands of a high-ly-trained team of brilliant individuals for whom his care was paramount. But that was little comfort as his fear of what was being done to him grew.

The ECG signal quickened in concert with his heartbeat. The ten electrodes stuck to his chest connected him to the machine and tugged unpleasantly at his skin. Even worse were the twenty-one electrodes covering his shaved scalp, connected by wires to an electroencephalogram machine that measured the electrical activity of his brain.

They made him feel like a lab rat in an experiment. Which, he realized uncomfortably, was precisely what he was.

His gaze traveled the length of the long tube that culminated in a transparent, plastic syringe filled with a clear fluid. The syringe emptied as the fluid entered the median cubital vein in his upper right forearm. It felt cold and he fought back a surprised gasp. The chill swept like a wintry draught along the length of his arm and entered his chest.

Benoit struggled to control his breathing, his heart now

racing as his fear escalated. The coldness permeated his brain. This time, he couldn't control the gasp that burst from his dry mouth.

A white-coated man with thinning brown hair and intense dark eyes checked the syringe was empty before removing the needle from Benoit's arm. A biochemist, his name was Pierre Lacoux. He smiled reassuringly. "It's okay. Everything is fine."

"It feels like ice entering my head."

"Because the fluid is colder than the temperature of your blood," he explained. "Injecting the compound at lower temperatures keeps it stable and produces the best results in our test subjects. It won't harm you and the sensation won't last long."

Behind Lacoux, several white-coated figures fussed over a set of trays standing on a trolley with wheels. Upon entering the room, he had been informed that this was a crash cart containing medical equipment to be used in case of cardiac arrest—a defibrillator, suction devices, bag valve masks and advanced cardiac life-support drugs.

At the time, Lacoux's explanation was meant to be reassuring; Benoit would receive the best possible care. Now, the presence of the cart added to his unease.

A tall, powerfully-built figure moved into view, his large frame dwarfing the slender Lacoux. In contrast to the scientists in the room, Devin Halle looked extremely fit, with a flint-hard face. He wore military fatigues and was studying him with concern. "How do you feel?"

He fought back his fear. "It feels like the mistral is blowing down from the Alps and through my head. But apart from that, I feel no different."

"The drug will take time to have an effect," said Lacoux.

"And it'll be incremental. This is the first treatment in a program that will take months. We'll stop and monitor the effects before we increase the dosage. We won't take any unnecessary risks."

He gave Benoit an encouraging smile, then turned to study a series of wavy lines with peaks and valleys, appearing on a computer screen attached to the EEG machine.

"What do those lines mean?"

"The electrodes attached to your skull are sending electrical impulse data from your brain to the recording machine, which converts the electrical impulses into the visual patterns you can see on the screen. What you are looking at is the electrical activity in your brain, shown as a pattern of waves. Increased activity is indicated by a faster wave pattern.

"We're monitoring the effect the drug compound has by recording these patterns, which we'll compare with your normal, pre-recorded activity levels. It's perfectly safe."

Benoit did not feel safe. He noted how, despite his friendly demeanor, Lacoux's intense eyes gleamed with anticipation as they studied his subject, reminding him of a pit viper he'd encountered as a child while hiking in Martinique. His parents had fallen behind him and he had been alone when he came across the serpent lying in the middle of the trail. The snake had transfixed him with the same black, glittering eyes. Eyes that had held the twelve-year-old Benoit frozen with fear as the snake coiled before striking.

Too scared to move, he could only watch helplessly as the serpent's diamond-shaped head lunged. The strike fell short of his ankle, but only just. As it coiled to attack once more, he had forced his shaking legs to move. He'd backed away, seized a heavy branch and killed the reptile with a blow to the head.

He had stood over the lifeless creature for a full twenty minutes, remorseful at what he'd done, but proud of overcoming his fear.

It had been his first kill. Many more had followed later in his life, all in combat and all deemed necessary military targets, but each had left him with the same hollow feeling of regret.

He remembered how, when his parents had finally arrived, they'd been badly shaken by what had happened. The snake, they informed him, was deadly. It was called a fer-de-lance; French for tip of the spear.

At the time, it had only been a story he would tell his friends back home in Marseilles. Now, the memory became poignant—the snake symbolized what he was about to become for France.

The concern on Halle's face deepened. "We can find someone else to do this."

"No. I'm the best choice." He felt his competitive instincts stir at the thought, helping him control his fear. Those same instincts had driven him through years of intensive combat training, forging himself into the elite warrior he had become.

He had risen through the ranks to become a commandant, leading his own battalion in the Fourth Foreign Regiment of the French Foreign Legion, from which he was chosen to lead the most sophisticated operational trial in France's military history—the Surobi FELIN trial.

These instincts had led him to place his life in the hands of this dark-eyed scientist, Lacoux, who studied him as eagerly as he would a mouse in a laboratory.

"I couldn't do this." Halle looked around at the medical equipment, distaste on his hard face. "I'm curious. Why did you agree to take part in this experimental program?"

"For the benefits it will provide France. And I won't ask one of my men to undergo something I refused to do myself."

"You're still the same man I remember from all those years ago, Jacques," Halle smiled. Though he now worked for the DRM, the French Directorate of Military Intelligence, which controlled the program and had appointed him to oversee it, he had previously served with Benoit in the Legion.

He was a man whose judgment Benoit trusted and as Lacoux moved away to talk to a technician, he seized the moment now to ask him a question that troubled him. "Do you think this program is immoral?"

"I understand the importance of it." He chose his words carefully. "But like you, I'm a soldier. I don't fully understand this science. And what I don't understand, I don't trust. But I strongly feel that if we don't do this, others will."

"Yes." His anxiety eased a little.

Halle reached into his pocket and pulled out a rectangular green and red badge embroidered with a gold grenade from which spread seven flames. "I brought something for you."

Benoit took it from him with a smile. It was the emblem of the French Foreign Legion.

Halle's face creased into a grin. "So you won't forget who you are."

He reached up and clasped the other man's hand tightly. "Thank you, my friend."

The emblem revered by Legionnaires helped quell his anxiety. He felt his fear subside, replaced with a confidence that soared with each passing second that he felt no ill-effects from the experimental drug compound.

The brain-freeze had passed and his head was bathed

in a warm, tingling sensation. He felt exhilarated, just as Lacoux had told him he would. He was certain the program would work.

His mind raced ahead, planning for the next phase. "Are you selecting the team for the operational trial?"

"Yes."

"I want them selected only from my battalion in the fourth."

"You know they'll have to leave the army."

A sour taste filled his mouth. The warmth inside his head had intensified. It felt alarmingly hot. Sweat beaded on his forehead. "I understand that's how it must be, that no one can know of France's involvement." His throat felt dry and his voice grated. "But I don't like it."

Like many long-serving field operatives, Benoit harbored a deep-seated mistrust of military commanders who risked soldiers' lives from the safety of a comfortable office. He had an even lower opinion of the secretive figures from the DRM, who provided the political and strategic thinking behind the activities of the French Armed Forces from the confines of their Paris headquarters.

He resented that, unlike commanders in the field, they held no accountability or care for the soldier on the ground.

After an intelligence failure had resulted in the deaths of five of his men in Afghanistan, he had sworn he would never again allow anyone who served under him to be thrown to the wolves by administrators supposedly serving France's interests. He had refused to participate in this program until he was given written assurances that the soldiers chosen to take part in it would be looked after.

But that was on a piece of paper. Benoit was a man of honor, for whom a man's word was a stronger commitment than a document prepared and signed by faceless individuals.

He sought that from Halle now. "I want your word that my men will be looked after."

"The men will be fine."

"Then give me your word, as a former Legionnaire, that my men won't be abandoned. I—" He broke off, the heat inside his head flaring as though a furnace door had swung open. Searing pain flamed through his skull.

He gasped, his back arching from the bed. The beep of the ECG intensified to a screech that filled his ears. He twisted from side to side, his thrashing movements rattling the machines attached to him by green wires.

"Bring the cart! Now!" Lacoux cried. He seized Benoit's shoulders, struggling to restrain him.

"What's happening?" Halle shouted.

"The drug is firing too many of his synapses at once, overloading his brain. He's seizing. Help me. Hold him down!"

Benoit felt Halle's weight press him back to the bed. He fought against the quaking of his arms to seize the man's forearm. "Look after my men. Take care of them. *Merde!*"

The violent jolting of his limbs shook the bed. His hands jerked open and closed. The badge with the emblem of the French Foreign Legion fell from his grasp and tumbled to the floor. His body convulsed as his head filled with agony. His brain felt like it was being consumed by roaring flames, then mercifully, everything faded to black.

CHAPTER 1

KARL SHEPHERD SAW the worry in his father's eyes and his alarm flared. "Dad? What is it? Damn it!" He resisted the urge to shake the laptop screen before him.

His father's image on it had frozen. It was a common problem out there in the Amazon rainforest, where thunderstorms often disrupted the satellite signal.

After a few seconds, his father resumed talking. "…Cassie. We had to take her to Mountainside Hospital. I've been trying to get in touch with you but—"

Shepherd interrupted. "Dad, you cut out. What happened to Cassie?"

His father's image flickered, then the screen went black.

"Shit!" Shepherd waited a few more seconds, then jumped to his feet and hurried from the communications room in search of help.

Hearing voices, he jogged toward them, down a corridor into a large room where he found all the residents of the drug research facility they had named the Inn. It was a lean team of nine scientists and three naturalists; all that could be sustained in this remote environment.

He was surprised. Usually at one p.m. they would all be hard at work in the laboratories, not in the recreation room. "What's going on?"

John Alderton, head scientist and the Inn's leader, turned to him with a grave expression on his face. "We were about to come looking for you. We need your help."

"First I need someone to fix the satellite link. I'd just found out Cassie's in hospital when it failed. I don't know what's happened to her. We need to fix the damn thing now!"

"Cassie?"

"My six-year-old daughter."

Alderton looked concerned. "I'm sorry. But it could take hours to fix it, if we can at all, given the storms building around us as the rainy season approaches."

"Don't you have someone who can look at it?"

"Only Pierre can." He gestured toward Pierre Lacoux, who was huddled in discussion with a group of people.

Shepherd made to head toward the dark-eyed scientist when Alderton halted him. "I'll get Pierre to fix the satellite but we have a more urgent matter to attend to first."

"But I need to know what's happened to Cassie."

Alderton placed a reassuring hand on Shepherd's shoulder. "Does she have family with her?"

"Yes but—"

"They will take care of her. There's nothing you can do for her from here. I promise you we'll try to fix the link later. But I need your help right now."

Reluctantly, Shepherd accepted he was right. "What's happened?"

"Jouvet is overdue from a field trip into the rainforest. I'm sending out a search party to look for him."

Mark Jouvet was a molecular biologist and like the rest of the science team, was prone to losing himself in his work. "Is that necessary? He could've just lost track of time."

"He was scheduled to meet with me an hour ago. We were to prepare for a meeting with Atione this afternoon to brief them on his discovery of the Alzheimer's cure."

Shepherd felt a stab of concern. Atione was the New York-based biotech company that had established the Inn to search for new drugs in the rainforest.

As their second season out there drew to a close—the

Cameron K. Moore

Inn could only be occupied during the Amazon dry season from May to October—the scientists were under increasing pressure to justify the massive expenditure behind the venture, especially after an underwhelming first season.

The Alzheimer's cure was their first major discovery and could keep them funded for years. Jouvet had discovered the cure by using spores extracted from a new plant species found in the rainforest. He wouldn't have forgotten the meeting.

Alderton gestured toward a slender young woman who was busy issuing instructions to several men. Allie Temple was an immunologist and the Head of Operations at the Inn; a role that made her Alderton's second-in-charge. "Allie will lead the search party. She wants to keep the group small and has selected the fittest people here, which includes you."

Allie waved for him to join her and Paul O'Connell, who was standing beside her clutching a backpack. "Good. Let's go."

"Just the three of us?" O'Connell settled the backpack across his wide shoulders. He had trained at UCLA and Oxford, had spent years working in a lab in Paris, yet still hadn't lost his brash Brooklyn accent. "Who's going to guide us? We need one of the naturalists with us."

"I've sent Mancini to find Ben. They'll both join us."

"You want Ben? Jesus, Allie. Why not Marlowe?"

"Because Ben is younger and fitter. Now let's go. I want to test our comms in the rainforest before we head in deeper. We'll wait for Ben and Mancini at the head of the trail."

She led them from the facility along a wooden boardwalk traversing a large grassy expanse to a mud-strewn trail which disappeared into the rainforest.

Shepherd glanced back toward the Inn. Since his arrival,

he'd spent most of his time inside the facility and it was strange to see it from this perspective. It was a large rectangular building with a wooden exterior and an interior made from specially prepared materials designed to keep its laboratories and living quarters climate-controlled.

Inside, it was like the other high-tech labs he had worked in and it was easy to forget the remoteness of its location. But from this vantage point, it looked small and vulnerable as the dense jungle pressed in around it, providing him with a sharp reminder of how isolated they were.

Disconcerted, he turned away and followed Allie into the jungle. Immediately, the bright sunlight of the clearing was replaced by dark shadows. He shivered despite the heat, feeling the oppressive presence of the rainforest surrounding him.

He halted on the track and glanced around. The Amazon rainforest felt primeval, looming above him like a vast green wave poised to crash down on them.

He looked up, hoping for a glimpse of sky, but the canopy allowed only a glimmer of light to enter. The intertwined branches above and the wall of vegetation on either side of the trail made him feel trapped in a tunnel of shifting shadows.

To distract himself, he watched as Allie grabbed the two-way radio clipped to the waistband of her cotton pants, which were already coated in mud. She had vivid green eyes that shone with an intelligence he found attractive. Her auburn hair was tied back in a ponytail. She had an athletic build with long legs kept hidden beneath the ever-present pants she wore to keep the clouds of insects that swarmed throughout the jungle at bay.

"Alderton? Can you hear me?" Allie waited a few seconds, the pause filled with the drone of mosquitoes and cicadas that vibrated the heavy, humid air. Macaws, parrots and monkeys screeched, mingled with the strange cries of animals unseen in the undergrowth.

The radio crackled.

"You're coming through loud and clear, Allie. Good luck. Make damn sure you're back by nightfall. I won't risk losing anyone else by sending people out after dark."

"Understood. I'll check in when we reach the Devil's Pond."

"Copy that, Allie. Out."

She re-clipped the radio to her pants and peered through the half-light as a newcomer hurried to join them. She frowned. "Where's Ben?"

"On his way," David Mancini answered, swatting irritably at a mutuca fly crawling on his cheek. He swept the crushed insect from his hand. His swarthy, Italian features were flushed with the heat. "He was asleep in his room when I found him. He had no idea Jouvet is missing. He said he'd catch us up."

Allie's frown deepened. "He was asleep? It's the afternoon."

Mancini rolled his eyes. "He's a trust fund kid. What do you expect?"

Shepherd checked his watch. He had to activate its tiny light to read the numbers in the gloom. 1:12 p.m. Near the equator, darkness fell quickly. It would be night by 6:30 p.m. "We don't have much time."

Allie didn't reply, but her stiff posture betrayed her growing anxiety.

"Sorry!" Ben Burg appeared through the gloom, running down the path toward them. In his early twenties, he was one of the Inn's naturalists and the youngest person there. His boyish features were apologetic beneath the long brown hair plastered across his forehead. "Took me longer than I thought to get ready." He patted the backpack slung across his shoulder.

Allie's voice was terse. "How long will it take us to get there?"

"A couple of hours." Reading the expression on Allie's face, he added, "We should be back before nightfall."

"Okay. Let's move."

They traveled in silence, driven by a collective sense of urgency, yet subdued by the overwhelming presence of the jungle. Sweat rolled down Shepherd's body, sapping his energy and attracting scores of mosquitoes, black pium flies, fleas, yellow-and-black-striped mud-dauber wasps and a seemingly endless species of moths that fluttered around his head.

The insects crawled over his body, climbing into his eyes and ears, biting, stinging and sucking as they went. At first he resisted, flapping his arms at the annoying invaders. Then he gave in to the inevitable, walking along with his head bowed as the tiny creatures burrowed under the damp cotton of his blue shirt and faded khaki pants, drinking his salty perspiration.

He looked ahead, past Ben's shoulder, his eyes follow-ing the tiny trail snaking its way through the jungle. Their path was narrow, muddy and clogged with leaves. Hanging branches and lianas snagged at him on either side.

Shepherd was the newest member of the research team at the Inn, having arrived only two weeks before. He was still acclimatizing to this hostile environment and although he was in shape and had a large, muscular frame, he was finding the going tough.

He was also anxious about Cassie. Not knowing what had happened to her left him fretting. Distracted by his fear, he failed to notice the obstruction ahead that first Ben, then Allie, had avoided. "Shit."

He sank to his knees in the thick, warm ooze of a mud pool. It got into his boots and squelched between his toes as he struggled to haul himself forward. He dragged one foot from the mud, took a step forward and almost fell as his second foot popped from the boot, leaving him stranded, stork-like. "Son of a bitch."

Allie turned back to help. "Need a hand?"

"Yes."

She placed his hand on her shoulder, seized his ankle and guided his foot back into its home, then pulled his leg from the mud.

Still clutching her shoulder, he stepped out of the mud. "Thanks."

She studied him, mistaking his worry for Cassie as fear of the intimidating rainforest. "It's daunting when you first come out here, but you soon get used to it. Stay close to me. I'll point out what to avoid."

His ego prickled. A former U.S. Army Ranger, he had received intensive training in jungles prior to becoming a doctor. "No need." He strode ahead.

She fell into step beside him. "Is everything all right?"

He forced his worry for Cassie aside. "Yeah. Like a damn sauna out here." He wiped beads of sweat from his face. "And these bugs!" He flicked a beetle from his close-cropped black hair. "How do you get used to them?"

"You don't. But you'll learn how to cope with them. Just try to ignore them."

Shepherd spat out a weevil that had worked its way into his mouth. "Not sure that's possible."

"We're falling behind. Let's hurry."

They hastened to catch up to Ben; a shadow on the trail ahead. Shepherd's long-legged stride was no match for Allie's experience in the rugged terrain. While he trudged from one pool of mud to the next, her practiced eye and natural athleticism allowed her to negotiate obstacles. She had no trouble staying at his shoulder and was breathing easily, while he was gasping for air.

"Where are we headed? Do you know where he was going out here?"

"When he missed his meeting with Alderton, we checked the Inn's log book. He signed out at six a.m., saying he was heading to the Devil's Pond."

"Which is what?"

"One of the sites we use for field research, where the naturalists found the new plant species from which Jouvet derived the Alzheimer's cure. Ben said they'd run out of it, so we think Jouvet must've decided to collect more before his meeting."

"Why wasn't one of the naturalists with him? I was instructed not to enter the rainforest without one."

"The logbook had Ben scheduled to take him."

Ben slowed on the trail, his slender frame rigid with tension. "I wasn't! We spoke yesterday and I told him I had some of my own research to work on today but that I'd take him out first thing tomorrow. I don't know why the logbook says otherwise. Maybe he entered it wrong. But Jesus! He shouldn't have gone without me."

"No one's blaming you," Allie said.

"O'Connell sure is," Ben retorted, looking at the bulky figure further back along the trail with Mancini.

"I'll deal with him. Let's focus on finding Jouvet."

Shepherd stared uneasily around at the jungle. "What

do you think has happened to him?"

"Plenty can go wrong out here," Ben replied. "What did they tell you when you first arrived?"

"Not much. There wasn't a need. As a replacement for your guy who fell ill, I'm here to finalize his work, not do field research."

"Okay," Ben said. "The rainforest surrounding the Inn is huge, over a million square miles. The Inn is located near the border of Brazil and Peru, in one of the most remote regions in the world.

"The jungle," he waved a hand, "is pristine and pre-historic. That's why the Inn was situated here in the first place—it's full of undiscovered plant and animal species just waiting for you scientists to experiment on in your search for new drugs.

"But it's also hostile. There are plenty of creatures out here capable of making a meal of us."

Shepherd had done his research before coming here. "Such as jaguars, caimans, anacondas."

"That's right."

"And it's not just the larger predators," Mancini called from back down the trail. The toxicologist's voice brimmed with enthusiasm. "There are also venomous creatures like the wandering spider and the bushmaster."

Shepherd knew of the bushmaster. The viper was one of the most dangerous snakes in the world. "What happens if you get bitten?"

"Simple answer—don't," Ben said. "One of the first things you have to realize is how isolated this place is. It'd take days to get a boat here and carry you back to Manaus. There aren't any rescue helicopters there either.

"The Inn has a variety of antivenoms and a lot of you

guys have medical degrees, but with the neurotoxins some of these creatures pack…" He shook his head. "So if you do get into trouble, it's serious. And trouble is never far away out here. The jungle's unforgiving. You're just another animal, part of the food chain."

A screech rang in the trees. Shepherd's head jerked around.

"A howler monkey," Ben said.

He nodded, eyes still probing the jungle.

Allie checked her watch. "How much longer, Ben?"

"Another half-hour, max."

"Too slow. We can do better than that."

She took the lead. Twenty minutes later, they arrived at their destination—a small, natural clearing near a varzea lake; a dagger-shaped body of water scything into the jungle.

"The Devil's Pond," Ben informed Shepherd. "A huge caiman lived here last season. Lunged out and took a tapir close to where a team of scientists were working. Scared the crap out of them. We think it's moved on, but it keeps people on their toes."

"Jouvet!" Allie shouted over the din emanating from the rainforest. The rest of the search party spread out, walking the fringes of the clearing, calling for the missing scientist. The squawking of startled birds was their only answer.

Shepherd and Allie stepped cautiously along the muddy edge of the leaf-coated varzea. He looked around for any clues as to what might have happened—signs of a struggle, items of clothing or field equipment, anything that could reveal Jouvet had been there.

His eyes fell upon a black plastic container at the edge of the open space. It was a foot square and nestled in leaf litter. "What's that?"

Allie saw it at the same time. "The logbook. Each of our field research sites has a waterproof, animal-proof container like this with a logbook inside. These logbooks serve the same purpose as the one back at the Inn. Our people are required to record their arrival and departure times at the site, any intended stopover points, and ETA back at the Inn."

Allie unfastened the heavy plastic clip and hauled out the thick notebook, which was fraying at the edges and covered with muddy fingerprints. She turned to the most recent entry. "M.J. arrival seven twenty-five a.m.," she read out. She peered at the scrawl. "Dept. eight a.m. the Point."

"Crap." Ben was looking over her shoulder. The rest of the search party gathered behind.

"Why would he head to the Point?" Allie wondered.

"Where is it?" Shepherd asked.

"Our naturalists have established two sites for field research—the Devil's Pond and the Point. The Point is the more remote of the two locations."

Ben frowned. "He didn't discuss heading out there with me."

"How long will it take us to get to it?" Allie asked.

"It's another couple of miles. Although the terrain is relatively good, it's another hour."

"I need to notify the Inn." She plucked her radio off her waistband and strode to the center of the clearing for better reception. "Alderton? It's Allie. We've reached the Pond… Hello?"

Shepherd heard a crackle of static but there was no response.

"Damn it." She moved to a different position. "Alderton, it's Allie. Can you hear me?" She waited a minute, then tried again. This time, accompanying the static was a long, low rumble of thunder.

Ben stared up at the sky. "The weather must be affecting the comms."

Lightning flashed above them, thunder boomed and rain deluged, soaking them to the skin. They hurried to the cover of the trees. The rain pounded deafeningly on the leaves.

Allie shouted to be heard. "We need to make a decision. I can't get through to the Inn, so this is our call. Do we go on to the Point, which will take another hour, or do we head back?"

"Jesus, Allie. It'll be dark before we get back to the Inn," said O'Connell.

"I know. Alderton won't send a second team out tonight. If Jouvet is injured, we'd be leaving him in great danger." Water trickled down her neck. Rain tumbled in sinuous rivulets through the canopy to the forest floor. "I think we should go after him."

"This is not just your decision," O'Connell snapped. "We all need to vote. I want to get Jouvet back safely. He's a member of my team, goddammit. But I don't want to risk anyone else's safety by traveling at night. We should return to the Inn and send another search party at first light."

"We have Ben with us," Allie said. "I think we can do this. And it'll give us the best chance of saving Jouvet."

O'Connell glanced dismissively at Ben. "He's just a kid. It'd be different if Marlowe was with us." Charles Marlowe was head naturalist at the Inn.

"Well, he's not."

"Which was your decision." O'Connell's pale blue eyes bored into her before flickering around the rest of the group. "What do you think, Mancini?"

O'Connell was the science project leader at the Inn and as such, Mancini and Shepherd's immediate boss. After a short pause, Mancini announced, "I agree with O'Connell."

"What about you, Shepherd?" O'Connell shouted over another rumble of thunder.

"I think the decision is Allie's. Alderton made her leader."

O'Connell snorted. "Clearly, that was a mistake."

"Maybe we should ask for Ben's view," he suggested.

Ben's face tightened as everyone looked at him, but his voice remained confident. "I can get us there and back, even in the dark. We have supplies and flashlights. I think we should go on."

"We don't have the rifle," Allie said. "I didn't think we'd need it."

"If we stick together, we should be fine."

"This is ridiculous," O'Connell said.

"We're going on," Allie announced. She locked eyes with O'Connell and held his glare until he turned and stalked off.

"Lead the way," she said to Ben.

CHAPTER 2

AFTER AN HOUR of trekking through difficult terrain, a brightening of the light revealed they had almost reached the Point. It was a grassy clearing about ten yards ahead.

"Christ!" Shepherd stumbled and fell face first into a puddle. He thrashed about before rolling to his side, spitting water. He rubbed the dirt from his eyes, then pushed his heavy frame from the ground. The mud yielded with a wet farting sound. He squatted, wiping a hand across his face.

He got to his feet and flexed his left knee, feeling the thick scar tissue stretch across his kneecap. The old injury was the result of an IED that had decimated his former platoon in Afghanistan. It had been reconstructed but continued to plague him; a haunting reminder of the worst time of his life. He bent the joint again. "Damn it!"

"You okay?" Allie asked.

"Just dandy." He paced gingerly, almost overbalancing.

She gripped his arm to steady him.

"Thanks." He rubbed his knee, nodded he was okay, and they followed the others into the clearing.

Jouvet wasn't there. Ben retrieved the Point's logbook, but it contained no entry to indicate he had arrived.

Shepherd put up his hand to shield his eyes from the dazzling light. At the far end of the clearing, sunbeams danced off the surface of a river, its brown waters swirling at the foot of a steep cliff, nearly thirty feet below. Beyond stretched undulating green as far as the eye could see.

"That's the Madre De Dios," Ben informed him. "The river you traveled along to reach the Inn. The nearest civilization to us from here is Manaus, nearly a thousand miles away."

The waterway was half a mile wide at that point, and with the recent rain, was churning and tossing, sweeping branches, logs and unfortunate animals along in its powerful embrace.

Thunder rumbled in the distance, and he could see ominous black mushroom clouds building on the horizon.

"Jesus," Ben said. "Look at that. No wonder Marlowe is concerned. He told me he was worried the storms could develop into a *derecho*. That's the worst you can get."

"We can worry about that later." Allie tried her radio once more. A voice spoke, but it was garbled and disintegrated into crackling static as the heavy atmosphere played havoc with the sensitive equipment.

Shepherd peered around the clearing. Where the hell was Jouvet? The empty logbook didn't mean he hadn't been there; the scatterbrained scientist may have been too absorbed in his work and forgotten to record his arrival.

But if he had been there, he would have been collecting samples. There should be signs—footprints, his backpack, specimen containers, plant-cuttings. The field research sites had been selected for their rich biodiversity, relieving the scientists of any need to penetrate the surrounding jungle. Surely Jouvet wouldn't have been stupid enough to do that without a naturalist.

He studied the ground. The rain had left behind dark pools of water, mud and scattered patches of dirt and leaves on the grass.

Shepherd checked his watch. 5:30 p.m. It would be dark in less than an hour. "Any sign he's been here?"

"There are some footprints," Ben replied. "But they could be his, or ours, or left by earlier expeditions."

"Look for any signs he might have entered the jungle," Allie instructed.

Allie, Ben, Shepherd and Mancini spread out along the perimeter. O'Connell remained in the center of the clearing. "This was a ridiculous idea." He slung his pack to the ground and sank to his haunches. "He's not here. For all we know, he might've made his own way back to the Inn."

"We followed the main route," Ben said. "He would've run into us."

O'Connell wiped mud from his face and flung it away in disgust. "If you'd done your job and been with him in the first place, this wouldn't have happened."

"O'Connell," Allie said. "This is not the time."

"Bullshit. This is a fucking *waste* of time."

Shepherd wandered away and examined the ground near the cliff edge, but could discern nothing to suggest Jouvet had been here. Then he noticed some impressions that might have been left by a person near the lip of the slope down to the river.

Crouching for balance, he chanced a look over the cliff. Had Jouvet fallen? Channels grooved the dark surface, but they were more likely to have been made by falling branches, or animals. But still... He watched the water sweeping away to his right.

"Jouvet might've fallen in the river," he said. The rest of the group gathered alongside him.

"What makes you think that?" Ben followed the line of his pointing finger, frowning doubtfully.

"Anything could've made those marks," Mancini said.

"Or Jouvet could've made them," Allie said. "I think we should check."

"How?" O'Connell demanded.

"If he fell in, the river would've swept him around to the right. We should follow it as far as we can and see if he made his way to the bank. He could be lying there hurt."

"If he's fallen in, he's gone," O'Connell said.

"We have to look," Allie said.

"We won't get lost as long as we stay near the river." Ben squinted at the sinking sun. "We should stay together, too."

"This isn't a good idea," O'Connell said. "We should head back to the Inn."

"This is the last place we have to check." Allie kept her voice even despite her obvious growing frustration. "We need to give Jouvet every chance."

O'Connell's pale eyes studied her for a few seconds. "I think your inexperience is showing." He looked at the rest of the group. "It's time for wiser heads to prevail. We need to put the safety of the group ahead of one individual." He pointed to the lengthening shadows. "If we leave now, we can minimize the time we spend out here in the dark."

"We're talking about a colleague's life!" Allie said. "I believe that justifies the risk."

"That's enough, Allie," O'Connell said. "It's time to go."

"Fine. Leave if you want to." Her tone hardened. "But I'm going after him." She plunged into the rainforest.

Shepherd hurried after her, concerned she would get lost. Immediately, he was enclosed in a circling wall of leaves, lianas and branches. He had experienced rainforests before in the Philippines and Belize, but nothing like this. He felt like he was in another world. The humidity intensified as if the leafy curtain blocking his view in every direction was giving off steamy moisture. Branches reached out to claw at him.

His stride was reduced to a laboring shuffle. The swarming clouds of insects thickened, the air vibrating with their ceaseless drone, and he fought to keep them from his eyes, ears and nose. He glanced behind himself. All trace of the clearing had vanished.

He halted, daunted by the rawness of this alien environment. How could they make their way through this? "Allie! Stop!"

She ignored him and pushed ahead.

He hesitated, knowing he couldn't keep up and not wanting to get lost. He felt a flare of anger at her impetuosity.

He heard the cracking of branches and swung around. With relief, he saw Ben emerge from the tangled lianas and thickly corded vines, squeezing past the moss-covered bulk of tree trunks, their buttresses radiating like wooden arteries.

Together, they caught up to Allie, who at Ben's insistence, finally stopped, her back still stiff with anger. Both men were breathing hard with exertion.

"You shouldn't have taken off like that," Ben said. "You could get lost."

"You need to control that temper of yours," said Shepherd. "It could get us all in trouble out here."

She glared at him, then composed herself. "I shouldn't let O'Connell get to me like that. But he's wrong. If Jouvet is out here, we have to find him *now*."

"I agree, but we need to stay together. We don't want to lose someone else out here."

"The others are right behind me," Ben said. "We should wait."

Mancini and O'Connell appeared. O'Connell gave Allie a frustrated glance, which she ignored. She turned to Ben. "Where's the river?"

"This way." Ben led the party, constantly looking around as he pushed vegetation aside. He almost looked at home.

Allie looked at her watch. "Ten minutes out, then we turn back."

Shortly after, they reached the riverbank. Shepherd

glimpsed its raging waters through gaps in the foliage, which reinforced his growing realization that if Jouvet had fallen in, they had almost no chance of finding him.

The group stopped at regular intervals to shout his name. A couple of minutes passed, then Shepherd lurched to a halt as he heard a coughing grunt. "What the hell was that?"

"Jaguar," Ben said.

"Shit." He knew that the jaguar was the apex predator in the rainforest. It killed by crushing the skull of its victims in its jaws. "What the hell do we do?"

"It should leave us alone if we stay together."

He noted Ben's voice had lost some of its confidence. His own confidence shaken, they kept moving.

Five minutes passed and he was starting to feel that this was a waste of time. He regretted pointing out the marks in the bank. He'd caused them to waste valuable minutes.

He stared down a steep, muddy bank to the water forty feet below. Further out, the current raced irresistibly along, but at that point, an inlet had been formed in the bank, where the flow curled in slow eddies.

Snagged on a jutting branch, an unusual object bobbed in the torrent. At first, he dismissed it as the body of a hapless animal caught in the flood. A tapir, perhaps. Then the object rolled and he spied white flesh as a limb flopped.

Shepherd's stomach tightened. It was a human body.

CHAPTER 3

BEN STARED DOWN the bank. "What do we do?" Despite the heat, his face was pale.

"We need to retrieve him." Allie placed a tentative foot on the slope.

"He's dead," O'Connell said. "It's too risky to go after him."

"We can't just leave him."

Shepherd eyed her in concern. The riverbank looked treacherous. It was a hell of a risk to go after the body.

"This is crazy," O'Connell said. "You can't go down there."

Her voice was cold. "Just watch me." She stepped over the lip of the cliff.

"Allie!" Shepherd cried.

Ignoring him, she found a firm foothold and stared down the bank to the water forty feet below. She inched forward. Almost immediately, her right leg slipped and she fell on her side, clutching a trailing vine to stop her slide. "Shit."

She seized a sturdy branch and tugged it tentatively. Satisfied that nothing was about to crawl or rush out at her, she hauled it from the jungle. Using it as a crutch, she was able to make her way down the slope.

Ten feet above the water, she paused, as if to take stock. Above her, the rainforest loomed, continually moving as if alive. She looked vulnerable now she was separated from the rest of the group.

"Wait, Allie!" Shepherd called. He crawled backward over the edge, probed for a foothold and slipped in the mud. "Damn it!" He scrabbled to regain his footing.

Ben threw out a hand to help him and he grunted his thanks. He steadied himself and kicked a toehold into the steep bank, lowered himself further, and hacked another toehold. He let go of Ben's hand and his weight carried him in a wild skid through the mud. He flung out his arms and dug in with his feet, halting his slide.

He looked at Allie, one side of his face coated with mud. "Just wait!"

But she turned away and kept moving. He was still twenty feet above her, edging his way down, his bulk threatening to cannonball him down the treacherous bank.

Ben shouted encouragement and directions on where to place his hands and feet. "Hang on! I'll come down and help you!"

"I need you to stay there and tell me where to put my damn feet."

Ben propped himself at the edge of the bank, watching anxiously.

Allie clambered down the remaining ten feet and was almost at the river's edge when she slipped and tumbled into the water. She surfaced, floundering as the river tugged at her.

"Hold on!" Shepherd called. He launched himself down the bank on his back, one leg and arm thrown out in a futile attempt to control his rapid descent, and plunged into the water.

Fully submerged, he struggled to find his feet, but they kept sliding in the mud. He was unable to see in the silt-filled water. He could feel the river pulling at him. Even in the small inlet, the powerful current threatened to sweep him away.

He was just about to panic when a hand gripped his shoulder and steadied him. He kicked his legs until he found a secure foothold on a submerged log and stood, spitting water and wiping dirt from his eyes.

Allie was beside him, balanced on the same log, murky water swirling around her waist.

Shepherd gazed at the river uneasily. It was difficult to see what was in it, and he knew only too well that such a protected place would make a perfect home for caimans, anacondas or any other of the river's inhabitants. The eddying water was also full of branches, vines and clumps of vegetation torn from the rainforest further upriver.

Sharing his disquiet, Allie said, "We can't stay here. We need to get the body onto the bank to confirm its identity."

He looked at the object floating before him. The corpse was lying face down, semi-submerged. A cloud of mosquitoes and dragonflies hovered. Black flies crawled over the parts of the body that were exposed to the air. The white flesh he had spied from above was the wrist of one outflung arm, where the shirt sleeve had pulled back.

Shepherd swallowed the bile in his throat. It had to be Jouvet. Who else could it be?

Allie looked devastated. "Let's get him out of here."

He reached out gingerly and touched the corpse's arm. It felt rigid. He could see the swarms of tiny fish darting beneath the surface. Below them, he spied larger shapes moving menacingly through the murk and wondered uneasily if they were piranhas. Or worse.

He felt tiny tremors as the body was repeatedly struck from below and realized they had to get it out of the river fast. A needle-shaped fish emerged from a hole in the cotton sleeve, a piece of flesh gripped in its mouth.

Shepherd fought back the impulse to gag and took a firm grip of the arm. Tiny fish and insects erupted from the body. Through the sleeve, the flesh felt like cold marble. He hauled at it. The corpse held tight, snagged. Another sharp tug and he felt it shift an inch. Another tug and it moved some more. He heaved with all his might.

The corpse came free and barreled into him, knocking him off his feet. The log he had been standing on rolled beneath him and Allie disappeared below the surface. He scrambled to his feet, his legs sinking into thick ooze. She surfaced, coughing and spluttering.

"Allie! Shepherd!" He looked up to see Ben pointing frantically. Shepherd turned and saw what at first appeared to be a log being carried along by the current. Then he realized the log was moving against the flow and toward them. He saw knobbed ridges, a scaly tail. A caiman.

"Move, Allie!" he shouted. "We have to get the hell out of here!"

He grabbed the corpse, intending to tow it out of the river. Beside him, Allie tried unsuccessfully to clamber to her feet. She over-balanced and disappeared beneath the water.

He reached out with his other arm and hauled her upright. "What's wrong?"

She gasped. "My leg. It's caught under the log!"

The caiman moved closer, only thirty feet away. She yanked to free her leg. It held fast.

He released the corpse, took a deep breath, dived and heaved at the log. His hands slipped on the mud that coated it. He came up for air then immersed himself again. He searched around her foot, found the projecting stump of a branch, and hauled. The log shifted a little before settling back into place.

He surfaced. From the corner of his eye, he saw the caiman had reached the mouth of the inlet. It slowed as if assessing its prey.

He dived, grasped the log, found a firm foothold and heaved with all his strength. He felt the log quiver, then it ripped from the mud and burst from the water, along with him. He rolled beneath its weight.

The water churned as he staggered to his feet, the log still gripped in his hands. "Move!"

The caiman was only two feet away. They had no chance of reaching the bank in time. He swung the log like an ax, striking the creature on the snout. It jerked away.

The two of them climbed onto the bank, dragging the corpse with them. They fell to their knees, panting. He felt his body trembling with adrenalin. It took several deep breaths before his heart rate slowed.

Beside him, Allie coughed and spat out a mouthful of dirt and water.

Shepherd's throat felt lined with silt from the river. "You always so reckless? You took a hell of a risk. Why didn't you wait for help?"

"O'Connell pissed me off. Thanks." Her eyes roved the swirling waters. "We should move before that caiman comes back."

He turned his attention to the corpse. With Allie's help, he managed to roll it over in the clinging mud.

Allie breathed. "Oh, my God."

Shepherd's eyes absorbed the horror of the face. It was a gory, shattered mess that the silt and weed couldn't hide. The wound was so massive it looked like a section of the skull had exploded. It took him a few moments to recognize what remained of Jouvet's features.

Surveying the damage, he felt his stomach tighten with shock.

"We have to move," Allie said.

He glanced over his shoulder and saw the caiman torpedoing toward the bank. Allie struggled to her feet, trying to lift Jouvet's body.

"For God's sake, Allie! We have to leave him!" He shoved her up the slope as the caiman crawled out of the water with a throaty hiss that belched a fetid stench of rotting flesh.

Allie fought for purchase in the mud. Her feet gripped and she half-clambered, half-limped up the bank, her right ankle bruised and bleeding. Ben was waiting a few feet above her with outstretched hands. Seconds later, Shepherd followed over the lip of the riverbank.

The caiman seized Jouvet's body and dragged it into the water.

Allie sounded sick. "Did you see his head wound? What creature could have caused that?"

His voice was grim. "It wasn't made by an animal."

CHAPTER 4

SHEPHERD STOOD APART from the group that had gathered. As soon as they had arrived back from the fateful search, Allie had rushed to inform Alderton of the tragic outcome. At his request, she had then gathered all the Inn's inhabitants in the recreation room.

The rec room was where everyone met each evening to discuss theories or unwind over a drink. Allie had livened its dull, whitewashed walls with posters of the New York Metropolitan Museum of Art and of the Louvre in Paris. Usually, when they drank in there it was loud and boisterous, full of arguments and bad jokes as they blew off steam.

Now, the atmosphere was subdued. Jouvet's death had shocked the small community and they conversed in muted tones as they waited for Alderton to arrive.

Shepherd was silent, still stunned by what he had seen. He had shared his misgivings with Allie as they'd journeyed back to the Inn. She had asked him to keep them to himself until she had reported what they had seen to Alderton.

His suspicions as to what Jouvet's injuries meant had grown with each passing mile. He knew a difficult decision confronted Alderton—was it time to evacuate the Inn? He felt conflicted at the thought but knew that for Alderton the conflict would be far deeper. The Inn was his brainchild.

Allie had told him it was Alderton's idea to establish the research facility deep in the heart of the Amazon rainforest. He had pitched to the Atione Board the idea of establishing a research facility to hunt for new species of plants and animals that might exhibit medicinal properties or traits that would result in new drugs.

Atione operated in a ruthless industry and were under considerable financial restraint. The board saw the highly speculative venture as a means of generating new revenue streams and agreed. But Alderton was under immense pressure to deliver on his promises.

Their recent discovery of the Alzheimer's cure was at a delicate stage, with intensive work needed to finalize their research. The result would be a staggering medical breakthrough and generate billions in revenue to Atione. But to accomplish it they needed more time, which added to the tension in the room.

A murmur ran around the group when Alderton appeared. A tall distinguished man in his early sixties with a full head of thick, silver hair, a hooked nose and piercing eyes, he had a powerful presence, one that momentarily silenced the group as he briefly surveyed them from the entrance to the room.

He strode into the recreation room and the crowd erupted.

"Alderton! What the hell is going on?"

"Have you spoken to Atione?"

"Those bastards at head office had better not be telling us to leave." Shepherd recognized O'Connell's nasal tone. "My team have to go through all of Jouvet's work. We can't leave yet."

Alderton held up his hands and the hubbub eased.

"Jouvet's death is terrible news. I'm sure you're all as shocked as I am. He was our colleague, our friend. He'll be greatly missed." He surveyed them somberly. "I know the risks you take by being out here. Your safety is my first priority. Which is why we need to evacuate the Inn for the season."

"Jesus fucking Christ!" O'Connell snarled.

"What about our work?" asked Lacoux.

"We can't leave now!" O'Connell said. "Jouvet's death was an accident. He knew the risks. He shouldn't have been out there by himself."

"My God." The lines creasing Charles Marlowe's forehead deepened as he frowned. "He was your colleague!"

O'Connell's pale blue eyes fixed upon him. "Why the hell wasn't one of your people with him? Jesus, you're meant to look out for the scientists."

"We don't know yet—" Marlowe began.

Ben interrupted him. "I was meant to take him out tomorrow morning. He should have waited until then."

"The logbook has you scheduled to take him out this morning," O'Connell said.

"The logbook is wrong!"

"You slept in, you lazy little bastard. It's a disgrace you're here at all. Everyone else has worked their asses off to get here. But not you. You have your wealthy daddy to thank for that."

O'Connell turned to Marlowe. "You should've listened to me. I told you it was a risk keeping him here. He should've been sent home on the last supply boat. Now a crucial member of my team is dead and it's Ben's fault!"

"That's ridiculous," Allie said.

"Don't be naive, Allie."

"Jouvet should have come to me or Parker if he couldn't find Ben," said Marlowe. "He knew the rules. There's nothing we can do if your people don't bother to inform us of their field trips. This isn't the first time this has happened."

"That's because going through your team is a waste of time!"

"If our team was larger, we wouldn't have to prioritize these trips," said Ben. "The rest of our team has left because your research is nearly finished. There are only three of us left now."

"I don't care about your problems. You're here to support the science team and—"

"Enough!" Alderton's piercing blue eyes silenced them. "I understand you're upset. This has been a big shock for all of us. But now is not the time for recriminations."

"We can't leave now," said O'Connell. "Jouvet was part of my team. His death is dreadful, but his work is too important to abandon. We're at a critical point."

He fell silent beneath the intensity of Alderton's gaze. "You think I don't know that?"

"That's not what I meant."

"I know what his breakthrough means. But I also know that the rainy season is coming in early. The risk is too great. There are also other factors to consider." His eyes were now grave. "Jouvet was shot."

"What?"

"That's insane!"

"Good God!" Marlowe cried. "But we don't have his body. How do you know?"

"Allie saw it. Before they were forced to leave him, Allie saw that Jouvet had a bullet wound to his head."

All eyes turned to her.

"That's right," she confirmed. "I saw it when we rolled his body over."

"It may have been suicide," Marlowe said. "He was under a lot of pressure from Atione. It could've been too much for him."

Allie frowned. "I don't think so."

O'Connell snorted. "What the hell would you know?"

Shepherd spoke for the first time. "I was with Allie. I saw the wound. It was a massive exit wound to the face. Close up it was unmistakable. The bullet was fired by someone standing directly behind him."

"What the hell do you know about gunshot wounds?" said O'Connell.

"I was once a military medic. Believe me, this was not a suicide."

Now they were all quiet, looking at him then at each other.

"Who could've done this?" Marlowe asked. "We know pirates operate along the rivers. Was Jouvet in the wrong place at the wrong time?"

"It's a possibility," Alderton said. "Or perhaps he ran into a party of native Indians out hunting."

"The Yanoama are the nearest tribe, and they're almost a thousand miles away," said Marlowe.

"Which is why we need to leave."

A tension-laden silence descended upon the group as they digested his words.

"Jesus," O'Connell breathed. "You think one of us did it?"

Everybody swapped nervous glances tinged with suspicion. The longest were reserved for Ben and Shepherd. He shifted uncomfortably, feeling every bit the newcomer.

"What does Atione say?" Marlowe asked.

"The comms are still down," Alderton replied. "I haven't been able to contact them."

"I'll go out and check the satellite," Lacoux said.

"Later," Alderton said.

"So what are we going to do?" Lacoux asked.

"We're going to leave. As soon as I can get through to

them, I'll tell Atione to send the supply boat."

"That could take days."

"Yes. Which is why I want everyone to remain here in the rec room. Allie, Marlowe and I will search everyone's rooms."

Grumbles of derision spread amongst the group.

"You can't do that," O'Connell growled. "That's an invasion of our goddamn privacy."

"You're welcome to complain to Atione."

"Then start with Ben's room," O'Connell said. "He was the one listed as being out with Jouvet."

"Jesus!" Ben cried. "Are you nuts? I didn't kill him!"

"We'll be searching everyone's room," Alderton said.

"And if the search shows up nothing?" Shepherd asked.

"Our next step will be for Marlowe and myself to interview everyone to verify their whereabouts in the hours before we first noticed Jouvet was missing."

"Are you sure you don't want me to check the satellite? Shouldn't we be calling for help?" Lacoux's voice sounded strained.

"After we've checked your room," Alderton said.

CHAPTER 5

AN HOUR LATER, Shepherd was seated by himself at a bar in the corner of the rec room, rapping his knuckles softly against its wooden bulk.

Like everyone else, he was dismayed by Jouvet's death, but it was his worry for his daughter back home that fueled his anxiety. Cassie had special needs. He had curtailed his career ambitions to give her the support and attention she required. This was the first time he had left her for an extended period, something he bitterly regretted as he pondered the meaning of her grandparents' last message.

Lost in his own thoughts, he remained oblivious to what was going on around him until raised voices grabbed his attention. He surveyed the room. The small crowd had degenerated into two groups—the scientists on one side and the naturalists on the other. They were arguing, their anger fueled by a half-empty bottle of Schnapps on the bar beside him.

"Who could've done this?" Chase Parker asked. The naturalist's pale skin was blotched with mosquito bites. Usually quiet and intense, he looked agitated.

"I can't believe it was one of us," said Mancini, taking a large swig from his mug. "I mean, we all stand to get the rewards from Jouvet's discovery. He made the breakthrough, but we've all been involved. What incentive would anyone have?"

"Some were more involved than others," Parker said.

"That's right. The scientists *were* more involved."

"That's bullshit," Parker said.

"Is it?" Mancini swept back his thick mane of dark hair.

"Look, we all acknowledge that you naturalists found the plant species. But that's the extent of your contribution. The scientists have done all the subsequent work. We analyzed it and experimented on it. It was our expertise that identified its remarkable properties." He gulped from his mug. "If it was left to you, it would've been classified as a new species and that's all."

"You don't know what you're talking about!" Parker snapped.

"I understand you're desperate. You're thirty," Mancini sneered. "Most of your peers have already made a name for themselves. But that doesn't mean you can take credit for something you didn't do."

Parker lunged toward him. "You fucking—"

Ben grabbed his arm and eyed Mancini. "Without us, you would've had nothing to experiment on. And we do way more than list species in a book."

"I have no interest in anything *you* have to say," Mancini said. "You don't deserve to be here in the first place."

Ben glared. "I deserve to be out here just as much as you do."

"You're only here because your father's rich."

Before Ben could reply, Franz Klaus interrupted his conversation with Lacoux to intervene. He was a biochemist with alert blue eyes, silver hair and a weathered face creased like parchment. He, Alderton and Marlowe were the patriarchal figures at the Inn. "Calm down, please. This is a stressful time for all of us. Let's not make it any worse."

Shepherd fought back his exasperation; they were squabbling over career recognition when there were far graver matters to worry about. His longing for home intensified.

A large form slipped onto a stool alongside him, his

grace belying his considerable bulk. His voice was a deep baritone. "You look lonely, sweetie. Let Big Jannie buy you a drink."

Despite his heavy mood, Shepherd grinned. Jan Hlasek was the same age as him—mid-thirties, had a razor-sharp mind and wit to match and liked to flirt. "You're not my type, Jan."

He pouted and swept a hand through his thick blond hair. "You get above yourself. My taste runs to tanned, blonde Swedes, like Erik back home."

"How long are you going to keep that man of yours waiting? You've been here nearly five months. New York is a big place full of rich, attractive men. I'm sure he won't be lonely for long."

Jan's pout turned to a smirk. "Big Jannie is irreplaceable. You know that." He moved behind the bar and mixed himself a cosmopolitan.

Shepherd rolled his eyes at the pink cocktail clutched in his bear paw of a hand.

"Don't you judge my taste. What do you like to drink? Beer?" Jan shuddered delicately.

"You know I don't drink."

"There's a lot I don't know about you, sweetie. Like why you haven't made a move on Allie, for example. She's smart, attractive and right now, single. Back in New York, she's way out of your league. Here, the jungle can play tricks on the mind. It gives you a chance. Take it while you can."

Shepherd squirmed. "I hardly know her."

"Such a waste." Jan sighed.

Shepherd glanced around the room. His attention was caught by O'Connell, who was sitting by himself, staring into space. "He looks pissed."

Jan shrugged. "He hasn't been happy since Allie was given the Head of Operations role over him."

"Do you know why Alderton didn't give it to O'Connell?"

"The word is that Alderton thinks he isn't a team player. He's a good scientist, but not the one Alderton wants as his successor."

"What do you think?"

"I think O'Connell is a pompous ass."

An argument erupted in the group. Parker and Mancini stood toe to toe, yelling at each other.

Klaus moved in between the two men, pushing them apart. Ben grabbed Parker by the arm and dragged him back.

Mancini, yelling at Parker, struggled to get past Klaus, who herded him to the other side of the room. Parker shrugged free of Ben's grip, gave Mancini a final glare, then turned away.

"Mancini likes a drink," Shepherd said.

"Mancini is a narrow-minded ingrate."

"Isn't he your lab partner?"

"That doesn't make us friends. His proud Italian manhood is offended by how I choose to live my life." Jan sipped his cosmopolitan. "Now *there's* someone with a bit more class," he said as Allie strode into the room.

She hurried to Lacoux and spoke to him urgently, her face tense. All conversation in the rec room hushed as everyone turned to watch them. Shepherd heard her mention the VSAT, which he knew to be the Inn's satellite station. Lacoux nodded and left the room.

Allie joined the two friends at the bar.

"Hello, lovely," Jan greeted her. "Time for a bevvy?"

"No time, I'm afraid. Shepherd, can you come with me?" At the sound of Jan's delighted chuckle, she frowned.

Parker and Ben approached. "Where did Lacoux go?" Ben asked.

"I sent him to fix the VSAT."

"Really?" Ben asked. "Does that mean you've searched all our rooms?"

"Not yet. Marlowe and Alderton are continuing. I'm here to get Shepherd. We're going to search the laboratories and the area outside the Inn."

"Why Shepherd? Why not Ben or me?" Parker demanded. "We know this place better than any of you."

Mancini joined them, his eyes bloodshot, his dark features flushed from the alcohol he had drunk. "I think you naturalists have done enough." He seized the bottle of Schnapps.

"Go screw yourself, Mancini," Parker snapped.

Jan snorted into his cocktail.

Mancini glowered. "Something you'd like to say?"

Jan swirled his drink. "Only that you need to learn how to handle your liquor."

"I'm not the one drinking like a girl."

Jan smiled. "Does it upset you to see me drinking with a real man?" He placed a hand on Shepherd's shoulder. "Are you a little jealous, perhaps?"

"Don't drag me into this," Shepherd muttered.

Parker snorted with laughter.

Mancini stepped angrily toward Jan. He halted when Shepherd slipped off his stool and straightened.

Allie jumped between the warring men. "While Alderton and Marlowe search the rooms, I'm going to search the laboratories, then the fringe of jungle sur-rounding the Inn. But I don't want to be outside at night by myself. The only rooms we've finished searching are

Lacoux's and Shepherd's. Lacoux is needed to fix the VSAT. So that leaves Shepherd to assist me. That's the reason why."

Mancini went to say something but clearly thought the better of it as Allie folded her arms and raised her eyebrows at him.

"I'm confident Lacoux will have the comms up soon." She glanced at Shepherd. "But in the meantime, we have to go through the labs. The rest of you please stay here. We'll give you an update as soon as we can." She gestured for Shepherd to follow her.

Ignoring another chuckle from Jan, he hurried in her wake.

CHAPTER 6

SHEPHERD PAUSED AT the entrance to the scientists' laboratory. "What are we searching for?"

Allie squeezed past his large frame. "I'm not really sure. Anything that looks like it doesn't belong."

"You really think the killer would hide his gun in here?"

Allie shrugged, but the doubt in her eyes resonated with his own mood.

The lab reflected neat efficiency, with workbenches holding laptops arranged in orderly lines and metal cabinets containing notebooks and journals.

It was filled with gleaming equipment including bio-cabinets, autoclaves, protein crystallography and nano-dispensers, several mass spectrometers, electronic microscopes, a high-speed centrifuge and a gas chromatograph.

It was strange to see the lab empty. It was so quiet he could hear the hum of the expensive machinery. Usually, it was a hive of activity, with scientists scurrying around, rushing to finalize and record their experiments, preparing samples for analysis or sequencing, tapping furiously at their laptops, or bouncing ideas off each other. O'Connell would be striding around, barking instructions, peering over shoulders, advising or rebuking.

"Let's start with the workbenches," Allie said.

They opened drawers and cupboards, sorting through the masses of notebooks and smaller equipment including microscopes, beakers, test tubes and specimen jars. They found nothing amiss.

"Let's search everyone's work site next."

Although they shared the equipment according to their

specialty, each scientist had their own post in the laboratory where they prepared and carried out experiments, left their laptops and stored personal items and protective clothing such as face masks, protective eyeglasses and lab coats. Two-way radios were left on the benches, as it was a requirement that each lab contain a radio in case of emergency lockdown.

After a few minutes, she announced, "I've found nothing. How about you?"

"No luck." He withdrew his head and shoulders from one of the cupboards with a thud and a muffled curse. He rubbed his head. "I'm not built to explore some of these cupboards."

"Just don't damage any of the equipment." She smiled.

"You're not planning on taking any of it apart, are you?" He looked at the array of apparatus lining the walls of the lab. All were highly sensitive and expensive.

"We'd need Lacoux for that. He has an engineering degree in addition to his Ph.D. in biochemistry. We're damn lucky to have him. He's the only one who can fix the satellite."

Shepherd straightened, stretching his lower back and flexing a knee. "Does the satellite fail often?"

She sighed. "It has of late. The weather causes problems, disrupting the signal. The heavy rain sometimes damages components in the station itself. But the insects are the main problem. The VSAT makes a good home for them."

"But usually Lacoux can fix the problem?"

"Most of the time. We've only needed a specialist shipped out here once in the past two seasons."

"What happens if he can't repair it? Is there a backup plan?"

Allie bit her lip. "If Lacoux can't fix it, we have a problem. Our only backup is the sat-phone in Alderton's office, but it's unreliable at the best of times. Now, with the approaching rainy season, the weather is working against us."

"Christ. How will we evacuate if we can't get through to Atione?"

"Atione will send the supply boat to investigate."

"When?"

"It's protocol for either myself or Alderton to report in weekly. But there have been several instances when we haven't been in touch for more than two weeks due to repeated comms failures." Allie seemed reluctant to share this knowledge. "If Atione doesn't hear from us, it'll be at least two weeks before they grow concerned. After a few more weeks, they'll probably get the supply boat to investigate. But it'll still take days for them to get here."

"So we could be stuck for a least a month." His mind filled with an image of Cassie. "Exactly how big a problem are we talking about?"

"We'll be fine."

"Allie, I'd like to know."

She drew a breath. "During our last status meeting with Atione, they informed us that thunderstorms had been detected to our north, with their Doppler radar indicating they were building. They felt the rainy season was starting earlier than usual and they wanted us to evacuate before the first of the season's storms struck."

Shepherd's brow furrowed. "It rains here all the time."

"These are different. We're talking about intense tropical storms. They pack powerful winds, along with the risk of lightning strikes and flooding. The water levels in the Amazon River and its tributaries can rise dramatically, generating currents known to sink boats. There'd be no chance of getting the supply boat out here. If we missed our departure window, we could be trapped for months."

Shepherd felt his face drain of blood.

Her eyes filled with concern. "Are you okay? It won't come to that. We'll be fine."

"I need to use the comms." His voice was flat, hollow-sounding.

"We'll all be able to use them when Lacoux gets the VSAT fixed. Let's focus on what we're doing for the time being. I really need your help."

He composed himself. "Okay. Look, Jouvet's murder. What do you think we're dealing with? Could this be related to the Alzheimer's cure?"

"I guess it's possible. It's a miraculous discovery, one that will establish the reputations of everyone involved. The team could even share a Nobel Prize. So there's been a lot of jostling to be associated with working on it.

"The people who work here are highly motivated individuals driven to succeed. They've sacrificed a lot to be out here given how remote this place is. All of them, including myself, want this badly."

"But wouldn't killing Jouvet be harming the chances of developing the cure?"

"Yes. He discovered it and has been doing most of the experimentation to refine it. It's why he was under so much pressure. Atione have been demanding that work on it be finalized before we're forced to leave."

"So we're back to square one, with no idea why he was killed."

"Maybe. Maybe not. The presence of the rainforest exacerbates existing tensions. You haven't been here long, but believe me, it can really get to you.

"At first it's the little things, the endless insects, the

constant heat, the noises. Then the sheer presence of it, the immensity of it, can overwhelm you. Eventually, it can break you down. It's a form of depression, like cabin-fever.

"We had to send several people home last year because of it." She sighed. "I hate to think it was someone I've worked with, but it's possible someone snapped. Maybe they overreacted to something Jouvet said or did."

"O'Connell, perhaps? He's certainly got a temper."

"O'Connell is a bully, but a murderer? I don't think so. I think he's aggressive in his pursuit of results. He pushes his teams extremely hard. But I rate his work highly. So does Alderton. He almost gave him the Head of Ops role; said it was a close call between us.

"I don't know what swayed him in the end. But he certainly thinks O'Connell is a brilliant scientist. It's why his sometimes deplorable behavior is excused—he has a strong track record of getting results."

"Ben? He was scheduled to take Jouvet on a field trip."

"I can't see it. Ben's just a kid who's been spoilt all his life. I think all he's guilty of is being lazy. He's a repeat offender in that respect."

"Why is he tolerated, given this is such a small team?"

"Because of Marlowe's influence. Marlowe is the best naturalist in the business. He thinks Ben has potential and has been pushing him. Otherwise, Alderton wouldn't have kept him, regardless of who his father is. Ben has talent. He just needs to focus and apply himself."

"Unlike everyone else."

"The rest of us are obsessed with what we're trying to achieve. I just can't imagine any of us killing Jouvet. But I guess it's possible that he had a falling-out with someone."

"Enough to follow him all the way out there and shoot him? That seems more calculated than a falling-out between colleagues."

"I don't know. The sooner we can get home and let the authorities sort it out, the better. Meanwhile, we need to keep searching."

He looked around. "Why don't you check the bio lab while I check around all the equipment?"

Allie hesitated. He wondered why. "You all right?"

"Absolutely." She turned to the suits hanging from the far wall. "Why don't you check the readings first while I get dressed?"

Inspecting the bio lab required a hazmat suit. It would take her a few minutes to put it on, and having him check the digital display to ensure the lab was safe to enter would save time.

"Okay." A distant rumble of thunder reminded him of the satellite. He prayed Lacoux would have it working soon.

His mind started to wander, filling with more images of Cassie. What had happened? Why was she in hospital?

He strode to the far end of the room and stopped outside the door of the bio lab. It looked more like the hatch on an aircraft, with a gleaming, gray metal exterior covered with digital displays and yellow warning labels.

He quickly scanned the displays glowing a soft red on the metallic surface. The numbers barely registered. "It's fine."

Allie placed the hood of the suit over her head. She shuffled past him to the bio lab door and placed a hand on the latch.

Her hand froze. "Shit!" She pulled her hood off and climbed hurriedly out of the suit.

"What is it?"

She pointed. The illuminated figures read .02.

Shepherd's throat went dry. "Jesus!"

The oxygen levels inside the chamber were 0.02%. At that level, anyone entering the bio lab would be unconscious in three seconds and dead within three minutes.

"How the hell can that have happened?" he said. "I thought there was an alarm for dangerously low oxygen levels."

"There is. And we test it frequently. Which makes me think the digital display is faulty. It's happened a few times before. Once, it indicated that the oxygen reading was too high, which had us worried about the fire hazard. Just one spark in an oxygen-rich environment...

"Anyway, Lacoux thinks it's something to do with the wiring but hasn't been able to isolate the fault." She took a deep breath as if to compose herself. "Didn't you look?"

"Yes, but I didn't notice anything was wrong. I guess I wasn't paying enough attention." He should have picked up the reading; it was standard safety procedure across most laboratories. But he'd been distracted by his concern for Cassie. If Allie had relied on his clearance, she could be dead by now.

He groaned in anguish. "Christ, if you'd entered... Goddammit!"

Allie reached out and placed her hand on his shoulder to reassure him. "It's okay. I think it's just the display that's at fault. We need to notify Alderton immediately and get Lacoux to look at it."

"Yeah, sure. I'm sorry. Thank God you checked."

"Alderton will suspend any further searches in the lab until Lacoux has given his all-clear. He'll send me to get him. I don't want to head outside by myself and I don't really want to get one of the others. But if you're not feeling up to it..."

"No. I'm fine. Really."

"Then let's go."

CHAPTER 7

IT WAS NEARING 9:00 p.m. as they left the Inn and headed for the VSAT station. They had informed Alderton of the faulty bio lab. As Allie had predicted, he had instructed them to get Lacoux immediately.

Consumed with his worry for Cassie, Shepherd was silent as they made their way to the VSAT station. Generator-powered floodlights stood around the complex. A network of boardwalks ran to the head of the main trail back to the river ten miles away, out to the supply hut and the VSAT station, and around the perimeter of the grassy space surrounding the Inn.

The floodlights were lit now, piercing the inky blackness of the night. The wind had picked up and was whining through the immense trees, which cast shadows that danced across the clearing. The tangled understory thrashed. Strange calls and shrieks punctuated the restless chattering of the jungle.

The VSAT station was situated several hundred yards from the main complex on a low rise, giving it the best chance of receiving an uninterrupted signal. At least, that was the intention. But the prehistoric environment worked to its own rhythm, influencing everything within it. Shepherd hoped Lacoux would have it fixed soon.

Allie must have mistaken his silence for fear. "I don't like being out here at night either. The jungle has a different feel to it. More hostile."

He didn't reply.

"You're not one for chatting, are you?"

He forced himself from his worrying. "Sorry."

He felt her eyes on him. Clearly, she wanted to talk, perhaps to distract herself from the brooding menace of the darkened rainforest surrounding them.

"We've hardly spoken since you arrived here two weeks ago. You don't socialize with the rest of us."

"I've been busy trying to get up to speed with your research."

"So I've heard. And we all respect you for that. But in such a remote environment, team harmony is vital. I like to get to know everyone on my team and to be honest, you remain an enigma."

"You have access to my personnel file."

"Yes. I know you were in the army for eight years. They granted you a leave of absence during which you obtained a medical degree from Harvard before returning to the army as a medic. After a year, you were honorably discharged from active service.

"You then joined the United States Army Medical Research and Materiel Command. Four years later, you left to pursue a career in private industry and worked with several small start-ups before joining Atione two years ago."

Shepherd smiled. "You seem to know all about me."

"It's not enough."

"Really? What else would you like to know?"

"I want to know more about *you*. Not your career."

"Such as?"

"When I searched your room earlier, there was a picture of a little girl riding your shoulder. Is she your daughter? She's beautiful."

Shepherd filled with pride. "She is. She takes after her mother, thank God."

"What's her name?"

"Cassie."

"You must be missing her."

His mood darkened once more. "Every single day."

Allie noticed his worry. "Is everything all right back home?"

He hesitated. "No. Cassie's with my parents. They'd just told me she was in hospital when the comms failed. I don't know why she's in hospital or how serious it is."

Allie's brow furrowed, her eyes filled with concern. "That's terrible. What about her mother? Is she with her?"

"Cassie's mom died four years ago."

"Oh! Sorry."

He saw her chagrin. "Don't be. You couldn't know. My wife's name was Claire. She was killed in a car accident. It took us a long time, and we'll never forget her, but Cassie and I are doing okay now."

"Maybe Cassie just had a little tumble. My nephews and nieces are in hospital all the time with various bumps and bruises. I have two older brothers."

Shepherd wasn't convinced. "Maybe." Then he sighed. "Cassie has Childhood Disintegrative Disorder, also called Heller's syndrome. It's a developmental disorder that occurs in children who've had previously normal development, then appear to regress.

"About a year after her mom died, she started to show losses in language, social skills and adaptive behavior. The disorder is lifelong with long-term impairment of behavioral and cognitive functioning."

Shepherd felt the familiar lurch in his stomach. He'd been devastated when they'd first been given the diagnosis. Then he'd thrown himself into his work. "That's why I'm out here. After Cassie's condition was diagnosed, I specialized in neurodegenerative diseases in the hope of finding a cure. Working for Atione allows me to pursue my research while spending more time with my little girl."

He smiled at the memory of playing hide and seek with Cassie at their home in New Jersey. Her excited squeals that always gave her hiding place away. His smile faded. "This is my first trip away from her since her condition was diagnosed. I didn't want to leave her, but she has her mom's stubborn streak. She convinced me she was fine, that she had her nonna and poppa to look after her. And her condition has been relatively stable for several months.

"In the end, I couldn't pass up this opportunity, because the Alzheimer's cure you've discovered may also have potential as a cure for CDD."

"Both are neurodegenerative disorders."

"That's right. But with Cassie's condition, she's at risk of seizures. She hasn't had one before, but with CDD, they generally increase throughout childhood, peaking in adolescence.

"I'm worried she's had one. I should never have left her," he said, more to himself than to her. "I'll never forgive myself if something's happened and I wasn't there for her."

Allie's voice filled with confidence. "Lacoux will have the VSAT up and running again soon. As soon as we get in touch with Atione, I'll make sure you get to call your family. Is Cassie in good hands with your parents?"

"She is." Shepherd found his mood lifting as he thought about that.

"Then let's stay positive and focus on what we can do here. Okay?"

"Yeah. You're right. Thanks."

"Anytime." She smiled.

"How much further?"

She looked disorientated as another gust of wind sent shadows swirling across the clearing. Then she pointed. "It's up there, beyond the supply hut."

The boardwalk ended as they reached the supply hut. Constructed on stilts to prevent flooding, the small, square building contained the food, water and other essentials delivered by boat every three months. They rounded it, the ground heavy underfoot after the recent rain.

Shepherd slipped in the mud and winced.

"Are you okay?"

"I'm fine. Just clumsy."

He gave his left leg a shake, then resumed walking. But now he had a slight limp.

It was another hundred yards before they reached the end of the clearing, beyond which snaked a trail through a short expanse of jungle to another, smaller clearing where the VSAT was perched. The satellite dish antenna was three feet in diameter, with a low-noise blocker and a transmitter. A lone floodlight lit the area and cast a shadow toward them.

"Where is he?" Shepherd asked.

Allie squinted. "I see him." Then she stopped in surprise.

Lacoux was crouched beside the VSAT, his back to them. He appeared to be fumbling with the equipment and talking to himself.

They moved close enough to see he was hunched over an iPad, talking to someone on the screen.

"What's he doing?" Allie hissed.

"What's wrong?"

"Lacoux should have alerted Alderton or me immediately upon fixing the VSAT. Protocol requires that all communication with the Inn be made through either of us."

Over the rumble of thunder in the distance and the droning of insects, Shepherd could hear snatches of conversation. Lacoux was almost shouting in his effort to be heard between gusts of wind. He was speaking French. "Do you understand what he's saying?"

"Some of it. I studied the language in high school." She listened, her face taking on a concerned look. "He sounds panicked. 'They found Jouvet. I had to— He was going to—Tell Benoit they have to move now. *Merde*. Can you hear me? Can't wait—'."

Lacoux nodded vigorously at the person onscreen. "Tell them to move immediately!"

He closed the onscreen window before removing a cable and disconnecting the iPad from the VSAT.

"We need to find out who he was talking to," said Allie.

A deep sense of unease settled over Shepherd. Who was Benoit? What did Lacoux mean? Why did they have to move now?

"Wait." Shepherd grabbed her forearm, intending to pull her into the jungle. He wanted to observe Lacoux some more; find out what he was up to.

But she shrugged his hand away and strode forward. "Lacoux! What the hell are you doing?"

Shepherd cursed and slipped into the jungle, circling through its fringe toward Lacoux. Through tiny gaps in the dense foliage, he saw the man spin around to face Allie, eyes wide in surprise.

"Who were you talking to?" she demanded, striding toward him.

He pulled an object from the waistband of his pants. Allie jerked to a halt in shock as he straightened, pointing a gun at her. Despite her obvious fear, she kept her voice calm and measured. "Put the gun down. Let's talk about this."

She glanced around, realizing Shepherd was no longer behind her. She looked isolated; vulnerable.

Shepherd kept moving until he was behind Lacoux. He crouched silently, listening.

"I don't know what's going on here, but let's discuss it," said Allie. "Why don't we head back to the Inn?"

Lacoux swiveled and fired into the VSAT. It exploded with sparks and a billowing coil of smoke. Then he turned back to her. His finger tightened and Shepherd realized he was about to shoot her. Allie started to run.

He burst from the jungle and was upon Lacoux before he could move. He jerked his arm up into the air, wrenching it behind him. The gun fell free.

Lacoux fell to the ground, thrashing. Shepherd's forearm crushed against his throat and he jerked spasmodically, then went limp.

CHAPTER 8

SHEPHERD DRAGGED LACOUX'S semi-conscious form into the rec room and deposited him on the floor, on his back. Allie followed, carrying the iPad.

Alderton dropped his meal on the table before him with a clatter and jumped to his feet. "What is this?"

"This is the man who killed Jouvet. I need rope. Fast!" said Shepherd.

"Allie?" Alderton demanded. "What's going on?"

Allie's green eyes were cold with fury. "Lacoux killed Jouvet. He tried to kill me too."

"My God! Are you all right?"

"Yes. Thanks to Shepherd."

Lacoux stirred and Shepherd knelt on him to hold him to the ground. "I need rope."

"Grab some, quick as you can!" Alderton ordered Ben, who was gaping at the scene. He pulled himself together and sprinted off to the supply hut.

"What on earth happened?" asked Alderton.

"We caught him using the VSAT. I challenged him and he pulled a gun. He destroyed the satellite and he was about to shoot me but Shepherd jumped him." She placed Lacoux's mud-covered iPad onto a table, then glanced at their captive. "That son of a bitch!"

Alderton looked stunned. "I'm so sorry, Allie. If I'd suspected it was Lacoux, I never would have sent you out there. Thank God you're okay. Lacoux destroyed the VSAT?"

"He shot it. It exploded."

"Christ!" O'Connell kicked a chair. "You mean to tell me we're trapped?"

"We still have the sat-phone," Alderton replied.

"We'll never get a connection with this weather closing in!"

Alderton didn't answer.

"What are we going to do with Lacoux?" Parker asked.

"We restrain him. Then we try to find out what happened," Alderton said.

"How can we restrain him?" Parker's voice rose anxiously. "This is a research facility, not a prison. Where do we put him?"

Lacoux stirred. His head swiveled from side to side as he gathered himself, taking in his surroundings. His dark eyes were focused, but they contained no fear, instead, they were simmering with anger.

He tried to lurch to his feet, cursing Shepherd, who grappled him to the ground again.

"Where's that damn rope?" Shepherd snapped.

O'Connell joined him and they anchored Lacoux beneath their combined weight.

Ben reappeared, brandishing a thick coil of rope.

Shepherd tied the man's wrists together, jerking them tightly behind his back, then looped the rope around his ankles. He thrashed and rolled, but his efforts to get to his knees failed.

O'Connell eyed him, then looked up at Shepherd. "You've done that before."

He ignored him, focused on a more urgent matter. Back at the VSAT, Lacoux had been talking about someone called Benoit. *Tell Benoit they have to move now.*

Lacoux was a killer. He'd delivered an urgent message to someone, then destroyed the VSAT to isolate the scientists. Why?

While Allie had checked Lacoux's iPad, he had hauled

him up and slapped him to a semi-conscious state. Then he had hustled their prisoner back to the Inn as fast as he could manage, intent on interrogating him to find out what the hell he was up to. "We need to interrogate Lacoux immediately before he gets settled. He was reporting to someone. We need to find out who and why. He killed Jouvet and was prepared to shoot Allie. This is a ruthless son of a bitch."

"I fully intend to speak to him," Alderton said. He was now flanked by Marlowe and Klaus, with everyone else crowding behind them. "But we can't leave him on the floor."

"We have nowhere to keep him secure," Parker said. "If he escapes, he could kill any one of us."

"Calm down, please," Klaus said. His brow furrowed, then his blue eyes gleamed. "Put him in the small meeting room beside your office. He can't do any damage there and it would keep him confined until we have a chance to talk to him."

"Good idea," Alderton said. "Can you keep trying to get through to Atione on the sat-phone?"

"Of course." Klaus hurried away.

"O'Connell, I need someone to fix the bio lab's digital display. Can you do that?"

O'Connell looked down at their prisoner. "What about him?"

"Let me deal with him. You're the only other person who can fix the bio lab. I need you there."

O'Connell hesitated, then turned on his heel and strode off.

Alderton glanced at Marlowe. "You and I will talk to Lacoux."

"Let me talk to him," Shepherd said.

Alderton looked surprised. "I think it more appropriate that Marlowe and I conduct the interview. We have far more experience dealing—"

"It's not an interview. It's an interrogation. Allie said he mentioned someone called Benoit. We need to find out who that is."

"This is the responsibility of the senior staff. I will not argue over this."

"Look, before I studied medicine, I was with the Army Rangers. I know how to interrogate."

Alderton folded his arms. "So do I. And I'm not discussing this any further."

"Then I want to sit in," he insisted.

"I do too," Allie said. "I want to hear what he has to say."

Alderton relented. "Fine. Take him to the meeting room and secure him. We'll meet you there." Then he glanced at Marlowe. "Let's go to my office and prepare our strategy."

* * *

"I SHOULD BE interrogating him," Shepherd said, rapping his knuckles in frustration against the wall outside the meeting room door. Inside, Lacoux was tethered to a chair.

"Alderton is one of the best negotiators I've ever met," Allie said. "He was the one who raised the additional funding for the Inn when things were tight after our first season. I watched him deal with plenty of slimy crooks calling themselves venture capitalists. He bested them every time. Give him a chance."

"He won't make Lacoux talk without any leverage." His knuckles drummed faster. "Believe me. I've dealt with people like Lacoux before."

"Where?"

"While I was with the army. We had some problems with insurgents. We needed information and we needed it fast. Like we do now."

She looked startled. "I thought you were a medic."

"It doesn't matter. What does matter is that we get Lacoux to talk."

"I want to know why he killed Jouvet, but if he doesn't tell us, we can hand him over to the authorities in New York. Let the experts deal with him."

"We don't know how long we're going to be stuck out here."

Allie gazed in exasperation at his knuckles, now a blur of motion. "Why do you do that?"

He rested his fists against the wall. "Sorry. Old habit. I stuttered as a child. This was a trick my old man taught me to help me control it. I grew out of the stutter, but have tapped my knuckles ever since when I'm frustrated."

A cough emanated from the meeting room. Allie frowned and returned to the subject.

"Alderton will sort this out."

"We're trapped here with a murderer."

"Klaus will get through to Atione."

"When?" Shepherd demanded. "Days? Weeks? How long do you think we can hold someone like Lacoux? If that's what his damned name is. We don't know who he is or why he's here. But believe me, he's here for a reason.

"He killed Jouvet and when he was found out his first instinct was to destroy the VSAT, then kill you. This guy is not a strung-out scientist having a nervous breakdown. He has a reason for being here and was prepared to kill for it. We need to know what it is."

His knuckles started their tapping and he stilled them. "The longer we have to hold someone like him, the more danger we're in. We need to know what we're dealing with."

Allie frowned. "Don't underestimate the power of this place to push people to the edge. We did a thorough background check on Lacoux before hiring him. His references were impeccable. He's also demonstrated that he's a brilliant scientist."

She glanced toward the meeting room. "There's been no indication of anything untoward over the past six months. He got along with everyone until now. For all we know, he might've had a falling-out with Jouvet over the cure, then panicked. Under that sort of stress, he might've been calling someone back home for help. When he saw us, he snapped."

"Sorry Allie, but that's crap."

Alderton and Marlowe emerged from Alderton's office and strode briskly toward them.

"How are you going to approach this?" said Shepherd. "What role will each of you play in that room?"

Alderton looked frustrated. "I'm not going to stand here and be questioned by you!" He brushed past him and entered the room.

"You are both to observe only," said Marlowe. "Do you understand?"

"Yes," Allie replied, with a warning glance at Shepherd.

"Just make sure that's the case." Marlowe disappeared into the room.

"Damn it!" Shepherd said. "Stupid, arrogant fools."

"Do you want to watch or not?"

He shook his head in irritation and followed her into the meeting room.

CHAPTER 9

THE ROOM HAD a spartan feel to it. The ceiling and walls were a bland white. A brown wooden table occupied the center of the room, two black metal-framed chairs positioned before it, with another on the opposite side. A whiteboard used by the scientists for brainstorming hung on the wall behind the table.

As a place to secure Lacoux, it was a good choice. The door was sturdy and could be locked, and there was little in it that he could use as a weapon if he somehow managed to get himself free. He was bound to the chair on the far side of the table. His hands were tied behind his back, his torso roped to the chair, his ankles lashed together.

Shepherd stood with his back against the wall beside the room's only entrance. His arms were folded as he fought to constrain his impatience.

Allie stood against the wall on the other side of the entrance. She shifted restlessly, her body taut with tension as she studied Lacoux.

Alderton seated himself on one of the chairs facing their prisoner. Marlowe sat beside him. They remained quiet, studying him, allowing a long silence to draw out. They were posturing to build his trepidation as to what was going to happen to him. It was an amateurish display that further fueled Shepherd's impatience.

Finally, Alderton spoke. "Why did you kill Jouvet?" He leaned forward aggressively, reminding Shepherd of a bald eagle, with his hooked nose, fierce eyes and gleaming silvery-white hair. He hoped the old man possessed the same predatory instincts as the raptor.

Lacoux was coated in mud and his face and neck were starting to show some ugly bruises from his scuffle. But his dark eyes were clear and impassive.

"Now is the time for you to speak up." Alderton's voice was crisp and authoritative. He leaned back, allowing the silence to build up once more.

Marlowe cleared his throat and spoke for the first time, his voice tense. "We will be handing you over to the authorities in Manaus, so this is the time for you to talk. If you help us, Atione will look after your extradition and legal fees."

Lacoux remained silent. A drop of blood from a cut lip ran down his chin, leaving a streak of red against the brown dirt. He seemed oblivious to it. He ignored Marlowe, his eyes fixed on Alderton.

Alderton held his gaze. He rested his forearms on the table before him, hands clasped in a composed grip. A minute passed and neither man moved, locked in a battle of wills.

Shepherd's impatience grew. He unfolded his arms and his knuckles started tapping softly on the wall.

"Talk to us!" Alderton demanded. "For God's sake, man! Help us to make sense of why you would do such a thing. Was it an argument? Were you and Jouvet fighting? I understand how this jungle can affect you. It can fray your nerves. If this was a moment of madness, one you now regret, then tell me. I'll do my best to help you."

Lacoux's expression remained impassive.

Shepherd's apprehension soared. By breaking the silence, Alderton had given Lacoux the upper hand. Surely he could see that?

"An act of madness I could perhaps understand," he continued. "But what I don't understand is why you had a gun."

There was another long silence, during which both men remained motionless.

"Let me spell this out for you," Alderton said. "In my report to the Manaus authorities, I will be providing an assessment of your character. I'm in a position to help you. I can explain that this was out of character, that instead of an extended jail sentence, you need psychological help. But you need to give me something to work with. Tell me what happened."

"If you don't help us," Marlowe said, "We'll let the Manaus authorities deal with you. You'll rot in a local prison. Can you imagine the conditions you will face? You'll die here. Help us and we'll help you, see that you're extradited to a fair hearing in the U.S."

Lacoux sat quietly.

"Good God!" Alderton thundered. "You've killed one colleague and turned your gun on another. I'm the only person who can help you. But you have to cooperate.

"If you think the French authorities can assist you, you're mistaken. You've murdered a U.S. citizen and you'll face U.S. justice for your actions. I can see to it that you're extradited and that the U.S. authorities pursue the death penalty in your case."

His tone grew measured. "You're an intelligent man, Lacoux. I'm sure you understand the position you're in. Only I can help you. I'll only do so if you talk to me."

Lacoux didn't respond.

Alderton sighed and shook his head. "I thought you were smarter than this."

The prisoner yawned. Alderton got to his feet and motioned to Marlowe. Without another word, they left the room. Allie slipped out after them.

Shepherd followed them out, closing the door behind him. "What the hell are you doing?"

"Always be prepared to walk away from a deal," Alderton said. "When the other party knows that, they lose their bargaining position."

"This is not a deal. We're not bargaining. We need to extract information."

Alderton glared. "I know what I'm doing."

"I don't think you do. Your theatrics in there aren't working. Using silence as a means of breaking him down might work in a boardroom, but not here. You gave him the upper hand by breaking the silence first. By continuing to use it as a parlor trick, you're playing into his hands.

"The longer he doesn't have to talk, the better for him. We need answers. Why did he kill Jouvet? Who was this Benoit he was talking about? Why do they have to move and to where? We need to know what he's up to, and we need to know it fast!"

Alderton drew himself up to his full height. His voice chilled to a temperature just above freezing. "If it wasn't for my negotiation skills, the Inn wouldn't be funded and you wouldn't be out here."

Shepherd tried to keep his voice calm. "This isn't a negotiation over funding. It's the interrogation of a murderer. An interrogation I strongly believe you don't have the experience and skill to carry out."

Alderton's patrician features flushed with anger. "Do not question my tactics! Now, step aside and let me do my job." He turned his back on Shepherd and instructed Allie, "I want the two of you to remain outside. Do not enter. Do not say a word to him. Do you understand?"

"We do." Allie frowned at Shepherd.

The two old scientists walked down the corridor, their silver heads gleaming under the Inn's halogen lights.

He fought to control his exasperation. "What do they think they're doing?"

"Alderton is right. If it wasn't for him, the Inn wouldn't have received funding. I was present in many of those meetings with venture capitalists and I've seen him use this tactic successfully before. He deserves our trust."

"Look, Allie. Alderton is your mentor and that's clouding your judgment. You need to put your relationship with him aside and take a good, hard look at how he's approaching this interrogation. Because he's going about it all wrong."

Allie's green eyes brimmed with anger. "Don't you dare question my judgment. Yes, Alderton is my mentor. But I know him and I trust him. Whereas I hardly know you at all. So unless you can come up with something more constructive than your damn opinions, you can get your ass back to the rec room and stay the hell out of the way."

Shepherd didn't move. "Lacoux will continue to ignore him. He's toying with us, for Chrissake."

"So what do you suggest we do? Torture him? Did you learn how to do that as an army medic?"

"Torture is useless. The subjects tell you what they think you want to hear."

The anger in her eyes was replaced with surprise.

"What we need is leverage," he continued. "Some evidence to shove in Lacoux's goddamn face. Something to shake him out of his comfort zone."

"Like what?"

"His iPad. Let's see if we can find anything on it we can use."

Allie nodded thoughtfully. "Good idea. I was able to

remove its password protection when we caught Lacoux at the VSAT. I left it in the rec room. If O'Connell's fixed the bio lab, get him to go through it and see if he can find anything Alderton can use."

He was reluctant to leave the interrogation, but he wanted to be doing something proactive. "Okay."

"I'm going to tell Alderton what we're doing." She hurried off.

Shepherd leaned against the corridor wall, fighting his anxiety. The Inn was cut off with no comms while a couple of amateurs were interrogating a murderer who was hiding something.

The confidence in Lacoux's dark eyes continued to trouble him. What the hell had he got himself into?

Shepherd wanted nothing more than to be home with his daughter. But he knew he was trapped until they sorted this mess out. The sooner they did so, the sooner he could be with her.

He pushed off the wall and headed down the corridor to the rec room.

Everyone leaped to their feet and crowded toward him, eager for news. He brushed by them and retrieved the iPad he found lying on a table.

"What's going on in there?" O'Connell demanded. "What's Lacoux telling them?"

"He isn't talking."

"What are they doing about the comms? Has Klaus managed to make contact?"

"I don't know." Shepherd showed him the iPad. "This is Lacoux's. Do you think you can find out what's on it?"

He took it, turning it over in his hands. "What the hell happened to it? It looks like it's had a mud bath."

"If you don't clean it properly, you could lose whatever's on it," said Ben. "I know how to do it. Let me look at it."

"You can't be trusted with it." O'Connell held the machine out of Ben's reach.

Ben pursued him. "Have you ever cleaned one before?"

O'Connell ignored him, poking clumsily at the slender machine with his large fingers.

Shepherd eyed him dubiously. "Do you think you can clean it?"

O'Connell turned it over once more. "I'm not sure."

"Then get Ben to look at it first. If anything pops up he can run it past you. Agreed?"

"Fine. Don't fuck it up." He handed Ben the iPad.

CHAPTER 10

THE NATURALISTS' LAB was large and rectangular, its walls lined with shelves containing an array of specimen jars, books and manuals. A stuffed jaguar crouched menacingly on a shelf along the wall to his left.

A long trestle table occupied the center of the room and served as a workbench. Ben was seated there, hunched over the machine before him.

Shepherd sat on a wooden stool nearby. He stretched and glanced at his watch. It was nearing six a.m. Ben had been working on the iPad for nearly half the night.

Shepherd got to his feet. "I'm going to check how the interrogation of Lacoux is going."

Ben didn't reply.

He found Jan standing guard outside the meeting room. "Alderton stopped the interrogation to let Lacoux stew for a while. I volunteered to take the first shift."

Frustrated at the lack of progress, Shepherd returned to the lab.

"Any luck?"

Ben was still hunched over the iPad. He didn't respond.

"Ben?"

He heard a snore.

"Jesus!" he strode forward and seized Ben's shoulder, giving it a firm shake.

"What's happening?" Ben looked around with bleary eyes, then they widened in alarm. "I fell asleep?"

"You did." Shepherd fought to control his anger.

"I'm sorry. Damn it!"

He reached out for the machine. "This was a waste of

time. I should've given it to O'Connell."

"No, wait. I can do this. Please!"

He hesitated, seeing the desperation in his eyes.

Ben spoke quickly. "I'm the best person to do this. Look, I know everyone here thinks I'm lazy, but I'm not. It's because they know my father used his influence to get me here. They don't believe I've earned my place out here like the rest of them have.

"And I guess I haven't, but for the first time in my life, I've found something I love to do; something I'm good at. I want to complete my thesis and become a fully-fledged naturalist."

Shepherd remained unconvinced. "That doesn't excuse your falling asleep."

"No, it doesn't. I know how important this is. The reason I fell asleep is because I've been working late each night trying to get my thesis done. The others won't help me, so it's up to me. Which is fine."

He stared earnestly at Shepherd. "Give me a chance to prove myself. That I can earn my keep out here. If there's something on Lacoux's iPad that can help, I'll find it." His youthful features were rigid with determination.

"Are you sure? We're relying on you."

His voice was firm. "Yes."

"Okay. What have you found so far?"

"After I cleaned the iPad, I was able to access Lacoux's files. The problem is there's a lot of them, all containing highly technical narrative and experiments. It's a painstaking process to go through each of them. Wait," he added, seeing Shepherd frown in disappointment. "It's slow going, but I'm making headway. I'm just being careful—I don't want to miss anything important."

"Just work as fast as you can." He sat on his stool making sure Ben didn't fall asleep again.

After half an hour, gripped with impatience, he slipped off the stool. "I'm going to speak to Allie. Let me know as soon as you find something."

He found her in the corridor outside the meeting room. Inside, Alderton and Marlowe had resumed their interrogation of Lacoux.

"How's O'Connell going with the iPad?" she asked.

Shepherd explained that he'd given the machine to Ben. He decided not to tell her Ben had fallen asleep. "He's finding it hard going."

Allie frowned. "Are you sure O'Connell shouldn't be looking at it?"

"Let's give Ben a chance first."

There was a shout from down the corridor. They turned to see Ben sprinting toward them, brandishing the iPad. "I've found something!"

He skidded to a halt and shoved the machine under Allie's nose. "Look!" He gasped, breathless with excitement.

She frowned in confusion. "What am I looking at?"

Ben pointed. "I found all these files with Lacoux's reports and notes. Most of it's over my head; lots of equations and stuff. But then I saw the name 'Toussen' repeated throughout his work. Aren't they one of Atione's competitors?"

"They are." She peered at the screen. The blood drained from her face. "Jesus. Good job, Ben."

"What is it?" Shepherd asked.

"Leverage."

* * *

ALDERTON'S FRUSTRATION AT his lack of progress was evident as they entered the meeting room. He was running a hand through his now unkempt hair and his features were rigid with tension as he turned in his chair and glared at Allie. "What is it?"

She showed him the iPad. "Lacoux was selling intellectual property to Toussen."

Alderton shot to his feet. *"What?"*

"Ben went through the iPad. He found this file, one that Lacoux must have been about to upload before we surprised him at the VSAT. It contains reports to Toussen summarizing Lacoux's experiments and the work performed by O'Connell's team.

"I need to go through it in more detail, but I bet it contains Jouvet's notes and experiments relating to the Alzheimer's cure."

Alderton's expression changed from astonishment to outrage. Toussen was a French biotech corporation. It had been hit hard by the global financial crisis, with funding for research drying up.

This information would allow them to manufacture the Alzheimer's cure using samples of the new plant species found by the Inn's naturalists. They could create patents worth billions of dollars while locking Atione out.

"You son of a bitch! I brought you out here, made you part of my team, and you betray me like this?" Alderton's face was beetroot red. "But we caught you! You'll be prosecuted for corporate espionage as well as murder. You've failed, you weak, insignificant fool!"

Lacoux strained against the ropes, his impassive façade dissolving beneath the anger now twisting his face. "I have not failed. You'll be dead soon." He looked at the others in the room. "All of you."

"What are you talking about?" Shepherd demanded.

Lacoux remained silent.

He reached across the table and seized him by the collar of his mud-stained shirt. "Talk, you bastard!"

Lacoux spat in his face.

He shoved him away and the chair tumbled backward. He strode around the table and crouched over him, jamming his forearm against the man's throat. "Talk!"

Lacoux struggled but kept silent.

"That's enough!" Alderton snapped. "I'll handle this."

Shepherd pressed harder with his arm. "You've wasted enough time already."

"Shepherd, stop!" yelled Allie.

He heard the shock in her voice but his disquiet intensified as he gazed into Lacoux's murderous black eyes. Fear swept through him. Something ominous was unfolding that would prevent him from getting home to Cassie.

He saw also that this man wasn't about to break. He stood and strode from the room, slamming the door behind him.

He hurried into the rec room and made a beeline for Mancini, who was seated by himself at a table. The man looked up, startled, as he loomed over him.

"I need your help."

CHAPTER 11

SHEPHERD THREW THE door open and strode into the meeting room, clutching a syringe.

Mancini followed more slowly. He also held a syringe in his hand.

Lacoux had been lifted back into an upright position on the chair. Alderton, Marlowe and Allie were standing over him.

"Why did you say we'll be dead soon?" Alderton said. "Who are you working for in Toussen? How much information about the cure have you sent them? Talk, damn you!"

All three swung around as he burst into the room.

"Shepherd! I want you out of here!" Alderton strode toward him.

He brushed past him, raised the needle and plunged it into Lacoux's shoulder.

The man flinched. "What the fuck have you done?"

Shepherd held the syringe in front of his eyes. "I've injected you with the venom of the Brazilian wandering spider." He gestured toward Mancini. "Our resident toxicologist assures me that it's the most venomous one on the planet. It contains a potent neurotoxin which causes loss of muscle control and breathing problems, which result in paralysis and asphyxiation. It causes intense pain and inflammation due to an excitatory effect on the sensory nerves."

"You're lying!" Lacoux spat.

He shook his head. "Mancini is very interested in what's about to happen to you. He's had only mice to work with before, haven't you, Mancini?"

The man nodded, his face pale.

"Of course, the spider itself could never deliver the amount of venom that I just injected into you. I reckon I gave you enough to bring down a bull elephant." He turned to Mancini. "With someone Lacoux's size, how long will it be before he starts feeling the effects?"

Mancini licked his lips nervously. "A few minutes."

"Will he die?"

"That depends on when he gets antivenom."

"Which Mancini is holding. If you tell us why you said everyone here will die, you get the antivenom. If not…" He shrugged. "It's up to you."

"Fuck you! You're full of shit."

Shepherd glanced at his watch.

"Shepherd," Allie said, "we can't do this!"

"We can and we will."

"I will not be part of this," said Alderton. "Mancini, give him the antivenom now."

"Don't you dare!" Shepherd gave him a warning glance.

"Give him the damn injection!" shouted Alderton.

Mancini looked like he wanted to disappear into the wall.

"Give it to me." Alderton gestured toward the syringe.

Shepherd blocked his path. "Don't interfere."

"Get the hell out of my way!"

He didn't move.

"Don't do this," Allie said.

Ignoring her, he turned back to Lacoux. "Mancini tells me that, aside from causing intense pain, the venom can cause priapism in humans. At least you'll die with a boner."

"You're fucking lying," Lacoux hissed. "You—" His eyes widened. A muscle spasmed in his cheek. It writhed and twitched like a giant worm. "Fuck you!" His eyes bulged.

"It's attacking your nervous system now. If you're going

to talk, you'd better do it fast. The antivenom will neutralize the venom, halting further damage, but won't reverse any damage already done."

Lacoux thrashed against the ropes. He was short of breath and his chest heaved as he struggled to force air into his lungs. Then he lunged back in the chair as a contraction rippled along the muscles of his jawline. "Fuck!"

"Stop this!" Allie demanded.

"Not until he talks."

"You can't do this!" Alderton was aghast. "Mancini, for God's sake, give him the antivenom!"

Mancini looked too scared to move.

Shepherd glanced at his watch. "It's been two minutes. You probably have another minute before the real fun starts." He gripped the man's injected shoulder and squeezed. "Does that hurt?"

Lacoux gasped, the chair swaying as he rocked away from his grip. He was breathing in ragged pants, his pale face perspiring. A muscle in the side of his neck bulged like a thick, knotted cord. A wail burst from his lips and he strained against the ropes. He was struggling to breathe. For the first time, there was panic on his face.

"You'd better talk fast. Who were you talking to at the VSAT?"

"Toussen!" Lacoux groaned, staring up at Shepherd with baleful eyes.

"Who is Benoit?"

Lacoux groaned again, his chest heaving.

"He's going to asphyxiate!" Allie shouted. "He needs the antivenom."

"You said tell Benoit to move now. Why? Where? What were you planning?" Shepherd kept his eyes locked on Lacoux.

"Mercenaries," he managed to say. "Sent by Toussen. Led by Benoit. They're coming." His mouth twisted into a smile, or a grimace, Shepherd couldn't tell. "Within hours."

He forced in a breath and the words spilled from his mouth. "They'll take the information they need about the cure, then destroy this place. If you run, they'll hunt you down. You're all dead." His eyes rolled. His lips were blue. The only sound in the room was his gargled moan as the last of the air collapsed from his lungs.

"Give him the antivenom!" Shepherd yelled at Mancini.

For a moment, he locked eyes with Allie and saw she was as stunned as he was. Finally, they knew Lacoux's plan, who Benoit was and chillingly, who was with him.

Mercenaries. Coming to kill them.

CHAPTER 12

FOR THE FIRST time he could remember, the rec room was silent as everyone absorbed what Alderton had just told them. It was raining outside and the early morning light was murky as it filtered through the windows, but it was enough to illuminate the shocked expressions on their faces.

An hour had passed since Lacoux had dropped his bomb-shell and collapsed. Mancini had injected the antivenom directly into a vein, while Shepherd had hastily administered CPR. The antivenom had worked rapidly and Lacoux was soon conscious, but in no state to tell them anything further about the mercenaries.

Alderton had run off with Marlowe to speak to Klaus and try to get an urgent message through to Atione, while Shepherd and Allie had remained in the meeting room to watch the prisoner.

They had sat silently, ignoring each other. Shepherd wasn't sure if she was more appalled by what he had done to Lacoux or by the magnitude of what the man had told them.

Alderton returned an hour later to check that Lacoux was secure. He had then gathered everyone in the recreation room.

Shepherd had seated himself at the bar, away from the rest of the group, where he could think. He felt dazed. All he'd wanted to do in coming here was assist in the development of a cure that could help Cassie. Now, he was caught up in a nightmare, one that could prevent him from ever getting home to her.

More than the fear of the approaching mercenaries, the thought of never seeing Cassie again chilled him. He sat quietly, grappling with his fears, fretting about what to do.

Allie stood at Alderton's side while he explained the situation. His words had the same effect as if he had lobbed a hand grenade into their midst. At first, there had been disbelief, then growing comprehension, and finally, a fear so palpable it had its own presence.

The ensuing silence lasted a full minute. It was Mancini who broke it. "What are we going to do? Do we even believe what Lacoux has to say? I mean, could he be making this up?"

"You saw him," Allie said. "He didn't tell us what he thought we wanted to hear. He was talking to save his life."

"Jesus fucking Christ," O'Connell said. "Do you feel the same way, Alderton?"

"Yes."

"So what the hell are we going to do?"

"Any word from Atione?" Mancini asked.

Klaus waved his gnarled hand toward the ceiling. A low rumble of thunder accompanied the hammering of the rain. "With this weather, the sat-phone is useless. I haven't been able to get through to Atione. I'll keep trying, but I don't have much confidence."

"Jesus," Mancini strode to a window and peered through. He turned to face them, his dark features tight with worry. "How soon will they be here?"

"Lacoux said a few hours," Alderton replied.

"That doesn't give us much time," said O'Connell.

"We need to discuss what we're going to do." Alderton looked shaken. His eyes had lost some of their certainty and his tall, usually relaxed frame was rigid with tension.

"What about the cure?" Mancini said. "We can't let these mercenaries take it. Not after all the work we've done on it."

"He's right," O'Connell said. "We can't let these bastards

take everything we've strived for. We need to do something."

"We have to run!" Mancini's voice rose.

"And go where exactly?" In contrast, Allie sounded cool and measured.

"We hide in the rainforest," Mancini said. "They won't find us. We take all our work and disappear."

"We're in the middle of the Amazon," Ben said. "There's nothing out there for thousands of miles. Where do you plan to go?"

"We don't have time to waste listening to you," Mancini snapped.

Alderton held his hands up for calm but was ignored.

"Well, you should!" Ben retorted. "You don't know what you'd be getting into out there."

"I think we should just get the hell out of here," said O'Connell.

"Ben is right." Marlowe's gray hair was rumpled, fatigue had deepened the wrinkles creasing his face, but his gaze was level and composed as he looked around at them all. "Mancini, there's nothing out there—only hostile wilderness. Leaving the Inn should be our last resort."

"We're at our last resort. We have only hours before these mercenaries get here. We need to leave now." O'Connell addressed his team. "I want you to start gathering all your research. As much as you can. I'll collate all our information on the cure." He glanced across at Shepherd. "That includes you."

He could see that Alderton was losing control. His people were arguing, making fear-driven decisions that suited themselves, not the group. They needed strong leadership.

Ignoring O'Connell, he turned to Alderton. "We need to coordinate what we're going to do."

"You'll do what I tell you," snapped O'Connell.

"Shepherd's right," Allie said. "First, we need to make a plan."

"We don't have time!"

"Silence!" Alderton's voice boomed. "I want you all to listen to me. We will not panic. And we will not run."

As a group they stilled, staring back at him. Waiting.

"We'll negotiate with them."

Allie frowned. "What exactly are you proposing?"

"We'll go out and reason with these mercenaries. More precisely, I'll negotiate with them. Marlowe and Klaus will come with me."

"Negotiate what exactly?"

"That they turn back and leave us alone."

"What do you intend to negotiate with?" Shepherd asked, his knuckles softly tapping on the bar.

Alderton smiled. "Atione has prepared for this type of situation. Recognizing the potential of the Inn, they now have small teams operating in some of the most dangerous places on the planet.

"They're participating in government programs and conducting trials, examining the outbreak of new diseases in third world countries, looking for possible cures. The risk of kidnapping by militant groups in these areas is high.

"As such, they've taken out kidnap insurance and established a contingency fund. Certain high-level Atione executives are permitted to use this fund to, where necessary, negotiate for the safety of its employees. I have such authority."

"You mean bribe them," Allie said.

"I mean, negotiate with them. Recently, one of our executives arranged with Somalian pirates for the release of several of our people. These mercenaries are no different from pirates."

"But how do you intend to draw from this contingency fund to pay them?"

"Atione will make arrangements. They'll arrange an electronic transfer to wherever these mercenaries request. Or they'll arrange for cash to be delivered to Manaus."

"What happens if they don't speak English? How can you trust them? How can you arrange a money transfer with the satellite link down?"

"Allie, if those idiots from Toussen can communicate with them, then I'm sure I'll be able to. The details will be worked out. The main thing will be to convince these mercenaries I can arrange for them to be paid more than whatever Toussen are offering. Everything will be fine."

Allie bit her lip anxiously, her face full of doubt. "Think this through. Where do you intend to meet them? How do we even know where they're coming from or when they'll get here?"

"The nearest town is Manaus. They must be coming from there, using the river. And there's only one access trail to the Inn. The jungle is impenetrable. They can't get here any other way. We'll intercept them before they reach the Inn. Because if they get here, we lose our bargaining strength."

"When?"

"Lacoux said they'll be here in hours. If we leave now, we can head them off."

"But these are mercenaries. You're risking your lives."

"And what do you propose to do instead?" said O'Connell. "I think Alderton's plan makes perfect sense."

"I don't hear you volunteering to speak to them," Allie retorted.

Before O'Connell could respond, Alderton did. "We're wasting time. We need to get moving. We can work out the details as we walk there. We'll need supplies. These negotiations can take a while."

Shepherd didn't like the direction this was taking. The more he thought this through, the more he felt that Alderton's approach was wrong. He got to his feet. "You can't negotiate with people like these."

Alderton eyed him impatiently. "What are you talking about?"

"These people aren't pirates. They're not opportunistic thugs who'll be grateful to take your money. They'll be professionals operating under a contract—one they're being well paid to deliver on. Men like these don't advertise. They are hired based on word of mouth and reputation for delivery. They won't risk that by breaking an existing contract. They will not negotiate with you."

Alderton's brow creased into a frown. "I know what I'm doing. Atione hired a former police hostage negotiator to train all of its executives in how to deal with exactly this type of situation. We'll be fine."

"This isn't a simulated training exercise. You have no real-life experience dealing with men like these."

Alderton sighed in exasperation. "Wall Street is a jungle—survival of the fittest and smartest, just like the Amazon. The same instincts and base motivations apply out here. They're mercenaries. Guns for hire by the highest bidder. As such, their motivations are transparent. I'll simply make them an offer they can't refuse."

"You're going to jeopardize the safety of everyone here. Listen to me!"

"I've already told you to stop questioning my tactics. I will not listen to you challenge me again! I value your advice in relation to neurodegenerative diseases, but *not* about working a deal. And right now, you're wasting my time!"

Shepherd fought his mounting exasperation. He kept his voice measured. "You're not working a deal. I've seen men like this before when I was with the military. I know how they operate."

"You were a medic. What the hell do you know about mercenaries?" O'Connell said. "I don't hear you coming up with an alternative plan."

"Before I was a medic, I was a soldier with the Army Rangers."

Alderton stared hard at Shepherd. "You mentioned these Rangers earlier. What are they?"

"Elite special forces within the U.S. army."

Alderton's gaze intensified. "That was at least a decade ago. During which time you've retrained as a scientist and spent your time working in laboratories."

"I remember my army training. And what I learned about men like these. Yes, it was a long time ago—but I'm the only one here with military experience."

"Well then—*do* you have an alternative?"

"I do. They're coming whether we like it or not. If we run, they'll track us down."

"So Lacoux says," O'Connell said.

"It makes sense. If Toussen is ruthless enough to hire mercenaries, they won't want anyone left alive who could point a finger at them."

"What are you suggesting?" Allie asked.

"We're alone out here. No one can get to us in time to assist. It's up to us. We need to defend ourselves; we have no other option. But we need to prepare now."

"This is ridiculous," O'Connell said. "You want us to fight? Are you crazy?"

"I've heard enough!" said Alderton. "There's too much at stake to listen to these ludicrous suggestions."

"You're an arrogant fool!" Shepherd snapped.

"Enough!" he cried. "We're talking about a cure for Alzheimer's. All the work we've done. This is my legacy! This is my decision and, by God, it's final."

He strode from the room, Marlowe and Klaus in tow.

CHAPTER **13**

SHEPHERD FOUND ALLIE in the comms room. It was little more than an hour later and Alderton, Marlowe and Klaus had departed the Inn.

After a final, futile, attempt to convince them to stay, he had rushed to find her. As he hurried into the room, she slammed the sat-phone down on the desk. "Shit!"

"No luck getting through to Atione?"

She swiveled to face him, her features taut and tense. "No. All I can hear is static."

"Alderton's making a mistake."

"I think so too. But he can't be budged when his mind's made up. I've been trying to call Atione for help."

"We don't have any more time to waste. We have to act now."

"And do what? We need to let Atione know what is going on."

"Even if somehow you managed to get through to them, what are they going to do? We're thousands of miles from anywhere. It's up to us."

She bit her lip and glanced toward the sat-phone "I should try again."

Shepherd's impatience mounted. "Jesus, Allie. The phone's dead. Do you understand what's happening here? These are mercenaries, for God's sake! Do I need to spell out what they're going to do?

"You're the person in charge now. You need to make a decision. We're sitting ducks! We can't delay any longer. You have to trust me on this."

Allie considered him. "Why should I trust you? I hardly

know you. I've known Alderton for years."

"Because I dealt with men like this while I was in the special forces. I know how they think."

"Did you deal with them the same way you dealt with Lacoux?" Along with uncertainty, there was now revulsion in her eyes.

"I did what I had to do. I didn't like it, but it was necessary."

"Would you have let him die?"

"No. At least, when he was unable to talk, I would've tried to save him. But I wanted him to think I would let him die."

Her green eyes interrogated him. Shepherd waited, acutely aware he was being judged—and that he needed her as an ally.

The uncertain expression on her face faded. "What do you suggest?"

Shepherd felt a surge of relief. "We defend ourselves."

"How? We're scientists. We have no idea what to do."

"I do. But we need as much help as we can get. We're going to build some traps in the jungle. Try to slow them down and give us more time to prepare our defenses here. We'll need one of the naturalists to guide us. And I need to speak to Mancini."

* * *

SHEPHERD HURRIED INTO the rec room clutching vials of a pale liquid Mancini had prepared for him. As he entered, O'Connell brushed past him, followed by the rest of his team. Jan hesitated, throwing an unhappy glance toward him.

"Get going," O'Connell growled as he bustled Jan toward the laboratory.

Allie stood in the middle of the room, accompanied by Ben and a reluctant-looking Parker.

"What happened?" asked Shepherd.

Allie's face was flushed with anger and frustration. "I gathered everyone and outlined your plan. I told them we think Alderton is making a mistake, but O'Connell wouldn't listen to me. He said he's not going to send his people into the rainforest based on what you think. His people are scientists, not goddamn marines and their time is better spent finalizing their work.

"At least Ben has volunteered to help." She gave the young man an appreciative smile. "How about you, Parker?"

Parker looked pale. "I—I think you're wrong," he said quickly. "I have work I need to finish. Sorry." He scuttled past Shepherd and left the room.

Allie couldn't hide her disappointment. "Damn."

"I know the jungle," Ben said. "I can get you out there."

"I'm sure you can." But her confidence sounded forced.

"Mancini's out as well. Said he had too much work to do in the lab." Shepherd surveyed the tiny team, fighting to hide his dismay. "We'd better get moving."

CHAPTER **14**

JACQUES BENOIT SQUATTED on his haunches and studied his palm-sized computer.

The tiny machine was called the Terminal Information System or TIS. He used it for tactical situation assessment. The TIS displayed schematics providing a layout of their target, maps of the region, and enabled him to exchange encrypted messages with the mercenary guarding their vessel back on the river and with the men in his squadron.

One of the mercenaries coughed and spat. "Fucking insects."

Benoit grinned. "They taste better than the food you were served back in the Legion, Henri."

He turned his attention back to the TIS. It was a tiny piece of equipment, almost insignificant compared with the sophisticated weaponry his squad carried, yet he still marveled at what it represented.

The TIS was a vital component in the French military's FELIN system with which his squad was equipped. FELIN was the French future infantry soldier system.

Benoit's mercenaries were connected via the FELIN Infantryman Information Network, the RIF, with each mercenary carrying a small personal radio transmitting voice and data communication, enabling GPS position tracking and information sharing within the squad.

FELIN made the French army the most sophisticated military force in the world.

But the powerful U.S., Russian and Chinese militaries each had their own future soldier programs. Technology was the new arms race, with each nation closely monitoring each other's progress.

Consequently, the French kept a component of their program hidden from scrutiny. This program was operated by Advanced Weapons Research, AWR, a secretive unit within the French Directorate of Military Intelligence, and utilized the services of several French private biotechnology companies, signed to lengthy and strict confidentiality agreements, with breaches treated as treason under French law.

Another cough was followed by more cursing.

There was a roar of laughter. "I'll bet that one tasted better than your mother's cooking!"

Benoit smiled. Even after their long journey in the oppressive heat, his men's spirits were high. He glanced around his squad. It was equipped with the latest technology developed under this program. Still experimental, this was its first operational trial. It had been only a matter of hours since they'd put feet on the ground in the rainforest, yet he was already confident it would take the French future soldier program not just into the next decade, but the next century.

He tapped the TIS. It displayed the real-time positioning of his men and through their launch's satellite system, provided a fix on their position via GPS. Or, at least, it usually did. Even the most advanced technology in the world was no match for the hostility of this remote environment.

He tapped again but the screen remained stubbornly blank. The TIS had been effective on the river, bringing them directly to the Inn's access trail. But it faded as they traveled beneath the jungle canopy.

One of his men glanced over. "Still not working? Just like those bastards at AWR to give us tech that doesn't work."

Benoit's smile broadened. "Have faith in the people running this op, Alain. Everything else they've provided is working fine."

He was unperturbed; they had prepared for this. Each of his men had memorized the layout of the Inn. They had detailed instructions on how to get to it and they had been able to get a fix on their coordinates before leaving the river. They also had two trackers with them, hired in Manaus for their knowledge of the region and skills in tracking prey through the jungle.

Of more concern to him was the fate of the man who had provided their information, Pierre Lacoux. Nothing had been heard from him since his last urgent message which had forced his squad to advance upon the Inn earlier than expected.

Lacoux had led the experimental program Benoit had undertaken and had saved his life when he'd had an adverse reaction to the initial administration of the drug compound. But rather than being worried about his welfare, Benoit was more focused on what it meant for this operation.

He rose to his feet. "Move out."

His men moved swiftly into formation. Two moved to the rear of the squadron, protecting the main body of men. Benoit led as point.

The two trackers waited in front, ready to scour the terrain ahead of them, looking for any hidden dangers along the trail.

He was proud of the efficiency of his squadron's response. He had pushed them hard and they were entitled to be tired and slower as a result.

Then he noticed one man was out of position. Devin Halle remained where he had been standing, a little apart from the rest of the squadron. The dark-haired Halle was peering at an object in his hand, sweat dripping from the chiseled planes of his hard face.

Benoit approached quickly. Absorbed in what he was doing, Halle didn't look up until he was standing immediately before him.

He nodded at the man's TIS; he was the only other member on the squadron who carried one. "Making another report to your masters at AWR?"

"I'm writing notes that I'll put into a report later. I can't send anything while we're under this canopy."

"Mine's not working either. Mind if I look?" His tone was friendly, but Benoit could see Halle's features tighten at the realization this was an order from his former commandant. He handed over his TIS.

Benoit scanned it quickly and read his words aloud. "'Bigger and stronger since the experiment. Faster.' You make me sound like Superman." His eyes flowed rapidly over the TIS. Then he laughed. "'Dramatic changes in mood… Yellow eyes.' You record shit like that?"

Halle sounded defensive. "My role is to record everything I observe whether I think it's important or not. That includes weather conditions, the heaviness of the terrain, the failure of our satellite comms now we're under the rainforest canopy. Anything that could act as a stressor, or impact the squadron's—and your—performance."

"*My* role is to take control of the Inn, wipe out the scientists and obtain the formula for the cure. A role that, right now, you're preventing me from doing."

He studied Halle curiously. Initially, he had been appointed to oversee the experimental phase of the program and select the men who would take part in this operational trial. But then he'd been embedded in the squad by AWR, even though he was an intelligence officer, not a soldier like the rest of the men.

He wondered—not for the first time—if Halle had another purpose for being there.

"I could have objected to your inclusion on the team. But you were a fine Legionnaire and I was assured your training remained up to date; that you wouldn't slow us down.

"I know you're here to report back to AWR. But you're also an active member of this squadron—you follow my instructions. We're ready to move and are waiting for you. Don't keep us waiting again."

To take the sting from his words, he gave Halle a friendly pat on the shoulder. "Make sure your report is balanced, my friend. Because even after our long hike, I feel strong and full of energy. I have to remind myself to slow down so the rest of you don't fall behind. I want you to include that in your report."

He grinned confidently. "This will be over very quickly. There's nothing that can stop us. Nothing."

He returned to his position at point, leading his men toward their destination.

CHAPTER 15

THE RAINFOREST SEEMED to fight them as they hurried along the trail carrying the spades and the machete they would need to prepare the traps for the mercenaries. Shepherd had also brought the Inn's rifle and carried it over his shoulder.

The oppressive heat and humidity sapped their energy with every step. Soldier ants clawed and bit at their skin as if sent by the jungle to slow them down.

Even Ben, who was most at home in this hostile environment, seemed to be affected, cursing as he wiped mosquitoes from his face and slapped away ants crawling over his body. "The rainy season's almost here. The humidity gets worse as the storms build up and it seems to stir all the insects into a frenzy."

Although Ben was their guide, Shepherd was their leader, directing them when to stop, showing them what he wanted and how to help him as they prepared traps for the mercenaries.

They had been at this for two hours and were working on what he said would be the last trap they would prepare. He directed Ben and Allie to dig a pit four feet deep, six feet wide, almost spanning the width of the trail. When finished, it would be the largest they had made.

"This is the first one the mercenaries will confront. It has to have the most impact. They'll be wary after this."

While they dug, he placed the rifle on a nest of branches to keep it dry. Then he fashioned stakes hewn from the jungle. When the pit had been completed to his satisfaction, he planted each stake in the mud at its base and applied toxin to each. He used a stick to extract the thick, paste-like substance from a large vial then, with excruciating caution, he wiped the paste on the tip of each stake.

Ben knelt beside him. "What toxin are you using?"

"A batrachotoxin Mancini prepared from a poison dart frog."

Ben scuttled back. "Jesus. I thought you were using a curare derivative that'd knock them out for a while. You know that can be absorbed through your skin, don't you?"

Shepherd nodded, trying to control the trembling in his tired fingers.

"Just how poisonous is it?" Allie was standing a few feet away, arms crossed as she stared uneasily into the dark pit. She was splattered from head to toe with mud.

"Is it from *Phyllobatesterribilis*?" Ben asked.

"That's what Mancini told me."

"Which is what?" Allie asked.

"The golden poison dart frog is one of the most poisonous animals on the planet. Its toxin makes the wandering spider venom look like chicken soup." He grinned at Shepherd. "Man, I still can't believe you injected Lacoux with it." He turned to Allie. "Mancini's been doing a lot of work on this stuff but he has to do it in the bio lab. Didn't you realize what it can do?"

"I knew he was trying to develop muscle relaxants, heart stimulants and anesthetics but I wasn't aware how toxic it is. I don't spend much time in the bio lab."

"Oh. Well, this stuff attacks the nervous system and produces heart and respiratory failure. It kills in seconds. Just two-tenths of a microgram is lethal in the human bloodstream.

"The toxin from just one frog is enough to kill ten men. Mancini has to be super cautious. Researchers have been killed when the toxin's been absorbed through their latex gloves."

"That's right," Shepherd said through gritted teeth. "So you might want to let me concentrate."

He finished applying the paste and sat back on his haunches, surveying his handiwork. Now the traps were set, he realized how exhausted he was. His heart was pounding, he was bathed in sweat from the humidity and he was covered in scratches and bites from the relentless swarms of mosquitoes, mites, leaf-cutter ants, wasps and myriad of flying beetles. His knee ached from hurrying along the heavy trail and crouching at each site.

He rocked back on his haunches, massaging his forehead to relieve a nagging headache.

"What do you call this?" Ben asked, staring in fascination into the dark hole.

"A tiger trap."

Ben wiped a thick strand of dark hair off his forehead. "How do you know all this?"

"The army." But he was starting to realize just how long ago that had been. Maybe Alderton had been right after all. He had struggled to remember how to prepare his traps. What had once been second nature now seemed foreign.

His difficulty in forcing himself to think differently, along with his growing fatigue and aching body, was clouding his mind with doubt. A decade ago, he would have barely raised a sweat after the same level of activity.

He had been a different man back then. A younger and fitter one. It was a stage of his life he'd thought he had left behind forever.

He was a father now. He liked medical research and he loved being a dad. He wasn't sure if he wanted to be the man he was as a soldier.

Then he thought of Cassie and realized that he would be that man if it was what it took to get home. But accompanying this realization was an uncomfortable thought—could he ever be that person again?

He shoved his doubt aside.

"Is this really necessary?" Allie asked as he and Ben covered the pit with branches, leaves and mud.

"What?" he snapped irritably, feeling a stab of pain in his left knee as he stood.

"That toxin. Aren't the stakes enough?"

"The stakes may only wound them. This way causes maximum damage."

"Maximum damage," she repeated. "You're going to kill them?"

"Yes."

"Jesus."

"I don't like it any more than you do. But this is necessary. What do you think these mercenaries are going to do? They'll murder everyone and their methods won't be any less brutal than this."

"Maybe Alderton will stop them." She eyed the tiger trap with dawning horror. "Alderton will be coming back this way! How will we prevent them from falling in? We have to warn them. Didn't you think?"

She stared at him and he could see the realization in her eyes. "You don't believe they will be coming back, do you?"

He didn't answer.

"We can't let them reach the mercenaries. I'm going after them," she said.

"No. I will. I was always going to go after them once we'd set the traps." He retrieved the rifle. It was a Winchester Model 70 bolt-action; a hunting rifle renowned for its smooth handling and accuracy.

Shepherd's father had owned one. As a boy, he had been entranced by the sleek walnut stock with cut checkering. It had almost dislocated his shoulder the first time he'd been allowed to use it on a hunting trip in Connecticut with his old man. Its .300 Winchester Magnum cartridges were capable of taking down a bear.

He tilted the barrel to allow water to drain from it, then inspected the bore to ensure it was free of obstruction. Satisfied, he slung it over his shoulder and hefted the machete in his hand. He looked at Allie. "It'll be safer if you wait here with Ben."

"I'm going!" Allie insisted.

"Allie, please. I'll move faster without you."

"I'm quicker along these trails than you are. You can either come with me or stay here. But I'm going."

"I'm not staying behind," Ben said.

He sighed in defeat.

* * *

BEN LED THE way, Allie at his shoulder. Shepherd soon found himself struggling to keep up as he slid and tripped his way along the trail. Both of them had far more experience moving along the jungle paths and it showed as they avoided unexpected holes, camouflaged roots and branches, that he seemed to blunder into with every step.

"Hurry up!" Allie urged over her shoulder.

Ignoring the stabbing pain in his left knee, he forced himself to move faster. How far behind Alderton's team were they? If they reached them in time, Shepherd would direct them back to the Inn. He would then go on alone, not to negotiate, but to assess the force confronting them.

He had put aside his concern for the safety of Alderton's

team as he'd focused on setting the traps. But now he had time to think, his worry flooded over him. Was there anything else he could have done to stop them? He knew he wouldn't forgive himself if anything happened to them.

Over the monotonous droning of brown cicadas, mosquitoes and flies, he heard a different sound. Men's voices on the trail ahead.

"Allie!" he hissed.

"I hear them! Hurry!"

"Wait!"

Ben and Allie halted.

"That must be Alderton," she said. "We've almost caught them."

"We need to be careful."

"You're wasting time. We can talk more when we reach them."

"Allie, listen to me." He kept his voice low. "We don't know what's happening up ahead. It sounds like they've stopped. I want to be sure of what's going on. Wait here. Ben, take Allie and hide."

"I don't think—" Allie began.

"Allie! For chrissake! Wait for me here."

She nodded reluctantly.

The two of them crouched behind the outflung fronds of a large fern. As hard as he tried, Shepherd could see no sign of them.

"Remain hidden. Wait thirty minutes, no more. If I haven't returned get back to the Inn as fast as you can. Make sure you avoid the traps we set."

He checked the rifle was secure across his shoulder, tightened his grip on the machete and set off along the trail toward the voices.

CHAPTER 16

BENOIT TRAINED HIS weapon on the tallest of the newcomers. Behind him, his squadron had unslung their weapons and spread out across the trail. Two men protected the rear, while others aimed their weapons into the jungle on either side of the trail in case of ambush.

Who the hell were these men? They didn't look threatening. They were old, with silver hair and lined faces. They looked exhausted, as if they had traveled far and fast to reach this point.

None carried visible weapons. Each looked fearfully at his mercenary force bristling with sophisticated weaponry.

They had to be scientists from the Inn. The intel AWR had provided had shown there were no other people for thousands of miles. But why were they out here?

He shouted in English, "On your knees, hands in the air! Now!"

The tallest of the three, a man with piercing blue eyes, spoke. His voice was calm and controlled. "We carry no weapons. We are emissaries from the Inn. We know why you're here. We've come to negotiate with you."

"I said down! Now!" His finger tightened on the trigger.

Halle, standing beside him, grabbed his shoulder. "You can't shoot them. We need to question them. How do they know we're here?"

Benoit shrugged his hand away. "You're here to observe, not to interfere. Now let me do my job." He turned his back on Halle and marched toward the scientists. He forced them to their knees and roughly patted them down for weapons.

Two mercenaries advanced further along the trail,

weapons raised. They disappeared into the gloom, then returned. "Clear," they informed him. "No sign of anyone else."

The tallest newcomer looked up at him. "My name is John Alderton. As you can see, we're unarmed. We're also tired and sore after our trek to meet you. Our knees are aching. Allow us to stand. Then let me offer you a proposal, one you'll find very attractive."

Benoit motioned them to their feet. "How do you know about us?" He slung his rifle over his shoulder, listening as Alderton talked.

From the corner of his eye, he observed Halle slip away to the back of the squadron where he started tapping on his TIS. Benoit felt his rage swell.

CHAPTER 17

THE TRACK CONTINUED in front of Shepherd for about fifteen yards before curving left into the jungle. The voices couldn't be much more than another twenty yards beyond the bend.

He wanted to limit the distance he would need to travel in the undergrowth as much as possible, but he was wary of staying in the open for much longer. Every couple of yards, he stopped and crouched, watching the shadows on the path ahead, looking for movement.

Five yards from the curve in the trail, he decided he had pushed his luck far enough and plunged into the jungle.

Worried about getting lost, he decided to stay as close to the path as possible. He poked a hole through the hanging curtain of vegetation until he glimpsed the trail, oriented himself, then pulled back and pushed through the fringe of jungle.

It was slow going. The branches clawed at him, snagging on his clothing and the rifle slung over his shoulder. Several times he was forced to unhook himself from thorns jutting from hanging vines. Often he was forced to use his machete, sawing at the vines to free himself, trying not to make too much noise.

Every couple of minutes he stopped, probing the foliage until he saw the trail. At each stop, he listened to the voices growing nearer. With every step he looked for places to put his feet, worrying that he might trip or break branches that could signal his presence.

And always at the back of his mind was the uncomfortable thought of the rainforest's hidden dangers. He reasoned that he would hear the approach of a large predator, but he fretted about lurking spiders and snakes.

He got his bearings, took a step forward, wiping away a clump of dirt that was stuck to his collar—and froze.

He heard movement in the jungle behind him. The cracking of branches. What the hell was it? A mercenary? An animal?

He raised his machete. There was more crackling. He saw movement. His hand tightened on the machete as he readied to strike.

"What on earth are you doing?" Allie slid her way from under the hanging lianas, Ben close behind her.

Heart racing, he struggled to compose himself. "Keep your voice down! Why the hell are you here?"

"I didn't want to wait."

"Jesus, Allie."

"I may be able to help Alderton."

He sighed, realizing there was no point arguing with her. "Then stay close and for God's sake, don't make a sound."

With Ben directing him, he found they were able to move more quickly. After another ten minutes, he estimated they had almost covered the last twenty yards. The trail had to be close. The voices were louder and more distinct.

"That's Alderton," Allie whispered.

They slowed to a crawl, cautiously parting vines and branches, careful not to make much noise. The endless drone of insects and squawking of birds helped mask their movements. The path came into view.

Shepherd saw Alderton standing in the middle of the trail, Marlowe and Klaus alongside him. The three men were mud-stained and weary, but Alderton was standing at his full, imperious height. It was his resonant voice that

Shepherd had heard, and he was gesticulating at someone who was out of sight.

He squatted for a better view. Allie and Ben knelt beside him. Shepherd felt Allie strain against his flank, as if she wanted to join her mentor. He placed his hand on her forearm, holding her in place, and she stilled.

He watched intently. Whoever Alderton was talking to remained out of sight. He struggled to understand what he was saying over the screech of a bird. Allie, however, didn't seem to have the same problem. Her head was cocked to one side.

Despite himself, he was impressed by Alderton's confidence. He showed no fear, appeared calm and, judging by the smile on his face, was even enjoying himself.

"Alderton has control," Allie whispered.

Then there was the low rumble of another voice.

Alderton nodded in response, his smile broadening.

"My God, he's actually negotiating with them." She shifted restlessly. "I should be with him."

"Just wait." He kept his hand on her forearm.

There was more low-pitched rumbling from the unseen man. Shepherd craned for a better look, but the other man remained hidden behind the screening vegetation. He wondered what they were saying, wishing fervently he could shoot the damn bird trilling beside his ear. Alderton was conversing easily, his manner relaxed. He motioned with his hands, fingers raised as if counting. He shot an enquiring glance at Allie.

"He's talking about the Inn," she muttered. "I think he's describing it, how many of us there are. Maybe he's bargaining a price per head. I think this is going to work. Alderton seems to have captured their attention."

He frowned. He didn't like Alderton giving up information like that.

"I think he's about to make his opening bid. Watch."

The scientist appeared to announce something, stepping forward as he did so, radiating charisma and authority. He disappeared from view.

"Can you see them?" Allie asked.

He shook his head. Only Marlowe and Klaus remained visible. Klaus looked around and Shepherd glimpsed his keen blue eyes. He looked tired, but not scared. He seemed to have complete confidence in Alderton.

There was silence from the trail. Shepherd moved his head, trying to get a better view. What was going on? Was the other party considering the offer? He wished he could see Alderton. What was he doing? Could this actually be working?

Allie leaned across to whisper in his ear. "This is a good sign. It means the other party is tempted."

More voices, harsh and demanding. Then silence. Marlowe and Klaus tensed. Alderton said something, his voice louder, deeper. This time, there was no response.

Alderton stepped back into view, fear on his face.

Shepherd's hand went to his rifle.

Alderton raised his hands and shouted. Again there was no response, but as Shepherd watched, another figure stepped into view. The man was huge, easily six-five. He was wearing a combat suit made from a black material that glistened like the carapace of a scorpion.

Beneath a black helmet, the mercenary had a hard face with swarthy skin beaded with perspiration. The whites of his eyes were a smoky yellow, almost amber. His nose had once been badly broken.

Two other figures stepped into view behind him, similarly clad in sleek combat outfits.

Shepherd recognized the Giat FAMAS F1 5.56mm

assault rifle and the FN Herstal Minimi 5.56mm light machine gun carried by each mercenary. His stomach tightened in dismay; rather than the grunts with AK-47s he'd hoped for, he knew that what confronted them was a sophisticated combat force.

Another figure appeared, head down as if examining the trail. Unlike the other men, this one was a native wearing stained black football shorts and a t-shirt with the faded blue and yellow colors of the Brazilian soccer team. A tracker. Another similarly dressed figure stood beside him.

As these new figures pressed forward, Alderton, Marlowe and Klaus stepped back. Alderton said something, lowering his hands, his features composed once more. Shepherd was filled with admiration for his courage.

The towering mercenary with the yellow eyes barked something at the tracker, who scrambled away. Yellow Eyes stepped forward. Shepherd saw to his relief that the FAMAS assault rifle remained slung across his shoulder. He eased his grip on the Winchester. It felt obsolete and puny now.

The man's left arm swung up. In his large hand, he clutched a PAMAS G1 9mm semi-automatic pistol. Alderton shouted. The pistol fired and Marlowe dropped to the ground.

Allie gasped and Shepherd clamped his hand across her mouth.

Yellow Eyes stooped, placed his gun to Marlowe's forehead and pulled the trigger. He straightened.

"No!" Alderton shouted.

Klaus turned to run but the pistol fired again. Klaus fell. He lay on his side, facing Shepherd, death in his unmoving blue eyes. His hair was matted with blood, the bright red a vivid contrast to the gleaming silver.

Alderton backed away, his face stricken with terror. He

turned and ran along the trail and out of sight. Yellow Eyes barked an order and one of his men loped after Alderton. There were more gunshots.

As the last echoes of the gunshots faded, the jungle was quiet, as if shocked into silence. Yellow Eyes examined each corpse, stooping and studying their eyes, then feeling for a pulse. He straightened and his smoky eyes swept the surrounding vegetation.

Shepherd held Allie close to him, willing her not to make any noise. She remained silent, her body rigid. Ben was frozen in place beside them.

The mercenary's arm hung at his side, clutching the pistol. He said something. The tracker started traversing the immediate area, studying the trail. Looking for other tracks. Signs of anyone else in the area.

He pulled back. They had to leave. His arm was still around Allie.

But she remained rooted to the spot, her face pale. "Alderton," she whispered.

Ben was on his knees, staring through the gap, his eyes wide, his face drained of blood. His chest was heaving and Shepherd worried he was about to throw up. He seized his shoulder. "Control it," he hissed.

He chanced another look at the trail. The tracker had vanished, but Yellow Eyes stood next to Klaus's body, talking to someone. More figures stepped into view. Shepherd did the sums. With the two trackers, that made a team of seven. A formidable force, but not as bad as he had feared.

There was the sound of other voices, and more figures came into sight. Two. Then three. Soon, he had counted thirteen mercenaries. Streamlined and compact in their combat suits, they reminded him of a troupe of deadly black army ants. Yellow Eyes barked an order and they started to move, heading along the trail.

Time to go. They had to get back to the Inn. Fast. He shifted back, drawing Allie with him. For a moment she strained against him, as if wanting to help Alderton. Then she seemed to gather herself. She glanced once more at the bodies on the trail, then turned away quickly.

She bumped into him and as she stumbled back, her foot landed on a branch. It broke with a loud crack.

They froze.

Through a tiny gap in the vegetation, Shepherd saw Yellow Eyes take a step toward them.

He removed the rifle from across his shoulder but kept his finger resting on the trigger guard. He would only fire as a last resort. He might kill this mercenary, but the rest would be on them in seconds.

Yellow Eyes took another step and he shrank back, feeling vulnerable. He heard the air whistling through Yellow Eyes' shattered nose like the warning hiss of a rearing cobra.

Shepherd had known fear before, but he had been younger then and had processed it differently. Crouching there, hidden in the shadows, with limited means of protecting the people with him, he had never felt so afraid in all his life.

Yellow Eyes moved closer to the jungle. Another step and they would have to run. His mind raced. Could they lose them in the rainforest? Maybe with Ben's expertise they could.

With a crack of branches, a pair of brightly colored macaws burst from the canopy overhead, squawking loudly in protest at their presence. Leaves and twigs fluttered to the ground in their wake.

Yellow Eyes swiveled rapidly, tracking the possible threat with his PAMAS G1 before dismissing it. He spun back toward the jungle, listening as more birds screeched over-head. He turned away, walking toward his men.

Shepherd exhaled. With Ben leading, they edged deeper into the rainforest.

CHAPTER 18

THEY RETRACED THEIR steps until Shepherd felt they were far enough from the trail to stop. Allie slumped to her knees, her shoulders heaving in racking sobs. Ben doubled over and gulped, then scrambled behind a tree. Shepherd heard him vomiting.

"Allie?" He crouched beside her. She didn't respond. He placed his arm hesitantly across her shoulders. She collapsed against him and he held her tightly.

After a while, her sobs eased. "Oh, God. Oh, fucking hell. Alderton…" She drew a deep, shuddering breath. "They killed them. Jesus… they killed them."

Shepherd kept holding her. "I'm so sorry." He felt sick, his mind raging that he should have done more to stop Alderton.

He forced himself to focus. He had to think of the living, not the dead.

Allie coughed, then caught her breath. "What are we going to do?" Her voice was hoarse and her face filled with fear as she looked around. "Where are they?"

"They're back on the trail. We're safe here." *For now.* Those trackers worried him. He gave her a few seconds as she gathered herself.

The shaking of her body stilled and color returned to her face. The grief in her green eyes was replaced by a spark of anger. "Those murderous bastards." Her voice was still hoarse but full of steely determination. "We have to warn the others."

He could see why Alderton had chosen her as his next in charge. "Yes, we do. And fast."

He studied Ben, who looked like he was still in shock. "The mercenaries are ahead of us now. Is there another way back?"

"I don't know," he replied dully.

"Ben, we need to get to the Inn before them. You're the most qualified person to get us there."

"Sure," Ben muttered. "Yeah… sure. Um, there is… ah, I need to think, I'm not sure. Oh, shit. They're all dead." He swallowed, looking like he was about to vomit once more.

"Ben!" Shepherd's voice cracked like a bullwhip. "I need you with me. We're relying on you. I know you can do this."

He remained silent for several seconds before nodding. "Yeah. Yeah, maybe…" His eyes stared sightlessly at the jungle, before focusing upon Shepherd. "Okay. I've got it. There's another trail leading off from the main one. I remember we passed it not far back. Parker and I have used it before. It's much smaller and it winds more, but it loops back to the main trail just before the Inn. If we can get there before the mercenaries…"

"Good. Can you get us to it?"

He looked more confident now. "I think so."

"Then let's go."

CHAPTER 19

BENOIT STRODE IN front of the marching squadron. Halle joined him. "How do you feel?"

Benoit frowned. "What do you mean?"

"You always hated killing when we were in the Legion."

He made a dismissive gesture. "Shooting the old men was necessary. We have what we needed from them."

"It didn't seem to bother you the way it once would have."

"Don't overestimate my patience. I understand that you have to monitor my performance, but there are limits to my tolerance."

"I need to know."

"I did what I had to. Nothing more, nothing less. Now, enough!"

Halle must have realized the subject was closed and changed tack. "For Lacoux to have been captured, he must've made a mistake. Which means the intel he provided could have holes. It changes our mission spec."

He gave Halle an impatient glance. Halle held his glare. He was as tall as Benoit, with the same powerful build, and was one of the few men not intimidated by his presence.

"It doesn't change a thing." He motioned at Alderton, who was being hustled along by a pair of mercenaries behind them. The terrified old man had tried to escape after the death of his two colleagues, but warning shots directed near his feet had halted him.

During the subsequent interrogation, Benoit learned Lacoux had been captured, the scientists had discovered the mercenaries were coming, and that Alderton had come to negotiate.

"Alderton said Lacoux destroyed their satellite. The rest of their comms are down. They're isolated."

"They weren't meant to know about us. This gives them time to prepare."

Benoit gestured at the squad behind them. "This is the most sophisticated force assembled in military history. They are nothing more than scientists. You really think it matters they know we're coming?"

"They can run," Halle replied.

"Which is why we have the trackers. Nothing we've learned from the old man changes the operation."

He hastened his speed, enjoying the strength provided by his combat suit, which made light work of the heavy conditions along the trail. Halle was similarly clad, but couldn't match the power of Benoit's stride and soon fell behind.

He slowed, a broad smile on his face, delighting in his physical superiority over the younger man. "You've got slower since you left the Legion."

Halle gave him a wolfish grin. "No, you've got faster." He breathed heavily with the effort to pull alongside, then ahead. "Whatever Toussen did—" He broke off abruptly as the ground beneath him gave way.

His left leg disappeared into a black chasm. His arms windmilled as he twisted to escape, his right leg scrabbling at the edge of the hole that had materialized from nowhere. But the weight of his backpack worked against him and he toppled backward into the dark depths.

Benoit's arm shot out and his fingers curled around the strap across his shoulder. At the same time, he anchored his feet on firm ground inches from the hole, then braced.

But Halle was tall and heavily built, encumbered by the heavy pack. He fought to control a hundred and forty kilograms of mass plummeting toward the jagged stakes jutting like shark's teeth from the bottom of the pit.

Benoit grunted with the strain as he arrested Halle's fall. His feet skidded forward, then held. Halle's weight threatened to pull him over the edge, but he crouched, taking the strain with his thighs and the shoulder of his outstretched arm.

For a moment they were poised over the gaping maw. Then he thrust with his legs and hauled them backward, levering Halle out of the pit, onto safe ground.

"*Merde*!" Halle gasped.

"It's a trap." Benoit beckoned the trackers. "There could be more. Search the area." He strode back to the pit. It was large—six feet square and almost four deep. Benoit knelt, studying the six rough-hewn stakes that cleaved the air.

Halle joined him. "Fucking tiger trap." His gaze was fixed on the stakes that, even with his combat suit, could have impaled his exposed head, neck, hands and feet. He looked at Benoit. "Thanks."

Benoit pointed. "The tips are discolored. A paste of some sort." He glanced up at Halle. "Poison."

The trackers returned.

"Any sign of other traps?" He asked in English, the only language he shared with the Spanish-speaking trackers. They shook their heads. "Could a hunting party have made this? Native Indians?"

The trackers chattered excitedly amongst themselves before one spoke up. "No, señor. No one live here."

"It appears our scientists have teeth." He marched toward the squad of waiting mercenaries and Alderton, who cowered before his towering figure. "Someone in your facility has military training, old man."

"No!" Alderton gasped. "They're just scientists!"

He dragged the man to the pit. He grabbed his hair and shoved his face toward the stakes. Alderton struggled but Benoit held him easily. "Then who the fuck made this?"

Alderton screamed. "I don't know! For God's sake! None of us could have made…" His voice trailed away. "One of my people did say he'd been in the army. A Ranger. But years ago! He's now a doctor, not a soldier."

Benoit swung him away from the hole and directed the trackers along the trail. "Sweep the path." He gestured to his squad. "We move. Now!" He strode along the trail behind the trackers who had spread out and were poking large sticks into the leaf-strewn track to test the firmness of the ground.

Halle fell into step beside him. "Lacoux's intel didn't mention the soldier. And not just any soldier, but a Ranger."

"No." Benoit was furious at this unexpected development, then his anger subsided as quickly as it had flared. In its place was a confidence so absolute that it made him feel euphoric. "It won't change the outcome. The new intel just means we need to move faster than we planned, give them less time to prepare."

He lengthened his stride, leaving Halle behind as he urged his squad to increase their speed. His men responded, as formidable and deadly as the troupe of army ants they resembled.

CHAPTER 20

SHEPHERD THREW OPEN the door and led Allie and Ben into the rec room.

Ben had been true to his word, leading them unerringly along the alternate path back to the main access trail. Allie and Ben had then waited, hiding behind the stilt-like roots of a palm tree while he'd scouted ahead to ensure they had arrived before the mercenaries.

When he was satisfied, they had rushed to get to the Inn as fast as they could.

Once inside they halted, gasping to catch their breath, coated in sweat and mud.

Shepherd was conscious they had little time to prepare before the mercenaries arrived. He prayed that his traps had slowed them down and, even better, killed some. He was anxious to start preparing their defenses, but just like Allie and Ben, he was exhausted from their flight through the rainforest.

He allowed himself a few seconds to gasp for air, realizing with chagrin that once he would have been able to complete the same hike with a hundred pound pack on his back and barely shift his heart rate.

Everyone leaped to their feet and crowded around, pelting questions at them.

"Where's Alderton?"

"How did it go?"

"Well? What's going on?" said O'Connell. He took in their bedraggled appearance and the haunted expression on Ben's face. "Shit."

Ben answered, his voice hollow. "They're dead. Alderton,

Marlowe, Klaus. The mercenaries murdered them."

"Jesus fucking Christ," O'Connell growled. "What the hell happened?"

"Alderton was negotiating with them," said Allie. "I thought it was going well. Then one of the mercenaries, I think it was their leader, shot Marlowe. In the head. Then he killed Klaus. Alderton tried to run, but another mercenary shot him. There was no warning. It was an execution."

"Fuck."

"They're going to kill all of us! What are we going to do?" Parker said.

Shepherd placed the rifle on a table. "The mercenaries will be here within hours. I set some traps that should slow them down, but we need to prepare to defend ourselves."

There was a long silence as they all contemplated his words.

"Bullshit," said O'Connell. "We need to get the hell out of here."

"Where do we go?" Mancini asked.

"It doesn't matter. What matters is that we're not here when these bastards arrive."

"I know you're all scared," said Shepherd. "So am I. But running would be a mistake. They're expecting us to run. If we do, they'll hunt us down. Our best chance is to stay and fortify the Inn."

"It's a big jungle," O'Connell retorted. "What are the chances of them finding us?"

"They have native trackers who know the area. Out there, we'll be exposed and defenseless."

A hopeful tone crept into Mancini's voice. "If we give them the cure, maybe they'll leave us alone."

"They won't," Allie said. "I saw them. What they did to

Alderton. They weren't prepared to negotiate. They're going to wipe us out and take what they want."

"Can't anyone help us?" Mancini asked.

"I've been trying the sat-phone. It's useless," Parker said.

Mancini turned to Shepherd. "So what do you propose we do?"

"We turn the Inn into a fortress. We barricade ourselves in and defend. They won't expect that—they're expecting a bunch of scientists. They think we're an easy target. We hit them hard while we have the element of surprise."

"You're nuts." O'Connell's pale eyes were piercing as he looked around at the group. "We need to head somewhere they won't be able to find us. We take everything we have on the cure and get the hell out of here." His gaze settled on Parker. "You're the senior naturalist. Our best chance to survive in the jungle is to have you with us."

"I don't know," Parker said nervously. "It'll be dark in a few hours. We'd have to get off the trails to shake their trackers. And to do that at night, on the run... We could easily get lost."

"You can handle it. We're going. Are you with me, Mancini?"

Mancini remained silent, his dark eyes appraising Allie and Shepherd. Then he made up his mind. "Yes."

"This is a mistake." Shepherd knew that somehow he had to keep them together. "I know you're scared. It's natural to want to run. But it's too late now. If we'd had a day's notice, maybe we could've kept ahead of them. But not now. After encountering Alderton, they'll realize we know they're coming so they'll move fast. You won't be able to get far enough away and you'll be tracked down. Believe me, staying and defending is our best option. We can do this."

"Shepherd is right," said Allie.

"Why should we listen to him?" said O'Connell. "He's only been here a few weeks! And in case you've forgotten, he's no longer a soldier but a scientist, just like the rest of us."

Shepherd kept his exasperation in check. He had to convince this man to listen to him. "Toussen will have hired and armed local militia to keep the whole operation at arm's length for deniability purposes. These mercenaries will be accompanied by someone Toussen trusts to oversee the operation and take charge of recovering the formula for the cure when they have control of the Inn."

"That's a nice lecture but it doesn't change my mind."

"What I'm telling you is that although they outnumber us, as a former Ranger, I've had greater training and have far more military expertise. And I know we can hold them off if we stay and defend."

"So you say. But I for one aren't going to put my life in the hands of someone I hardly know."

"I saw how Shepherd prepared traps for the mercenaries," said Allie. "We should listen to him."

"Fine. You stay. We're leaving. What about you, Jan?"

Jan didn't hesitate. "I'm staying."

"You're a fool." O'Connell turned his attention back to Parker. "I need an answer!"

"Don't do this," said Allie.

O'Connell ignored her, waiting for Parker's response.

"Will you give me recognition for helping to find the cure?" Parker asked.

O'Connell's pale eyes gleamed with triumph. "If you keep us alive."

"I need to gather supplies and my work."

"We're leaving in thirty minutes, so move your ass. You

too," he added to Mancini. "Collect your work and as much food and water as you can carry."

Shepherd filled with impatience. "Listen to me! We need to work as a team to survive. If the mercenaries split us up, they weaken us. Don't give them what they want."

He surveyed them, his gaze lingering on O'Connell. "Yes, I'm new here. You hardly know me. But before I trained in medicine, I was a soldier. More than that, I'm a father. I have a little girl at home in New Jersey waiting for me. And I'm going to do everything in my power to get back to her. That means staying and fighting because it's our best option. Don't run. Stay and fight. We *will* beat them."

O'Connell folded his thick arms. "We've made our decision. You're welcome to stay here and die, but the rest of us are going."

"I think that's a mistake." Allie looked around at the group. "I want to get all of you out alive. To do that, I believe we all need to stay together."

"Alderton was the only one who supported your promotion. One you didn't deserve anyway. Now he's dead, I don't see any reason why we should continue to listen to you, especially when you show how poor your judgment is by trusting Shepherd when you hardly know him!"

Allie's voice was cold. "Now is not the time for pursuing your personal ambitions. This isn't a damned interview for Alderton's role! You need to think for the good of the group, not just worry about your own ass.

"And I put my trust in Shepherd because of the expertise he proved he had out there in the jungle. He displayed skills that none of us have and I believe him when he says we can defend the Inn. But I also think that our best chance is if we all stay. Help me keep everyone together."

"I'm not going to help you commit suicide! We're going." He led Parker and Mancini from the room.

"The stubborn bastard!" Shepherd snapped.

"I'll go after him. He needs to listen."

"There's not enough time. We need to act for ourselves now."

"So what do you want us to do?" Jan asked.

"We need to barricade ourselves in and gather whatever weapons and ammunition we have."

"The Inn has storm shutters we can put up," said Allie. "They're made from a titanium-based alloy. They're supposed to be able to withstand the worst the Amazon can throw at them."

"Perfect. What about weapons?"

"We only have the one rifle."

"Are you sure? The construction workers who built this place didn't leave any weapons behind?"

"There were complications with obtaining the necessary permits from the Brazilian government. And Alderton never saw the need."

"There's the tranquilizer gun we naturalists use to collect animal specimens," said Ben.

"Get it," Shepherd ordered. "Grab Mancini before he leaves and ask him to load it with something fast-acting and nasty. Hurry! Jannie, I want you to find as much ammunition for the rifle as you can. Allie, we need to get those shutters up."

CHAPTER 21

SHEPHERD GRUNTED WITH effort as he heaved the heavy shutter over the outside of the window. He held it steady while Allie tightened the screws to fasten it in place.

The storm shutter was constructed of louvers which, when closed, formed a solid metal sheet. He rapped it with his knuckles. The titanium steel gave a reassuringly solid thunk.

He surveyed their handiwork. They had secured the storm shutters over both the Inn's windows, giving the facility an abandoned feel; the shutters were put up at the end of each season.

He looked above the jungle canopy to the clouds building in a towering wall and rolling ominously toward them. Black and ugly, lit up by flashes of lightning, they hinted menacingly at the fury and power they contained.

Full of foreboding, he followed Allie back inside.

O'Connell stood beside a small pile of khaki backpacks on the floor of the rec room, berating Parker, who had a black backpack slung over his shoulder. "Why the hell aren't you ready?"

"I need a few more minutes. We don't have enough supplies to last out there. And I still need to get a first aid kit together. I thought Mancini was gathering more supplies!"

Mancini rushed into the rec room carrying a half-full backpack. "I was helping Ben load the tranquilizer darts with batrachotoxin. This is all I had time to put together."

O'Connell towered over Parker. "You've wasted enough time already. We're leaving in two minutes. So if you're coming with us, you'd better have your ass back here by then."

Parker scurried down the corridor, gripping his black backpack anxiously.

O'Connell rounded on Shepherd, who was examining the inside of the shutters. "What makes you think these mercenaries won't just blow the goddamn place up?"

"Because we have something they want. They won't know where the information for the cure is until they've secured the Inn. And for that they need Lacoux."

"Lacoux!" Allie exclaimed. "What are we going to do with him?"

"Nothing for the time being. He's secure enough where he is. I want to keep him out of the way until we need him."

"You think those little shutters are going to hold back armed mercenaries?" said O'Connell. "You're crazy."

"They'll hold. You'll be safer in here with us. Running is not the answer."

"Bullshit."

Shepherd turned to Mancini. "Do you really want to run? Don't let him bully you into something you don't want to do."

Mancini shifted nervously but didn't reply.

"You don't have to listen to him. You can stay here with us. The more of us the better."

"Leave him alone," said O'Connell. "Mancini is coming with me. He's not stupid enough to stay here and die. Are you, Mancini?"

The scientist cleared his throat nervously. "Are you sure leaving is the right thing to do? I mean, it does look like Shepherd knows what he's doing. Perhaps he's right."

"You really think they can defeat heavily armed merce- naries with tranquilizer darts and one rifle? If you stay here, you'll be killed like the rest of them."

Mancini groaned. "Christ! I don't want to die!"

"Then stay with us," said Shepherd.

"Running is the easy option, Mancini," said Allie. "But it's also the wrong one. If we stick together, we'll get through this. Don't allow O'Connell to split us up."

"Shut the hell up!" said O'Connell. "He's coming with me."

This is your decision, Mancini," said Shepherd. "Not his."

Mancini looked miserable. "I—I think I'm going."

"Good choice," said O'Connell, before turning back to Shepherd. "Keep out of our way."

"You're a damned fool." But he knew he had no more time to waste convincing O'Connell and Mancini to stay.

When Jan hurried in with boxes of ammunition, Shepherd directed him to organize them in two neat piles, one beneath each window, with the top boxes open. Ben arrived with the tranquilizer gun and darts, which Shepherd placed on the ground alongside the rifle and ammunition.

The three men then built barricades against the two entrances into the Inn—one in the rec room and another at the rear of the facility. They used tables, chairs and machinery ransacked from the scientists' laboratory and the supply room.

When they were finished, Shepherd turned his attention to the shutters. "Can those be opened from the inside?" he asked Allie.

"Sure. What are you planning?"

He popped out the mesh insect screen covering the nearest window and slid the dust-coated glass pane open, exposing the outside shutter. "How does this work?" He tapped his knuckles against a dull gray louver.

She seized a lever on the side of the shutter, forcing it upwards. The louvers parted and the clearing came into view.

He grabbed the rifle and sighted along the barrel, poking it through the metal slats. "Perfect." He placed the rifle on the floor beneath the window and motioned Jan to join him. "The mercenaries won't be far away now. Keep an eye on the access trail. Let me know the moment you see any movement."

Ben eyed the small pile of weapons and ammunition dubiously. "That isn't much."

"It'll have to do." Shepherd positioned himself beside one of the windows and made sure the boxes of ammunition were within reach. He practiced, crouching by the window with his rifle raised in one hand, reaching for the ammunition with the other. "Not fast enough. Jannie, when the time comes, I'm going to need you to hand the bullets to me."

"Of course."

"What are you doing?" Ben asked.

"This is a Winchester bolt action rifle. Its downside is that it holds only four rounds. That means I'll have to reload regularly, which puts us at a disadvantage against the machine guns carried by the mercenaries. But don't worry." He patted the Winchester affectionately. "What this baby lacks in efficiency, it more than makes up for in accuracy and reliability. This is a weapon I trust."

He broke it down and hurriedly cleaned and loaded it.

O'Connell's pale eyes narrowed with derision. "You think you're going to hold the mercenaries off with that old piece of junk?"

"It'll do the job."

O'Connell snorted. "Good luck. You'll be lucky it doesn't blow up in your face. Jesus, Allie. Can't you see what a fool you're being? Why don't the rest of you come with us? If Shepherd wants to stay here and die, let him!"

"We're staying," Allie said.

Parker sprinted in with a bulging backpack.

"Finally!" O'Connell glared. "What's taken you so long? Have you got everything we need?"

"Yes."

"Then we're leaving." O'Connell seized the door handle.

"Wait! Listen to me," said Allie. "Look at how organized our defenses are. Can't you see that Shepherd knows what he's doing? Together we can get through this. Out in the rainforest, you'll be on your own. Defenseless. You might be able to hide for a while, but eventually, they'll hunt you down. That's if the creatures out there don't get you first. I'm terrified, but I know this is our best option. Stay with us."

O'Connell hesitated.

"I see something!" Jan's smooth features were tense as he peered through the window. "There's movement in the rainforest. In the shadows." He frowned, his cerulean eyes squinting. They widened and he stepped away from the window. "Oh my God."

Shepherd ran to his side, everyone crowding behind him.

At the head of the main access trail, several black-clad men had appeared. Like ants spilling from a nest, they flowed from the rainforest's depths and spread around the perimeter of the clearing.

O'Connell turned to Parker, his expression bitter. "You took too long, you stupid bastard! You've killed us all."

CHAPTER 22

"WE HAVE TO get out of here!" Mancini cried, darting toward the door.

Parker seized his arm. "Not that way. Through the labs!"

The only other entrance to the Inn was at its rear, on the other side of the laboratories, where a door led to the supply hut and the clearing beyond.

"Come on!" Mancini urged O'Connell.

But O'Connell didn't move. He stood grim-faced, staring outside. "We'll never make it across the clearing."

"But we can't stay here!"

"Jesus fucking Christ," O'Connell said.

Shepherd crouched beside the window.

"What do you want us to do?" Allie asked.

"I want you to look after them." He gestured toward the panicking Mancini and Parker. "Keep them calm. I want everyone at the back of the rec room away from the windows. Jannie, I need you to stay and pass me ammunition."

"I'll help," Ben said.

"Both of you keep down. That goes for all of you," Shepherd shouted. "They may have snipers."

"Shit," O'Connell muttered and knelt with Allie, Mancini and Parker behind the solid bulk of the bar.

An eerie silence fell over the Inn. The rainforest was quiet, disturbed by the new intruders. Shepherd could hear nothing from outside.

A sense of foreboding settled over him like an icy shroud. He hunched before the window, his broad frame tense as he stared outside.

He held his rifle below the window line, out of sight of

the binoculars he knew would be trained on them. Jan and Ben squatted beside the other window, Jan's hands poised over the ammunition boxes as he waited for his command. The .300 Winchester Magnum bullets gleamed under the Inn's halogen lights.

Ben held the tranquilizer gun, checked where to place his finger on the trigger, then threw it to his shoulder and practiced his aim. As Shepherd glanced across to make sure both men were staying low, he noticed Ben's hands were shaking.

Beyond the window, a narrow porch gave way to a set of stairs down to the wooden boardwalk which traversed nearly two hundred yards of muddy, grassy terrain before ending at the main access trail.

At the trailhead, several figures were crouched in the shadows. They had removed their packs, protecting them from the mud and rain by placing them in a neat pile on a stack of branches under a palmitto tree. Their weapons were trained on the Inn. Other figures hastened around the perimeter in either direction.

Allie scooted out from behind the bar and crouched low beside him. He felt a flare of exasperation. "I thought you were keeping an eye on the others."

"They're too scared to move. I want to know what's going on."

"Then stay down!"

"What are they doing?" she asked.

"Circling us in case we run."

He watched the figures disappear from view. The movement through the jungle stilled. The mercenaries at the trailhead remained in the shadows.

"What are they waiting for?"

"The traps we set alerted them that someone here has military training."

As he scanned the jungle in either direction his attention was caught by movement at the trailhead. A force of five mercenaries emerged from the jungle and advanced beside the boardwalk toward the Inn. They moved steadily through the late afternoon shadows, halting every ten yards, scanning the building before advancing again.

They had removed their packs and aimed their guns at the facility. Their weapons looked sleek, sophisticated and deadly, especially compared with the older, more cumbersome Winchester he held. The mercenaries were wearing black helmets. With dark visors pulled down, obscuring their faces, they didn't look human.

Shepherd released the safety on the Winchester. His jaw clenched and he felt perspiration beading his brow.

"Why aren't they firing?" Allie asked.

"This is just an advance force to probe our defenses, ascertain our strengths and weaknesses. Lacoux will have provided them with intelligence on us. They know the Inn is manned only by scientists, with no security detail for protection. They'll be aware we have the rifle but believe we have no expertise in using it. Their mission spec will state we're an easy target.

"But this is a confident move. I thought they'd observe us for a while after encountering our traps." His voice rose to address all of them. "They'll have snipers trained on us to provide cover for this advance party. As soon as I fire they'll respond, so keep your heads down!"

The mercenaries were halfway across the clearing now, moving fast. Their black combat suits glistened. Shepherd was grateful they weren't wearing heavy, bulky combat armor that would have forced him to aim for the far more difficult target of their heads.

In one fluid motion, he swept the rifle up to his shoulder. He directed it through the shutter and fired. The round thundered into an attacker's chest, punching him backward into the mud. The rest of the mercenaries threw themselves to the ground.

Shepherd worked the rifle bolt smoothly, ejecting the cartridge and chambering a new round, then fired once more. He had time to see his shot smash into the flank of a prone figure before the rest returned fire.

He jerked the shutter closed and sprawled beside Allie, reloading the rifle. There was a staccato cracking from outside, then bullets hammered against the heavy, wooden walls of the Inn. Allie flattened herself against the floor, gripping her head in her hands. Bullets clanged against the titanium shields before ricocheting away with high-pitched whines.

The explosion of sound seemed to last an eternity before there was a lull.

He rolled to the other window, knelt and opened the shutter. The mercenaries were sprinting toward the Inn, leaving two men behind on the ground.

He prepared to fire once more when his attention was caught by movement behind them. The fallen men stirred in the mud. They rose to their feet and ran to rejoin the main body of rapidly approaching mercenaries. Clumps of dirt and mud cascaded from their torsos. Their combat suits remained smooth and unblemished, with no sign of having been struck by the heavy caliber bullets.

Shepherd watched in disbelief. He'd shot them. Without heavy combat armor, the .300 Magnum bullets should have exploded through their bodies. He studied their gleaming black combat suits, trying to understand what the hell was going on.

A bullet smashed into the wall beside the window. He slammed the shutter and ducked away. The titanium louvers rang as more bullets struck them before ricocheting away. Sniper fire.

When a lull came, he cracked open the shutter, jerked the rifle through the window, took careful aim and fired. A mercenary's visor exploded. Blood and gray matter erupted through the back of his helmet. The man dropped, his body quivering on the ground. Shepherd slammed the shutter closed and threw himself to the floor.

"More bullets!" he yelled to Jan over the cacophony of retaliatory fire. This time, the explosion of gunfire was more sustained. A bullet plowed into the wall beside his head. He heard the earsplitting crack and felt the thud, but the wall remained intact. He sent a silent prayer of thanks to the Inn's builders.

Jan hurriedly tossed him a loose handful of bullets. Shepherd cursed as he juggled to control them. "Hand them to me, damn it! Don't throw them," he shouted as he quickly reloaded.

There was another lull and he rolled back toward Allie, his heavy knee thudding into her ribs. He opened the shutter and fired. This time he fired and reloaded several times before ducking once more and stuffing his pockets with loose ammunition handed to him by Jan.

More bullets slammed against the Inn. He waited several seconds, then scrambled to his knees. His rifle spat four times. There was the sharp crack of returning gunfire. He swayed back behind the wall before darting forward and shooting.

He kept firing and reloading, his hands a blur as he snatched cartridges from his pockets and snapped them into the magazine. He fired half a dozen shots then ducked away.

Sniper bullets cannoned against the louvers. Shepherd counted two shots. He waited, but the gunfire outside stopped. He waited a minute longer, then cautiously glanced outside. The mercenaries' advance had halted. He watched them disappear from the clearing, leaving two men strewn in the mud.

His tension eased for the moment. His face was covered in sweat. It rolled from his chin, dripping to the floor. His hand gripping the rifle trembled.

Allie cautiously raised her chin. "What's happening?"

Shepherd's throat was dry. His voice grated. "It's over. They're retreating."

CHAPTER 23

BENOIT ORDERED HIS men to retreat and watched the three surviving mercenaries withdraw from the clearing into the shelter of the jungle. They were followed by sharp cracks of gunfire.

He counted six in succession—heavy caliber, judging by the explosive reports and the splatter of blood around the skulls of the two dead men. They had underestimated their target.

A bullet smashed into a log beside him, causing an eruption of splinters. The men took cover behind trees. Only Benoit remained on his feet. He snatched the Giat FR-F2 7.62 mm sniper rifle from beside the prostrate figure of Alain Roche, their sniper, who had his head in the dirt.

He strode to the edge of the jungle. A gunshot spat into the mud beside him. He took aim and fired twice. The bullets clanged into the metal shutters. There was no return fire.

Benoit held his stance for a moment, staring at the pockmarked wall of the Inn. Then he lowered the FR-F2, spun on his heel and strode toward Alderton, who was lying on the ground, sheltering his head with trembling hands.

Benoit's rage threatened to consume him. His clenched jaw ached. Air hissed through his broken nose. Alderton looked up with terrified eyes as he loomed over him.

He seized him by the arm and swung him against a tree. Alderton groaned with fear, eyes wide and fixed on Benoit, who pinned him easily with one large hand.

He studied the man before him, taking perverse pleasure in the fear he saw on the helpless scientist's face. "You didn't tell us the soldier is an expert marksman," Benoit hissed in

English, his hand sliding from Alderton's arm to his throat.

Alderton gargled.

"Two of my men are dead." Benoit's hand tightened.

Alderton's face turned red and his eyes bulged. Benoit held him up against the tree for several seconds, then released him. Alderton slumped to the ground on his knees, hands pressed to his throat, gasping for air.

Benoit withdrew his PAMAS G1 and held it to the man's forehead.

"Don't kill me!"

"How many weapons does the soldier have? What else haven't you told us?" His voice rose to a shout.

"We only have one rifle!"

Benoit held the PAMAS G1 in place. "If any more of my men die, I'll kill you."

"We're just scientists. Let us give you what you want. Then leave us alone."

Benoit lowered the pistol. "Tell me more about the people in your facility. I want to know their backgrounds. Who else can handle a rifle?"

Alderton swallowed, but all that came out of his mouth was a dry croak.

"All I want is the formula for the cure," Benoit said. "I'll let you all live if you don't get in our way."

"You murdered my friends. How can I trust you?"

"Killing them was a mistake. We weren't expecting a welcome party. For all I knew, we were walking into an ambush." Benoit slipped his pistol into a pouch on the flank of his combat suit. "I know of your reputation. Toussen wants you alive because, I'm told, you're such an important scientist—one who could help them."

A gleam of defiance replaced the fear in Alderton's eyes.

"I will never help them."

Benoit smiled in amusement. "Then perhaps you can tell them that yourself. Now," his voice hardened once more. "Tell me everything you know about your people. Do they have other weapons?"

The man's fearful expression returned and he provided the detail Benoit wanted.

When he'd finished, he saw the pitying glances cast the old man's way by the mercenaries. His men knew he had lied to Alderton; no one could be left alive at the facility. There could be no witnesses to what was to occur.

The scientist had served his purpose now. There was nothing further to be gained from keeping him alive. They all expected him to kill the prisoner. Instead, he walked away.

He had other plans for Alderton.

CHAPTER 24

"IS ANYONE HURT?" Shepherd's heart was still pounding and his legs felt rubbery with adrenalin. With the attack over for the time being, he allowed himself to relax.

O'Connell, Parker and Mancini emerged from behind the bar.

"We're okay," O'Connell said. "What the hell is happening?"

"The mercenaries have retreated."

"They've gone?" Parker said. "It's over? Oh, thank God."

"It's not over. Do we have any water, Allie?"

She ran over to the packs still piled in the middle of the floor, pulled out a bottle and threw it to him. She then slid the packs across to the wall and out of the way. He drained half the bottle and splashed the rest over his face and neck. "Keep watch, Jannie."

"You don't think they've gone?" Allie said.

"No. They're reassessing now they've discovered someone here can use the rifle."

"So they'll attack again?"

"They know we aren't going anywhere. They'll take stock and be more cautious. They don't need to risk anyone else in a frontal attack." His mind returned to the image of the two mercenaries getting to their feet despite having been shot. He sifted through the possibilities, troubled by the realization that they were technologically more advanced than he'd thought.

"What is it?" she asked.

He told her what had happened. "I know I shot them, Allie."

143

"Then how could they get back up?"

"It has to be an advanced form of body armor. Nano-tech, maybe. Stuff I thought was still theoretical. Who the hell are these guys?"

"There's something you need to see." Jan pointed out an alarming number of empty ammunition boxes. "I was checking our supply. It looks like some of the boxes had already been opened. Not all of them were full. There's less ammunition than we thought."

"Shit," Allie said in dismay.

"We still have the tranquilizer darts," Ben said, getting to his feet.

"Keep down!" Shepherd hauled him roughly away from the window. "If they see a shot, they'll take it."

"I'm just trying to help!"

"I know. But you need to listen, okay?"

"Sure," Ben gave him a quick, nervous smile.

"What about the ammunition?" said Allie.

"Could there be more in the storage room?" Ben asked.

"I checked earlier," Jan said. "There's no more."

"We'll make do. I want everyone to stay calm."

He returned to his position beside the window and looked across the clearing to the trailhead, where he saw movement in the lengthening shadows. It would be night soon. They had maybe two hours of daylight left.

Allie joined him. "What will they do now?"

Before he could respond, there was a shout from the jungle. A man's voice. Deep and heavily accented, it sounded harsh and cold. "We want only the cure. If you come out now, you will be left unharmed."

The rec room was quiet as everyone absorbed what they'd heard. Finally, Parker broke the silence. "We should do as he says. It's our only chance."

"Stay where you are!" Shepherd commanded.

"I think we should go out there," O'Connell said. "You held them off. Perhaps it's made them believe this could be harder than they first thought. They could be prepared to negotiate now."

"It's a ruse. If we leave they'll kill us."

"You don't know that!" Parker said.

"There's no way we can hold them off again. We have to go!" said Mancini.

"Just wait!"

There was another shout from the jungle. "It seems I need to motivate you."

The others crowded behind Shepherd and Allie at the window. There was movement within the shadows at the trailhead. Then a figure was dragged several yards into the clearing by two mercenaries and forced to his knees, facing the Inn. The silvery gleam of his disheveled hair was unmistakable. Alderton.

Allie gasped. "Oh, my God!"

The two mercenaries left the scientist and retreated to the edge of the clearing, where they knelt, leveling their weapons at him. An execution squad.

There was another shout. "You have ten minutes. If you have not given yourselves up in that time, your scientist will be killed. This is your only chance to save his life and your own. After that, there will be no mercy. You will all be killed."

CHAPTER 25

"I THOUGHT YOU said Alderton had been shot!" O'Connell snapped.

"I thought he had been." Allie gazed at the kneeling figure. Even at this distance, the terror on his face was apparent, the tension written in his posture as he braced for a bullet between the shoulder blades.

"We have to surrender," Mancini said. "We can't let them kill him."

"We saw them murder Klaus and Marlowe," Ben said. "What makes you think they won't kill the rest of us?"

"Shut the hell up," O'Connell said. "We don't need your opinion." He shifted his focus to Shepherd. "Do you have a plan?"

Shepherd stepped away from the window, hands clasped behind his neck. "I need to think."

"We can't let Alderton die," said Allie. "I was prepared to stay and fight, but now, with Alderton out there… it changes things. I think we need to hand ourselves over to them. They kept Alderton alive. Maybe they'll let all of us live."

Shepherd was scarcely able to believe that Alderton was still alive. He'd heard the gunshots and been convinced that he had been executed like Marlowe and Klaus. He hadn't anticipated they'd kept a hostage.

He forced his rattled mind to work, thinking through their options. They could stay and continue to defend. They could hand themselves over to the mercenaries and let them take control of the Inn. Or they could use the cure to try to negotiate their, and Alderton's, release. But the more he thought it through, the more convinced he was that only one course of action was truly available to them.

He turned and faced the group. "Lacoux told us the mercenaries are here to wipe us out. I believe if we give ourselves up or try to negotiate, they'll murder Alderton anyway, then the rest of us. We should continue to hold our ground and defend."

"What about Alderton?" Allie snapped. "Are you saying we leave him out there to die? I can't do that!"

"I know this is hard. But we have to think of everybody, not just one individual."

"I want to get everyone home," Allie said. "That includes Alderton!"

"Trying to negotiate was his own stupid decision," O'Connell declared. "He has to live—or die—with the consequences. We need to think of ourselves now."

"Alderton was acting on our behalf. We can't abandon him!"

"Alderton was your mentor, Allie. He treated you like his daughter." O'Connell's pale eyes swept across the rest of the group. "Allie is too emotionally involved to make this decision on our behalf."

"That's ridiculous," Jan said.

"So what do you think we should do?" Mancini asked uneasily.

Shepherd spoke before O'Connell could reply. "Right now, we need to think this through."

"You're the one who backed us into this goddamn corner in the first place," said O'Connell. "If we'd run when I wanted to, we wouldn't be in this fucking mess! With Alderton as good as dead and Allie hopelessly compromised, I am effectively the leader now."

"I didn't see you volunteering to stand up as leader while the mercenaries were shooting at us," said Jan. "You were too busy cowering behind the bar."

"I didn't have the rifle! What was I meant to do? I believe Shepherd and Allie have made poor decisions ever since we knew the mercenaries were coming. We should never have stayed. We should've got the hell out of here like I wanted to. Now it's time for me to fix this goddamned mess."

"You're an idiot!" said Allie.

"And you're weak," he replied. "Leaders need to make tough decisions. You clearly are incapable of doing that."

"That's enough! All of you!" snapped Shepherd. "Using Alderton like this is a deliberate tactic to weaken our resolve and it's working. We held them off once, we can do so again. But we need to stay calm and work together."

"Don't you dare tell me we're not going to try to save Alderton," Allie said.

Shepherd hated what he was about to say, but knew he had to say it. "Allie, for once I agree with O'Connell. You're too emotionally involved. Alderton's your mentor and I know you want to save him, but it can't come at the cost of everyone else."

"You bastard! I supported your decision to stay. I put my faith in you and now you say you're not going to help Alderton? You're going to abandon him? I can't accept that! I want to get everyone out alive. So unless you can come up with another option, we'd better start preparing to negotiate with them. They want the cure. I'll go out there with a sample and negotiate our release."

"I know how difficult this is to accept. But you won't save Alderton by going outside. All you'll be doing is giving them another hostage."

"Then you'd better come up with another plan because I'm going out there."

O'Connell glanced at his watch. "This is bullshit. We've wasted five minutes. We need to make a decision."

"What do you suggest?" Mancini asked.

"Someone goes out to negotiate. If Allie wants to do it, let her."

Jan scoffed. "That sounds like a terrible idea!"

"They'll kill her," said Ben. "They're not going to negotiate. We should stay here."

"We're almost out of time. Allie has to go. Now," said O'Connell.

"The first time you agree with her is when you want to save your own ass!" said Jan. "Allie, don't do this. If O'Connell wants to negotiate, let *him* do it!"

"No. We need to act now."

Shepherd saw her mind was made up. He cursed her stubbornness, while another part of him admired her courage. His mind churned. There *had* to be an alternative. How could he convince her to stay?

The glimmer of an idea came to him. "Wait. There's another option. We use our own hostage, Lacoux. He's valuable to Toussen—they'll need him to re-engineer the cure, especially with Jouvet dead. The mercenaries will have been instructed to keep him alive. We can use that."

"How?" O'Connell said.

"We do a trade. Lacoux for Alderton. And tell them that once we have him, we'll consider giving ourselves up in return for our safe release."

"You said they wouldn't give us that!" O'Connell said sharply.

"They won't. But it will give us time to prepare for the next attack."

"Well, I think we should negotiate," said O'Connell. "If

we use Lacoux as well as the cure, we have more bargaining power. We trade Lacoux and the cure for our release. Remaining here and defending is our worst option; eventually, they'll overrun us."

"They won't let you leave," Shepherd said. "Allie, using Lacoux is our only chance to save Alderton."

She considered for a long moment, then nodded. "Okay. Let's do it."

*   *   *

SHEPHERD BROUGHT LACOUX from the meeting room, the muzzle of his rifle caressing the small of the prisoner's back. He pushed him to the middle of the rec room. "I need someone to take the rifle and watch him."

Nobody responded.

Finally, O'Connell stepped forward with a snort of derision. "Wimps. Give me that." He aimed the firearm at Lacoux's chest, the rifle steady in his arms. His eyes drilled the man as if challenging him to run.

Shepherd opened a shutter, cautiously standing to one side of it, and shouted. "We want to do a trade! Lacoux for Alderton." He saw the flare of hope in the old man's eyes and prayed this would work.

There was no movement in the shadows beyond the kneeling figure. "Do you hear me?" he bellowed. "A trade! You need Lacoux. We want Alderton. When we have him back safely, we'll regard that as a sign you'll keep your word and won't harm us. We'll consider giving ourselves up." He waited, his tension growing with each passing second. If this didn't work, he saw no way to save Alderton. *Come on,* he thought. *Take the bait.* But the rainforest remained still.

Then a large figure stepped into the clearing, his weapon

trained on the Inn. The visor on his black helmet was up. Shepherd saw the broken nose and strange eyes. Yellow Eyes. Shepherd guessed this was the mercenary leader, Benoit.

"I need to see Lacoux is alive."

Shepherd seized the rifle from O'Connell and shoved Lacoux toward the door. Jan and O'Connell shifted the barricade enough for them to access it.

Standing against the wall, he stretched out his arm, jerked the door open and prodded Lacoux into the open doorway. "You run and I'll shoot you."

"Fuck you." Lacoux remained motionless, several feet inside the facility, but clearly visible from outside.

There was a pause so long that Shepherd started to wonder what was happening.

"I want proof he is not wired to explode."

"There's no trap," Shepherd bellowed.

"Prove it. You have shown too much military training for my liking. Show yourself. Address me like a man. Do not cower in there like a dog."

"I'll decline." He untied Lacoux's hands. "I'll shoot you before you can get ten yards across that clearing. Strip!"

Lacoux began unbuttoning his cotton shirt slowly.

Shepherd strode back to the window and stared through the louvers, wondering why the mercenary leader just stood there. A show of contempt or something else?

His instincts started to gnaw at him. He looked at the two men kneeling with their weapons trained on Alderton. Where were the others?

He looked for movement in the deepening gloom but could see nothing. He looked back at Benoit and realized he was no longer studying Lacoux for any signs of explosives.

His mouth was moving as if he was talking to someone.

Movement in the clearing caught his eye. He turned his attention to Alderton, realizing he was no longer watching the Inn either. He was looking at Benoit, his head cocked slightly as if listening. He looked at the Inn and jerked his head repeatedly in the direction of the jungle behind the facility.

Shepherd thought of the mercenaries he'd seen surrounding the Inn earlier to cut off any escape. "Damn it!" He'd been outwitted.

Silently thanking Alderton, he scrambled away from the window and shoved the rifle back into the hands of O'Connell. "Shoot Lacoux if he runs!" Then he grabbed Mancini and bolted toward the corridor. "Jannie, I need your help. Right now!"

"What are you doing?" Allie shouted.

Shepherd didn't respond as he sprinted toward the bio lab.

CHAPTER 26

MANCINI EMERGED FROM the bio lab wearing a hazmat suit and clutching a metal canister in each hand. The blue suit looked bulky and uncomfortable, with the scientist constantly jerking his head to keep the hood and visor centered.

He hurried to Shepherd who was hovering just outside the bio lab hatch with Jan. Shepherd seized the canisters and turned them over in his hands. They were slim and made from gray titanium, with fluorescent red biohazard warning labels on each.

Allie rushed into the scientists' lab and ran up to him. "What's going on? Why did you leave Alderton out there?"

"I don't have time to explain." He studied the canisters. "What are these?"

Mancini pulled off his helmet. "Be careful! They're aerosols, full of batrachotoxin from the poison dart frog. Point and depress the lever and the toxin is released as a fine spray."

"Won't they be just as dangerous to the user?"

"Make sure they're pointed the right way." Mancini laughed nervously. "They have a range of several feet. If you wear gloves and a mask, you should be fine."

"Should?"

Mancini shrugged. "Best I could do."

Jan sniffed. "Which is not saying much."

"Don't you start."

"Enough!" Shepherd snapped. "I need you both to stop griping at each other." He turned to Mancini. "In this form, how long will it take for the batrachotoxin to take effect?"

Mancini glowered at Jan. "Anyone you spray will be dead

153

in seconds. Just make sure they don't vomit or cough on you. Any bodily fluids will have enough toxin to kill you as well."

"I'll try to keep that in mind. I want a backup plan."

"Like what?"

"Surprise me."

"I guess I can put what's left of the batrachotoxin I gave Ben into syringes. Will that do?"

"That'll do fine."

Mancini pulled the hood back over his head and re-entered the bio lab.

"What are you planning?" Allie said.

"I said I don't have time to explain!"

Her green eyes flashed with anger. Stepping in close to Shepherd, she hissed, "Tell me why you just abandoned us in there."

He struggled to compose himself. "Look, what you saw was a ruse. Benoit was playing us. I think his men are going to attack from the rear of the Inn, believing us vulnerable while our attention is focused on Alderton."

"Oh, Christ." The anger in her eyes was replaced with fear.

"If it hadn't been for Alderton, they would've had us. Now we have a chance. But we have to act fast. I need an explanation of how the emergency containment system works. Quickly, Allie!"

"Do you know anything about it?"

"I got a short induction briefing when I arrived, but nothing detailed."

"The emergency containment system is designed to ensure none of our pathogens can escape. The Inn's been constructed around an inner sanctum that can be sealed off to prevent anything getting in or out. That inner sanctum consists of the scientists' laboratory, and an inner core, the bio lab, where all the really dangerous pathogens are handled.

"In an emergency, airtight doors are automatically sealed shut, separating the sanctum from the rest of the facility. Within the sanctum itself, the bio lab is also sealed from the scientists' lab by its airtight hatch."

"Can the emergency containment be manually triggered?"

"There are manual override levers on the walls beside the airtight hatches that separate the rest of the Inn from the scientists' lab."

"And once triggered, how is it stopped?"

"There's a keypad outside each of the two entrances to the scientists' lab and one outside the bio lab. Entering an eight-digit code will end the emergency lockdown, or start it if it's not already commenced. Only Alderton and I have the code."

"Can you give Jan the code?"

"Yes, but why?"

He ignored her question. "There are only two entrances to the Inn? There's no other way the mercs can get in?"

"The only entrances are the one in the rec room and one on the other side of this laboratory."

The hatch behind them opened with the hiss of escaping air and Mancini reappeared, holding two small syringes with rubber stoppers on the end of each needle. He placed them in a slim metal canister which he handed to Shepherd. "This is a titanium container and will prevent the syringes from breaking. Don't remove them until you need them. And make sure you don't jab yourself, for God's sake. You'll be dead in seconds."

"Keep everyone in the rec room, Allie," said Shepherd.

"Leave Lacoux where he is for the time being. I don't want Benoit to think we're onto his game."

"But if he does, won't he call off his surprise attack?"

"Maybe, but that's not what I want."

"Why?"

"We're low on ammunition. We need to do something. We use Benoit's tactics against him."

"This isn't a good idea," Jan said uneasily.

"We have an opportunity. We need to use it."

"What about Alderton?" Allie asked. "We can't leave him out there!"

"I'll let Benoit think we've taken his men hostage, and use them and Lacoux to get Alderton back safely."

"Jesus," Allie breathed. "So what's your plan?"

"There isn't enough time to explain all of it."

Before she could protest, he added, "Just trust me. Please. What you need to know is that I'm going to trigger the emergency containment system which will seal you from this sector of the Inn. Keep a radio with you. I'll contact you. If I use the word Geronimo, it's safe to open the door. Okay?"

"Got it." She wrote the override code on a scrap of paper and handed it to Jan.

Shepherd eyed him with trepidation. "I'll understand if you say no, Jannie. Are you still with me?"

"At your side."

He grabbed a long, delicate test tube from a bench, stuffing it into his pocket, along with a pair of gloves and a face mask. "Then let's go!"

CHAPTER 27

"WHAT DO YOU want me to do?" Jan asked. They were in a corridor which ran thirty feet from the scientists' lab to a brown wooden door at the far end, which was now protected by a crude barricade of storage cabinets and heavy scientific equipment. The white walls and ceiling of the corridor glowed nakedly under the halogen lights.

There were three rooms on the left side of the corridor. The first, approximately five feet from the lab entrance, was a supply room containing spare test tubes, specimen jars, microscopes and an array of other scientific equipment.

The second, halfway along, contained the generators that powered the Inn. The third, six feet from the wooden door, was a storage room for broken instruments, hiking equipment, rain gear and anything the scientists didn't want to leave lying about in the laboratory or their rooms.

Shepherd surveyed the corridor, ceiling and floor, wanting to know every possible strength and weakness, but conscious they were almost out of time. "We have to hurry, Jan. What's above and below us? Quickly!"

A tiny furrow blemished his brow. "The Inn's roof is separated into sections. The section directly above the scientists' lab and the bio lab contains the air-conditioning systems and HEPA filters. It's sealed to make sure escaped pathogens can't penetrate the rest of the facility. The sections on either side are empty."

"Is it possible to move between the sections?"

"I don't think so. Heavy barriers are in place between them to prevent insects and animals getting into the systems and filters. The roof covering these sections is reinforced

157

steel to keep the worst of the weather out. The same goes for the ceiling directly above us."

"Okay. And below?"

"I'm not an engineer!" The furrow creasing his brow deepened. "The Inn was built on a concrete base. Something about the rainforest floor shifting with all the floods. They needed a solid platform for the structure so it wouldn't crack."

"What about the drainage system?"

"It sits directly below the laboratories and the bio lab and is used for liquid waste decontamination. There's a series of pipes leading to a twenty-thousand-gallon containment tank, which in turn is connected to a heat decontamination tank. It's how the Inn's liquid discharge is treated before being flushed into the sewer system."

Shepherd frowned. "Sewer system? Where does that lead to?"

"To a sewage tank, which gets picked up at the end of every season."

"Is there any way they could use it to get inside the Inn?"

"I don't think so. The hatch to the drainage pipes can only be opened from inside the lab."

Shepherd ran to the end of the corridor and with Jan's help, hastily removed the barricade. He then made sure the door was unlocked. Outside, a short path led to the supply hut. Then there was nothing but clearing until the jungle.

He rushed the thirty feet back to the entrance to the scientists' laboratory, swung open the metal door and stepped inside for a few seconds. He stepped back into the corridor and examined the keypad on the wall, just outside the door.

Jan watched him, his eyes full of trepidation. "What are you intending to do?"

Shepherd outlined his plan as fast as he could.

"This sounds dangerous. I'm scared for you, my friend." Jan gripped his shoulders. "Please don't do anything too foolish in there."

"I'll be fine, Jannie." But he found himself struggling with his fear. He'd been scared in combat before, but the faith he'd held in his training and experience had enabled him to master that fear.

Now he was confronting a different fear—the mind-numbing terror of a father who might never hold his child in his arms again. A fear that would overwhelm him and leave him unable to function, if he allowed it to. To deal with it he had to put all his trust in his past combat experience and the brutal training he'd received as a Ranger.

He tried to convince himself he was still that man. He forced himself to be confident. He could do this. He just had to keep his mind clear. To hesitate could be fatal. But he was finding it damn hard.

"What do we do now?" Jan asked.

"We wait."

* * *

SHEPHERD KEPT HIS eyes locked on the wooden door. The handle moved slightly. "It's time," he hissed.

Jan looked scared but in control. "Be safe," he whispered and hurried into the supply room, closing the door behind him.

Shepherd remained outside the entrance to the scientists' lab. Several long seconds passed and he wondered if he'd been mistaken. Then the door handle moved again and he realized he was right—the mercenaries were outside. They would have expected the door to be locked and the fact that it wasn't had made them cautious.

He felt a surge of adrenalin that left his heart pounding and his breathing ragged, followed by a wave of panic. What the hell was he thinking? He couldn't do this. He'd been stuck in a lab for too long. It was years since he'd trained as a soldier.

He stood frozen to the spot, fighting his fear. What if he couldn't remember how to fight? *So make it quick,* he urged himself. He had the aerosols. He could do it.

The door handle shifted a third time, then the door opened a crack. The odor of wet earth and rotting vegetation wafted in. He heard the trill of cicadas and mosquitoes and the raucous squawk of a parrot as it flew overhead. A howler monkey screeched; the harsh sound jolting Shepherd into action.

He slipped into the lab and swung the door wide open, turning off the light as he did so. He wanted them focused on what might be beyond that dark doorway, not on the supply room where Jan was hiding.

Ten feet to his right was the bio lab. The digital display on the closed hatch glowed in the darkened laboratory.

Shepherd leaned back against the wall. His heart still raced and the adrenalin surge had left his limbs feeling shaky. Tendrils of doubt circulated around his mind and he forced them aside, squeezing the aerosols for reassurance.

Using one arm, he cradled the canisters to his chest as carefully as the first time he'd held Cassie. With his free hand, he slid the gloves and face mask from his pocket. He fumbled with them, almost dropping the canisters. He crouched, carefully placed them on the ground, wiped his sweaty palms on his pants, then pulled on the gloves, before positioning the face mask over his mouth and nose.

He drew the container with the syringes from his pocket and opened it. The needles gleamed in the soft light from the digital display. He carefully removed the rubber stopper from one. The slightest scratch and the batrachotoxin would race through his system and produce convulsions, massive cardiac arrest, muscle paralysis and suffocation. Death would be almost instantaneous and agonizing.

With trembling fingers, he placed the stopper back on the needle, then slipped the syringe into his pocket.

He grabbed the aerosols and stood with his back against the wall. He could hear heavy footsteps in the corridor. They were slow, cautious, but moving toward him, lured by the open door, as he'd hoped. Once they were inside the lab, Jan would hit the emergency override, sealing the mercenaries in and protecting the rest of the Inn, while Shepherd attacked them.

He heard the creak as a door along the corridor opened. The storage room. The footsteps continued and the door to the next room creaked as it was shoved open. The generator room. He heard the low rumble of the generators inside.

There was silence, then the footsteps moved on. The supply room where Jan was hiding was next. Shepherd automatically started to tap his fists against the wall behind him before he remembered the aerosols and halted. Being deprived of the familiar method of controlling his nerves agitated him.

The footsteps moved closer. Two of them, Shepherd guessed. They paused outside the supply room. He waited a few agonizing seconds, but the mercenaries didn't resume their advance. There was a faint screech as the handle to the supply door was wrenched open. Shepherd's heart pounded. Already, his hastily formed plan was falling apart. By thinking he could outsmart Benoit, he'd placed Jan in peril.

He felt the hard shape of the test tube he'd taken from the scientists' lab in his pocket. He flung it against the far wall where it smashed with a tinkle of glass. The footsteps started again. Moving toward him. Fast.

The light spilling in through the open doorway was blocked as the intruders stepped into the lab. Shepherd flicked on the light and burst around the door. Their combat suits glinted under the halogen lights. The visors on their dark helmets were pushed up, light-intensifying image display units were placed before their eyes.

Both were over six feet and heavily built. They bristled with weaponry, each with a Giat FAMAS F1 5.56mm assault rifle shoved back over a shoulder, with FN Herstal Minimi 5.56mm light machine guns leveled before them.

The man nearest to him was covering his companion, who had taken several steps inside. Both froze in the sudden light, shoving their display units away from their eyes.

Shepherd charged the nearest man and sprayed him flush in the face. The man gasped, collapsing to the ground. His feet drummed on the floor.

Shepherd lunged at the second man and fired the second aerosol. The mercenary ducked, the mist jetting over his shoulder. Shepherd kept going, crunching the aerosol in an uppercut to the mercenary's jaw. The man's head snapped back and he staggered backward. His machine gun flew from his grasp and skittered across the floor. The suit seemed to stabilize him and he regained his balance.

Shepherd grabbed the syringe from his pocket, flicked off the rubber stopper and leaped at the mercenary, who was frantically reaching for his rifle. The mercenary swiveled and smashed his elbow into his face, sending his mask flying. He heard the gristly crunch as his nose broke, accompanied by an explosion of pain through his skull. He was flung several feet through the air, landing on his back on the floor.

Stunned, he scrambled to regain his feet. He managed only to get to his knees before the mercenary stooped and seized him by the arm. Shepherd rammed the syringe into the man's flank. He heard the crack as the needle snapped against the suit. The syringe was jarred from his grasp and fell to the ground.

The mercenary lifted Shepherd into the air. His shocked mind had time to register that the mercenary held him easily with one arm—then he was flung across the lab. He crashed to the floor, ten feet away and tumbled along the ground. He heard a crackle and pop as his left knee caved. Burning pain seared up the limb. His momentum slowed and he stopped, lying on his back, gasping. The mercenary loomed.

There was a metallic whirr and the heavy laboratory door slammed shut behind him. Bolts clunked into place and the seals hissed. Jan had done his job. A row of red lights bisecting the ceiling flicked into life and flashed. The mercenary looked around in surprise.

Shepherd scrabbled to get to his feet but his wounded leg wouldn't respond. He flopped about on his back like a stranded fish. He flung out a hand to stabilize himself and struck something hard. The syringe. His fingers closed around it. Then cold steel pressed against his throat. He stilled.

The mercenary stooped, dripping sweat onto his face. Scar tissue from an old wound twisted his top lip into a sneer. The blade bore down. He felt a lance of pain followed by the warm trickle of blood. Twisted Lip spat at him, growling words he didn't understand. He paused, sucking in deep breaths. Then he hissed in a language Shepherd did understand. "You're more valuable to me alive, motherfucker."

Shepherd felt a chill, realizing Twisted Lip's intentions. It would have been better had he been killed. Twisted Lip lifted the knife from his throat and, keeping a careful eye on him, retrieved his machine gun and shouted something that he thought was French, before reverting to English. "Get to your fucking feet."

He spat out some blood, then rolled slowly to his right, drawing his good leg up beneath him. He rose slowly to an awkward crouch, hands planted on the ground, his injured leg trailing uselessly behind him. He halted, head hanging. The fight had exhausted him. His shattered nose throbbed, the pain radiating to his sinuses.

He gasped for air, feeling nauseated. The knowledge that he'd been defeated, that he'd let the scientists down, made him want to slump to the ground.

He spat out the blood pooling at the back of his throat and gently brought his left hand up to feel his nose. His clenched right hand concealed the syringe.

"Over there." Twisted Lip gestured toward the far wall with his weapon.

Shepherd took a step with his damaged leg. The burst of pain in his knee halted him.

"Now." The machine gun slanted toward his groin.

He hobbled toward the far wall and slumped against it. Twisted Lip's black eyes assessed him, then flickered around as he took in his surroundings. "Where are we?" His voice was deep and guttural, with a heavy French accent.

"A laboratory."

"Where's everyone else?"

He shrugged, wincing at a pain in his shoulder.

Twisted Lip jammed his gun into his groin. He doubled over and groaned.

The mercenary hissed, "Where is everyone?"

"Outside. Another room."

Twisted Lip shoved him toward the closed door that blocked the entrance to the corridor leading to the rec room. He stumbled, his leg useless. He slumped against the door, gasping in agony, and was held there by the blunt snout of the machine gun in the small of his back.

"Open it," Twisted Lip snarled.

"I can't."

The barrel ground deeper, pressing against his vertebrae. "I'll blow your fucking spine through your stomach."

"It's—it's sealed," he wheezed. "It can only be opened from the other side."

"Then get them to fucking open it." Twisted Lip pointed to the radio clipped to Shepherd's waist. "Call them."

He slowly unclipped the radio, assessing his options. The titanium container with the unused syringe pressed against his leg but he knew he had no chance of reaching it. The broken syringe was all he had. He clenched it tighter, exhausted from the pain and the fight, feeling himself weakening by the second. He had to do something now.

"Call them!"

He hit the transmit button and raised the radio to his mouth.

Allie's voice rasped. "Shepherd? What's happening? Are you okay?"

He didn't respond.

"Are you all right? Shepherd?"

"Talk!" Twisted Lip rammed his knee into Shepherd's injured leg. He screamed in agony.

"Shepherd! What's going on?"

"Allie," he gasped.

"Tell her to open the fucking door!"

Allie spoke again. He heard the fear in her voice. "What's that?"

Twisted Lip seized the radio. "Open the door or I'll kill your friend."

There was a long pause. Shepherd heard the crackle of static over the radio. "Who is this?"

"The person about to blow your friend's brains all over this door if you don't fucking open it."

"Oh, my God. Shepherd…"

"Don't open it, Allie! He'll kill all of you!"

Twisted Lip seized him by the hair and slammed his head against the heavy door.

"You have three seconds. Then I kill him. And then I blow the fucking door open anyway and kill all of you. If you open it, I'll spare you and your friend here."

"Oh, Jesus."

"Three."

"I need more time! I can't open it from here! I have to get to the keypad."

"Two."

"One."

"Okay! Okay! Just let me do it."

"Time's fucking up!"

There was a metallic click from the far end of the laboratory. The red lights stopped flashing as the door on the other side of the room was shoved open. Jan's anxious face appeared. "Shepherd? Are you okay?"

"*Merde!*" Twisted Lip swung around.

Jan ducked away from the entrance.

Shepherd cannoned into the mercenary. Twisted Lip reeled before the suit balanced him. He swiveled, and unable to level his machine gun, he swung it like an ax at his head.

Shepherd ducked, and thrusting with his good leg, he launched himself upward and shoved the syringe into the man's mouth. He kept going, slamming the top of his head into the man's jaw.

Twisted Lip's teeth snapped and the syringe shattered. With his last remaining strength, he heaved Twisted Lip away from him, stumbling back as he did so. His injured leg locked and he crashed to the ground.

The mercenary coughed, spitting blood, teeth and glass shards. He jerked his weapon toward Shepherd's chest. "You fucking—" His finger tightened on the trigger, then he fell to the ground, clasping his chest and screaming. His shrieks faded to a gargled burble. His mouth worked like a fish gasping for air, his heels kicked. Blood and froth spewed from his mouth. The kicking stilled.

Shepherd remained slumped on the floor, panting as he fought the urge to throw up.

After a few seconds, Jan's tanned face reappeared in the doorway. "Shepherd?"

He managed a groan.

Jan crouched over him anxiously. "Sweetie!"

He didn't have the energy to move. His knee throbbed. Blood pooled in the back of his throat and he spat it out.

"Are you okay?"

He gurgled. "I'm fine."

Jan studied the prone figures on the floor and shuddered. "Sometimes I feel like I don't know you at all."

Shepherd struggled to his feet and tested his injured leg. The knee had locked and he knew cartilage and perhaps worse had been torn. His nose was broken and he could feel the blood clotting deep in his throat.

He took some deep breaths, trying to stop the shaking that had taken hold. It had nearly been a disaster. He had placed the entire facility in harm's way. If Jan hadn't appeared when he had...

Jan's face was full of concern. "I'm sorry. I didn't know what was going on in here. I waited as long as I thought I should."

"Jannie, you couldn't have timed it any better."

"I do know how to make a magnificent entrance," he agreed modestly. "But never put me in that position again."

"I won't." Leaning against Jan's shoulder for support, careful to avoid the blood and froth sprayed across the floor, he hobbled over and studied Twisted Lip's corpse. His black combat suit had an oily sheen. It was smooth and sleek, unlike anything he had ever seen before.

Then his attention was caught by the mercenary's helmet. He recognized it as the SPECTRA model used by the French military. The image display unit was the Sagem optronic system with light-intensifying camera. This was the futuristic FELIN system, the most advanced military system in the world.

The helmet used sensors that measured vibrations of the cranial cavity to transmit voices, eliminating the need for an external microphone. The bone-conduction technology allowed soldiers to remain in constant communication.

He'd made another mistake. He straightened abruptly, his knee collapsed beneath his weight and he stumbled. Jan caught and held him upright.

"We have to get back to the rec room. Now!" He grabbed his radio. "Allie! Open the door! We're okay!"

The radio crackled. "What happened? How do I know it's safe?"

"Geronimo. Open it, Allie! Now!" He threw his arm around Jan for support. "The mercs are using the FELIN system, Jan. It means they're in constant communication with each other."

"So? You stopped them."

"Benoit knows I killed his men—and Alderton is out there."

CHAPTER 28

BENOIT HEARD THE screams over the RIF and knew the surprise attack had failed. His men were dead. He saw the stunned looks on the faces of the mercenaries as they listened to the last gargled breath of their dying friend. Then silence.

He seized Alderton by the arm, forcing him along as he stalked back to the jungle.

Benoit motioned to the sniper, Alain Roche. "Fire and keep firing. Target the windows. Take out anyone you see."

Roche didn't bother to respond. Already in position, lying hidden in shadows at the edge of the jungle, he sighted and squeezed the trigger. The heavy weapon grunted. Roche kept firing.

Alderton twisted futilely in Benoit's grasp. "No! Stop shooting!"

Benoit pulled out his PAMAS G1 and held it to Alderton's forehead. "Your soldier must have had help! One man couldn't take out my men. Who else is in there? Who could have helped him?" The air hissed through his broken nose. "Answer me!"

Despite his fear, Alderton's voice was defiant. "There's no one who could do that. I don't know what happened!"

"Then you're useless to me." He motioned at Roche to halt firing, then marched Alderton to the edge of the rainforest. His legs collapsed beneath him in fear, trailing limply along the ground. Benoit threw him onto the dirt and looked at the facility for several long seconds, his yellow eyes laden with malice. Then he shot Alderton in the back of the head. Alderton's body jerked, then was still.

Benoit stalked back to the jungle. He instructed Roche, "Keep firing. Irregular intervals. Keep the fuckers guessing." He looked around at his men. "Whoever is leading the scientists is only one man. And maybe injured after Didier and Farben's attack. He'll grow tired and weak soon. That is when we attack."

His shocked and angered men were motionless as if mesmerized by the intensity of his gaze. "For now, I want you to rest. That is our advantage. We have the numbers. We have them surrounded. We can rest. They can't."

His men murmured their acknowledgment, then dispersed. The trek had been arduous and they seemed grateful for the rest as they slumped to the ground. All except Halle, who was busy recording his observations in his TIS. Absorbed in his work, Benoit could see that he didn't register his presence until it was too late.

Benoit snatched the TIS from his grasp. His eyes narrowed as they scanned the man's notes, then they fixed him with a smoky glare. "What is this shit? Excessive anger? Over-confidence that might have contributed to the loss of my men?" His voice rose to a shriek. "I want this crap removed from your report!"

Halle held his stare. "No. These are my observations. I will include them." He held out his hand for the TIS.

Benoit's fist tightened around the tiny machine as if to crush it. Then his grip loosened and he handed it back. His voice was calm once more. "These observations aren't objective. They are subjective, merely your opinions. Are you making this personal? You undermine me and take the credit for our success?"

Halle looked uneasy but kept his voice even. "This isn't personal. I'm just doing what AWR have instructed me to do."

"I'll be sure to make my own observations to AWR."

Halle shrugged. "Feel free. They'll want to debrief you anyway."

Benoit's rage faded just as quickly as it had flared. "I made the right call, given what we knew. It shouldn't have failed." He filled with absolute conviction. "We won't lose any more men."

Halle was unconvinced. "Instead of sending the two-man team into the facility in a surprise attack, we should have observed the facility longer to gauge the strengths of this soldier. And we should have kept Alderton alive to interrogate him further. The scientists are trapped. We hold the upper hand. Your move was reckless."

Benoit fought to control his anger. He knew the importance of Halle's report; he wanted to keep this man on side. "Unlike your masters at AWR, you've been out in the field. You understand what it is like to be in battle, how rapidly circumstances can change and how quickly you need to respond. Which is what has happened here, due to failings in our intel—intel that was provided by AWR. Your report needs to show that the fatalities are due to weak intel, not poor leadership."

He considered that. "I will include the intel failings in the report. My observations will be balanced. I'll capture both positive and negative aspects of the team's performance."

"Good." Benoit was satisfied. For now. But deep down, he felt Halle was becoming more of a problem than he'd anticipated.

Halle glanced toward the clearing. "What about the men we left out there?"

They couldn't do anything for their dead inside the facility, but the two men lying in the clearing could be retrieved under covering fire.

The Legionnaire's Code flowed through Benoit's mind—*In*

combat, you act without passion and without hate, you respect defeated enemies, and you never abandon your dead, your wounded, or your arms.

For a fleeting instance, Benoit felt like the man he once had been. Then the moment was gone.

"They're dead. Let them lie." He walked away, ignoring Halle's troubled gaze.

CHAPTER 29

THEY WERE HALFWAY along the corridor when Shepherd heard the gunfire, followed by screams. He gasped. "No!"

By the time they reached the entrance to the rec room, the gunfire had stopped. But as he clung to Jan's shoulder for support, he saw the damage had already been done.

The rec room looked like a charnel house. Blood was smeared across the floor from the window to nearby tables and chairs. Bloody footprints and scuff marks were etched across the floor where the victim had been dragged away from the window.

He realized what had happened—a sniper bullet. Heavy caliber, judging by the extent of the damage.

"Sweet Jesus," he whispered. He saw his distress mirrored in the pale, terrified faces of the group hiding behind the bar. He hobbled across to Allie, who was seated cross-legged on the floor, cradling Ben to her chest. Vivid red blood coated her hands and the front of her shirt, emphasizing the pallor of her face.

He crouched beside her stiffly, positioning his injured leg straight out in front. He was forcibly reminded of his days as an army medic and he prayed those memories would assist him now.

Ben's dark head was lolling to the side, his half-hidden face a deathly white.

"Ben? Can you hear me, Ben?" Shepherd patted the young man's cheek. He wanted him conscious.

He moaned.

"Keep holding him," he said to Allie. "Keep him upright." She tightened her arms, pulling Ben against her, which caused a groan to break from his lips.

"Get to the sickbay!" he yelled to Jan. "Bring me the first aid kit."

He returned his attention to Ben. His shoulder was covered with blood. Shepherd lifted the t-shirt and probed gently. The bullet had torn through the fleshy part of his shoulder. He prodded behind it, prompting another groan, but he persisted until he found the exit wound. The bullet was through. He breathed a sigh of relief. That would save him going in after it.

He sat back, ignoring his throbbing knee. As far as he could tell, there was no structural damage. It looked gory, with plenty of blood, but it appeared to be a glancing flesh wound only.

Ben had been lucky. The heavy-caliber bullet must have cannoned into the titanium shutter, diffusing its energy, before ricocheting into him. If it hadn't, it would have blown his shoulder and half his neck off.

Jan returned with the first aid kit. Shepherd rifled through it, pulled out what he needed and quickly bandaged Ben's wound to stem the flow of blood. He needed to get him to the sick bay to treat the wound more thoroughly, but he was satisfied the kid was okay for now.

He turned his focus to Allie. "What happened?"

"Ben was watching the mercenaries. There was gunfire and he didn't get the shutter closed in time. A bullet ricocheted in. There was this noise, and then all the blood. Ben was down. And… oh God… Alderton is dead. He… he shot him. Then just left him on the ground in the mud."

Shepherd felt he'd been kicked in the guts. He'd underestimated the mercenaries. Both their technology and the capability of their leader. Alderton's death was on him.

He pushed aside his anguish, forcing himself to think.

"Where's Lacoux?"

"He tried to escape when Alderton was shot. O'Connell hit him in the stomach with the rifle butt and dragged him back to the meeting room."

As she spoke, O'Connell hurried in, clutching the Winchester. "I tied Lacoux up and left him there. Thought we'd need the rifle back here in case they try something else."

"Good. Thanks." He felt relieved; having seen the mercenaries up close and personal, he wanted to talk to Lacoux and find out more about their technology. But that would be later; Ben needed his help now.

"How's the kid?" asked O'Connell.

"He's going to be fine."

The man's voice took on an accusatory tone. "Where were you? Ben shouldn't have been keeping watch. *You* should've been. You didn't tell us what you were doing. You just abandoned us. It's your fault Ben got hit!"

"The mercenaries launched a surprise attack from the rear of the Inn. Jan and I managed to stop it."

"How?"

"I'll explain later. Now I need to get Ben to the sick bay. Jan can help me, but I need you to stay here with the rifle in case the mercenaries attempt another attack."

"Fine. I'll protect your fucking fortress. But then I want to know what happened. And whether or not you're going to abandon us again."

Shepherd bit back his angry retort and turned his attention back to Allie. "I'm so sorry about Alderton," he said gently. "But we need to help Ben now. Jannie?"

Jan gathered Ben in his arms, cradling him gently as he strode toward the sick bay. Shepherd followed, holding Allie for support.

* * *

SHEPHERD SNIPPED THE bandage and stepped back to survey his handiwork. With Jan and Allie's help, he'd cleaned and dressed the wound before applying a heavy bandage.

Ben groaned. He was pale and in pain, but conscious. "Am I going to die?"

"No. But you were damn lucky."

"It happened so fast. I tried to close the shutter. Was anyone else hurt?"

"Everyone else is fine. I'm going to give you something for the pain, okay?"

"Okay. God, it hurts."

Shepherd injected him with morphine. "This will kick in after a few seconds. I want you to stay here and rest. Okay?"

Ben nodded. His eyes fluttered, then closed as he slipped into unconsciousness.

Jan moved him from the operating table to a bed, then left to update the others as to his condition. Shepherd remained by the bed, where he continued to observe the kid for several minutes.

Satisfied his patient was as comfortable as he could make him, he glanced at Allie, who was standing beside him. She hadn't said a word since they'd left the rec room. The freckles stood out across her cheeks and the bridge of her nose. There were dark rings under her eyes, which had a haunted appearance. He wanted to wrap her in his arms and comfort her, and that surprised him. He hadn't felt this way about a woman since Claire. "Are you okay?"

She looked up at him. The shock had left her face now. In its place was raw anger. "You left Alderton out there to die!" she said in a low voice.

The pain in her eyes seared through him.

"You said you'd help him. But you didn't!" Her voice rose. "We—I—trusted you! We should've negotiated. Told them we knew they were planning a surprise attack. We could've offered them the cure to prevent it and trade for Alderton's release. But you wanted to lure them in. You abandoned Alderton!

"Now he's dead and Ben is wounded. Damn you! Damn you to hell."

Shepherd felt sick. He tried to think of something to tell her, anything that would help ease her suffering. But couldn't. His exhaustion flooded over him and he felt consumed with pain to the point where he couldn't focus.

His anxiety to help Ben had kept him upright, but now he felt he couldn't stand on his wounded leg any longer. The air burbled through his broken nose and he could feel the congealed blood in his throat. All he knew was that he had abandoned Alderton. His initial assessment of their enemy had been inaccurate.

He'd assumed Toussen would hire local militia so nothing could be traced back to them; the operation would be seen as an opportunistic attack on a wealthy target by former Maoist guerrillas based in Manaus.

Shepherd had convinced himself that although they had the greater numbers, he, as a product of the U.S. Army, had the greater military training and expertise. Now, after seeing and experiencing the power of their technology first-hand, he knew his assumption had been wrong. Perhaps fatally so. Who the hell were these guys? Why did they have this technology?

He winced, feeling the ache in his knee. It served as a harsh reminder that he was a different man from the one he had been as a soldier. Different, and older.

He struggled to remain on his feet, unable to put any weight on his damaged knee. The pain was intolerable now. He could barely stand. "They have FELIN technology, Allie. I'm sorry, but there was nothing I could do for Alderton."

He staggered away from Ben's bed and sifted through the cabinets, collecting bandages, swabs and a syringe, which he filled with a local anesthetic mixed with adrenalin.

He seated himself on a chair in the corner of the room and pulled up the left leg of his pants. He probed the knee gently. It was swollen, the familiar, ugly scar tissue that covered it an inflamed, angry red.

His mind dragged back to another time, another hospital. *Claire.* He forced his mind back to the present. The injury to his knee was serious. He could tell from the structural instability that he had damaged the ligament. All he could do now was manage the pain and stabilize the joint. Later—if there was a later—it would require surgery.

He injected the contents of the syringe into the side of his knee. Sensing a presence, he looked up to find Allie standing there. The anger in her eyes was now mingled with concern. "Let me help."

"It's okay." He firmly wound the bandage around his knee in a figure-eight above and below the joint, to give it support. It felt stiff and it hurt like hell, but no longer flexed alarmingly from side to side.

His hands moved to his nose, feeling the broken cartilage. Pain resonated around his skull, followed by another gush of blood. He coughed and swallowed.

"Are you all right?" she asked.

"Been better," he admitted nasally.

The skin wasn't broken, which was a sign the injury wasn't as severe as it felt. Again, he might need surgery later, but for now, he had to do something to help him breathe.

He filled another syringe with a local anesthetic and injected it into the side of his nose. He waited a few minutes for it to feel numb, then probed the broken cartilage once more.

He'd done this to others before, but never to himself. He took a deep breath and held it, then clicked the cartilage back into place. There was a gristly crunch, and despite the anesthetic, he felt a sharp pain that seemed to grip his head in a vice.

Blood burst down the back of his throat and from his nostrils. He grabbed a towel and held it to his face, leaning his head forward. He waited until the bleeding had stopped and pulled the towel away. His nose felt swollen and numb, and he knew his eyes would be blackening, but he could breathe freely now.

He shifted his attention back to his leg. He tested the bandage then gingerly flexed the knee. The anesthetic was beginning to have an effect and the pain had dulled. He breathed deeply. The adrenalin was also kicking in; his heart rate was up, helping to combat his pain and exhaustion.

He got to his feet, testing his leg. The bandaged joint was stiff, but it was now stable.

He faced Allie. The concern had left her face, leaving anger simmering in her eyes. "Alderton didn't have to die."

"I'm sorry. But I had no other choice."

"You did! You could have asked us to help you. We're trained scientists, experts in problem-solving. We would have thought of something."

"Like what?"

"You said Benoit needs Lacoux. We should have used that, maybe threatened to harm Lacoux unless he called off the attack. Then perhaps we could have negotiated for Alderton's release using the cure."

"It wouldn't have worked. I thought it was worth trying to trade Lacoux for Alderton, but that changed when I realized what Benoit was really doing. I don't believe he would have called off his surprise attack just to save Lacoux.

"His main goal is to take the cure and wipe us out. If he loses Lacoux, he can just hand over everything related to the cure to the scientists at Toussen and let them analyze it. This way, at least we've got more weapons and the ammunition we need. It gives us a chance."

"There had to be another way! You should have involved us."

"There wasn't enough time."

"I think you're wrong. And I don't believe you're including us enough in your plans. We're a valuable resource, one you should be using."

"Jesus, Allie. That'd be wonderful if we were sitting around a table hypothesizing about scientific theorems, but in combat situations, things happen so fast there isn't time."

Her eyes narrowed to blazing green slits. "Don't you dare patronize me. No, I don't have your military training or background, but I'm Head of Operations, a position I got through working my ass off and my own intelligence. Despite what O'Connell says, nobody gave me this position on a platter—I earned it.

"With Alderton dead, I'm in charge of this facility. Everyone here is my responsibility and I want to get them all home alive. I deserve your respect and to be included in your plans. I'm trained to solve problems. And my problems are these fucking mercenaries, that asshole O'Connell, and right now, *you*. So you can either work with me or get the hell out of my way!"

"You have to trust me."

"Then we need to know more about you," she said. "We stayed because *you* told us we should. We trusted your judgment. But now I think we deserve to know why we should be listening to you."

Grudgingly, he realized she was right. Her trust in him deserved to be reciprocated. Perhaps he hadn't been inclusive enough.

He remained convinced that with his military training and skills, he was the only one who could solve the problem, as Allie had phrased it, posed by the mercenaries. But he also realized that his task would be easier if the scientists worked with him.

They weren't soldiers trained to follow orders. They were scientists with highly analytical minds, trained to ask questions. Which meant, perhaps, being more inclusive in his planning. "Okay. What do you want to know?"

"You told us you were with the Rangers. What are they? Some sort of Special Ops? Like the Otters, or whatever they call themselves?"

"SEALS," he corrected her. "No. They're navy. I was army."

"What did you do?"

"I was a platoon leader. In Afghanistan and Iraq."

"Is that how you hurt your knee?"

"Caught some shrapnel when an IED exploded. I was invalided out. The army put me through medical school. After I completed it, I worked as a medic with the Rangers for a while, but with my knee, I couldn't function the way I should. I was endangering others so I left."

"How do you know about that FELIN thing you mentioned? Because you were a Ranger?"

He hesitated.

"Damn it!" she snapped. "I need to know everything."

"After I left the Rangers, I worked for USAMRMC. While there, I was seconded to work at the Army Research Laboratories as a consultant. Specifically, the Weapons and Materials Research Directorate." He looked at her with weary eyes. "The goal of WMRD is to increase the survivability of the soldier, which was where I came in. I had unique skills. Medical knowledge and frontline combat experience.

"As a soldier and doctor with experience in combat conditions, I knew the extent to which the human body could be pushed. What it could survive. My role was to provide this advice. And I was good at it. Good enough for them to expand my role." He pondered whether to elaborate further, before deciding to continue. "Have you heard of the JASONs?"

"No."

"The JASONs are the scientists on the Pentagon's scientific advisory panel. In 2008, in a report to the Pentagon, the JASONs expressed concern about adversaries' ability to exploit advances in human performance modification, thus creating a threat to national security.

"The JASONs recommended that the American military push ahead with its own performance-enhancement research—and monitor what foreign militaries were doing—to make sure the U.S.'s enemies don't suddenly become smarter, faster, or better able to endure the harsh realities of war than American troops.

"Following their report, a small team within WMRD was formed to do just that. I was part of that team. We were sent around the world, under the guise of benchmarking and looking at global advances in this field, but in reality monitoring and keeping an eye on where the U.S. stood in the technological arms race. That's how I know about

FELIN. Do you have any more questions?"

"No. That certainly wasn't in your personnel file." She smiled.

He returned the smile tiredly. "The existence of the WMRD team is classified. You're now one of only a select few people who know."

The anger faded from her eyes and she checked her watch. "It's five-thirty. It'll be dark soon. What should we do?"

"We need to have a closer look at the technology the mercenaries are carrying."

* * *

BACK IN THE scientists' laboratory, Shepherd stooped over the body of the mercenary he had fought. He was still shaken by the power Twisted Lip had displayed; he'd been tossed around like a rag doll. Yet the mercenary, while large and in excellent shape, didn't seem overly muscled. He wondered if any human strength could have supplied that sort of power.

Images filled his mind of the mercenaries he'd shot in the chest and the way they had risen to their feet. What on earth were these guys wearing? He was surprised by how sleek Twisted Lip's combat suit was. The combat armor Shepherd had used had been bulky. So how had it stopped his bullets and the syringe?

As a Ranger, he had worn the Improved Outer Tactical Vest, a redesigned version of Interceptor body armor. It protected against 9mm ammunition and fragmentation. The IOTV was also equipped with front, rear and side armor plates, known as Enhanced Small Arms Protective Inserts. When worn together with the plates, the IOTV could stop 7.6-millimeter armor-piercing rounds.

The downside had been its bulk, inhibiting mobility. It had been damn heavy too, and many of the Rangers he had served with had chosen not to wear the armor plates. The suit Twisted Lip wore seemed every bit as effective as the IOTV but didn't appear bulky enough to contain armor plates.

He pressed his finger into the man's chest. It yielded with the consistency of silicon. He poked harder; a sudden jab. The suit hardened immediately, resisting the pressure. The mercenary was wearing a form of Kevlar vest and he realized what he was looking at. "Jesus."

"What is it?" Allie asked.

"Liquid body armor." At WMRD, it had been his job to understand this form of technology, but it had been theoretical then. He'd assumed it still was. Yet here it was, right before his eyes. A liquid body armor Kevlar vest.

He had seen experiments involving this form of tech. The key component in the liquid armor vest was shear thickening fluid composed of hard nanoparticles of silica, suspended in liquid form. During normal handling, the STF was deformable and flowed like a liquid. Upon impact, such as a bullet strike, it transitioned to a rigid material, preventing the projectile from penetrating.

This was highly advanced technology, but it still didn't explain the strength the man had displayed. Nothing about the suit did. There was no powered exoskeleton or energy source that he could see.

The only technology he knew of that could have explained that power was the HULC suit designed by Raytheon and used for lifting and carrying heavy goods and equipment.

But that was cumbersome technology and required a power source. Twisted Lip's combat suit looked nothing like it. That it could provide that much strength was beyond his comprehension and filled him with a sense of foreboding. What were they dealing with here?

Only one person could provide an explanation. "I think it's time we had a chat with Lacoux."

CHAPTER 30

THEY STOOD OUTSIDE the meeting room. "What are you going to ask him?" Allie asked.

"I want to know more about Benoit and the technology his men possess. The mercenary threw me around in the lab as if he were a machine. Yet they weren't wearing anything I know of that could have given them such power.

"And why do they even need such a sophisticated force? For all they knew, we were just a helpless team of scientists. A couple of pirates with guns should've been enough to overpower us. It doesn't make sense."

He seized the door handle. "It's time we found out exactly what we're dealing with."

"Let me lead the interrogation," she said.

He hesitated. He'd resolved to trust her and the rest of scientists more, but he was reluctant to relinquish the lead role after witnessing Alderton's efforts in interrogating Lacoux. "I have more experience in conducting interrogations."

"I've worked with Lacoux far longer than you have. I know him better."

He turned to face her. "What makes you think you can get him to talk? What will your approach be? You need to have a strategy in there."

"I think I can come up with one more subtle than your efforts with the spider venom," she retorted. "Lacoux is brilliant and arrogant. I'm going to use his ego against him."

Shepherd hesitated a moment longer then relented, deciding to trust her.

Allie pushed the door open and led the way into the meeting room.

Lacoux looked ill, his face gray. Despite the antivenom Mancini had administered, the wandering spider toxin had ravaged his body. The muscles along his jaw and down his neck were still twitching. The dark eyes that looked up at them were filled with pain. The rifle butt to the stomach delivered by O'Connell probably hadn't helped.

Allie strode to the table. Resting her hands on it, she leaned close to Lacoux and fixed him with a piercing stare. "Your plans to take over this facility aren't working out the way you expected them to."

Lacoux's black eyes bored into her, glinting with a confidence that Shepherd, standing beside her, found unnerving.

"You didn't anticipate being captured. I'm sure you thought the mercenaries would take us by surprise and overwhelm us in minutes. I'll bet you informed Benoit that we're isolated, vulnerable and easily taken." Allie let her words sink in. "You're in a dangerous position now. Maybe we won't be overrun after all. Or if we are, it'll be after a far greater fight than your friends expected. Many of them are dead."

Lacoux coughed excruciatingly, then grated, "Bullshit."

"It's the truth. They attacked and we held them off. I saw the bodies. It's not a sight I'll ever forget."

Lacoux dark eyes were now less certain.

"I'd imagine they're not thinking too highly of you at the moment—their men died because of the information *you* provided. Once they've taken what they want, you're no longer useful to them. Maybe you'll meet the same fate as Alderton." She let him consider her words. "Or I can help you."

"How can *you* help me?" he sneered.

"I can give you your freedom in exchange for information.

Tell us what we want to know and I'll let you go."

Lacoux's twisted face was inscrutable, but a faint spark of interest flared in his eyes. "What information?"

"Tell me about Benoit. Who is he? Why is he here?"

"It won't help you." His voice was full of contempt. "You don't know what you're dealing with."

"I think I'm dealing with a thief who'll do anything for money leading a team of mercenaries who haven't been able to overrun a bunch of scientists. Doesn't sound too impressive."

Lacoux's eyes flashed with anger. "He's more impressive than you realize! Benoit is the product of the most sophisticated military development program in the world. *My* program."

Allie had been right—Lacoux's weakness was his massive ego and her deliberate goading had provoked him into talking. But Shepherd also had the more uncomfortable realization that Lacoux clearly thought there was no harm in giving up information, meaning he believed that regardless of what he told them, the scientists would all be killed.

He followed Allie's approach and stroked Lacoux's ego some more. "Did you develop their suits too? I haven't seen anything like them. Amazing tech. What are they? What gives them such power?"

"The combat suits contain nanomuscles. Artificial nano-fiber muscles. They're up to two hundred times stronger than human muscle."

Shepherd was impressed; this was an astonishing leap forward in technology. But he kept his face impassive. "You took a soldier and armed him with the best tech your military has. Any grunt in one of those suits would be stronger. Benoit still doesn't sound that imposing."

"You fool," Lacoux hissed. "It's not the suit. Benoit has been biologically modified."

"That's impossible," he retorted. "How? What's this program you mentioned?"

"You Americans think you lead the world in everything. That your army is the biggest and best equipped. The same goes for the Chinese and the Russians. But France saw the future of warfare long ago and invested not in new weapons but in technology, establishing a future soldier program, the most sophisticated program of its type in the world. It'll make your army redundant. Toussen provides the biotech for it."

"What did you do to Benoit?"

"The program's not just about making our soldiers stronger and faster. It's about making them smarter. I developed a cognitive enhancing drug. I used it on Benoit, enhancing his mental abilities."

His black eyes studied them with derision. "You think because you held him back once that you've won? The military has spent millions on this program. This is the first operational trial of their prototype future soldier. They're monitoring Benoit to see how he performs, how he reacts.

"All you've done is provide a better test of their program than they could've hoped for. You may have slowed him down, but the outcome will be the same—you're all dead."

"Oh, my God," Allie whispered.

Lacoux's voice grew smug. "Now you understand."

"Experimentation with cognitive enhancement has been around for decades," Shepherd stated dismissively. "What did you use on Benoit? Modinifil? You're not impressing me, Lacoux. This stuff is old school."

"We moved beyond modinifil years ago. Instead, we've researched a new class of drugs that facilitate the physiological changes of brain plasticity. You may have heard of them," he said condescendingly. "Ampakines."

Ampakines were a class of compounds known to enhance attention span and alertness and facilitate learning and memory.

Atione had been investigating them as potential treatments for a range of conditions involving mental disability and disturbances such as Alzheimer's disease, Parkinson's disease, schizophrenia, as well as neurological disorders such as ADHD, among others.

"You know we've heard of them," Shepherd stated. "What makes them any better than modinifil?"

"Modinifil doesn't make the patient smarter—just a more efficient learner by reducing errors and the time needed to learn given material. But the drug compound my team discovered from ampakines actually enhances mental capabilities. It makes the subject more intelligent."

"How?"

"You wouldn't understand," he scorned.

"Try me."

"Let me put it into words you'll understand. If we look at the brain as a network of electric potentials, then we have ramped up the voltage in Benoit's brain. Upping the voltage has allowed for faster and better transmission of signals. Benoit's brain is now more wired than yours, or even mine."

"So this is the biological modification you were talking about?"

"Enhanced intelligence is one aspect of the compound of drugs we gave him. But the drugs Benoit received also affect the stress hormones his body's glands pump into his bloodstream in life-or-death situations. His body's normal biological cocktail has been re-balanced so he doesn't panic, doesn't retreat and keeps on fighting, even when the odds are against him and any normal person would give up."

His dark eyes filled with triumph. "That is why you can't defeat him."

Shepherd felt a coil of trepidation swirl in the pit of his stomach. Lacoux was enjoying this. He was toying with them, providing them with this information to instill fear.

"But why are you out here? What does this have to do with us?" Allie asked.

"Toussen promised the French military that no one else in the world is conducting this research with the results we've had. So Toussen maintains a strong interest in its competitors' research in this field. They infiltrate companies they perceive as having promising research."

"To steal their ideas," she accused.

"Yes. Or to sabotage. When we learned about the work Atione was doing, we arranged for Jouvet to be placed on your team. Then later, myself."

Shepherd glanced at Allie. "Didn't you guys do background checks?"

"Yes," she said defensively. "But nothing related to Toussen turned up."

"The military took care of each candidate's background story," Lacoux informed them. "There would be no trail leading back to Toussen or the French future soldier program."

"If Jouvet was working for you, why did you kill him?" Allie asked.

"He saw the potential in your new drug. But instead of seeing its benefit to the future soldier program, he wanted it to be used to treat Alzheimer's."

"How did you know?" Shepherd asked.

"We saw his behavior change. Rather than reporting regularly, his reports became less frequent and less informative.

I was sent to investigate. We discovered later that his mother has Alzheimer's. The weak fool was desperate to help her. The military became worried he'd tell you about their program."

"So you murdered him," Allie said.

"He was a traitor," Lacoux snarled.

"Why do you want our cure?" Shepherd asked. "You already have your cognitive enhancement drug."

Lacoux remained silent.

"Our deaths mustn't be as inevitable as you'd originally thought if you're worried now about what you might tell us," Allie said.

He looked scornful. "I'm not worried."

"Well, then. Why do you need our cure?"

"The cognitive enhancement drug is temporary. All our attempts to increase its lifespan have failed. In early versions of the compound, the effects lasted only a few days. We trialed it on mice, then on Benoit. We started with small amounts, monitoring his behavior and testing his IQ. But despite all our efforts, the effects diminished over time.

"For this operational trial, we have given him a larger dose to reduce any risk it will wear off too early. We estimate that with the amount we've given him, the effects should last for a few months. But they'll wear off.

"But Jouvet believed that your drug will be not only far more powerful than our compound but could lead to permanent cognitive enhancement." He smiled. "You see? Instead of being a cure for Alzheimer's, your drug will lead to the production of smarter, stronger future soldiers for France. Our military couldn't allow it to fall into the U.S. Army's hands—it would render all our own work redundant and shift the balance of military technological might to the

U.S. That's why you won't be allowed to keep it."

His gaze lingered on Shepherd. "Despite all your pathetic efforts, it'll be taken from you." Lacoux shifted his attention to Allie. "You think I'm worried about the intelligence I provided Benoit with? That he'll no longer view me as useful? *I* led the program that made him." His dark eyes grew cruel. "He won't kill his creator. He'll do everything in his power to save me. Just as he'll do everything in all his formidable power to destroy you."

CHAPTER 31

Benoit paced back and forth restlessly.

Halle moved alongside. "You look frustrated."

"I'm fine."

"Are you sure? We've suffered many setbacks."

Benoit fought to keep his growing impatience from this man. That the scientists had survived this long would look bad in Halle's report. Even worse, the deaths of four of his men could sway the military toward believing the trial was a failure. It was the last thing he wanted.

He had endured too much for this to be deemed a failure now.

Halle seemed to read his mind. "You've been through a lot. You almost died when the first dose of the drug compound Lacoux gave you overstimulated your brain. What did he call it? Excessive synchronous activity which resulted in violent epileptic seizures?"

Benoit kept his voice even despite his stirring of anger. "Yes. You also know that when the drug program recommenced, the doses were small, allowing my brain to grow used to it. Which it did."

The testing had gone on for six months, during which he had been put through a punishing physical training regime while being administered myostatins to increase his strength.

It was the success of both of these tortuous programs that he wanted Halle to focus on in his report—not the unanticipated resilience of the scientists. "The soldier in there will soon be dulled with fatigue. But I feel like I'm growing stronger. Back at AWR they told me that my fitness levels are those of an Olympic athlete."

"I read their report," Halle said. "It also mentioned side effects. Are you experiencing any?"

Benoit hid his irritation that he was again searching for negative aspects to the future soldier program. Of the possible side effects that Lacoux had warned him about, all he had experienced were nausea and a headache. The nausea had lasted a few days and had now faded. The headache seemed to be worsening, though not to an extent that concerned him.

"No. I feel exactly as Lacoux told me I would. Better, in fact—my new abilities are exceeding my expectations."

Which was why he found these unexpected setbacks so frustrating. He wondered how Halle felt about them, and what he would report.

For the first time since the operation commenced, Benoit felt anxious. Not for the outcome, which he knew was inevitable, but because he desperately wanted the trial to be considered a success.

The sensations he was experiencing were so exquisite, he felt euphoric. He couldn't imagine reverting to his old self. To being inferior. No, he felt like a god.

His impatience surged. He strode across to Roche and ordered him to fire.

CHAPTER 32

THE GUNFIRE BEGAN as Shepherd and Allie departed the meeting room, shaken by what Lacoux had told them. They heard loud cracks echo from the jungle, followed by thunks as the bullets smashed into the closed shutters.

In the rec room, Jan and Parker had thrown themselves to the floor, hands over their heads. Mancini and O'Connell were crouched behind the bar.

With Allie's support, Shepherd seized the Winchester and hobbled to the nearest window. He waited. The gunfire slowed. He opened the shutter, readied to shoot, then realized there were no mercenaries in the clearing. He held his fire, not wanting to waste their precious ammunition.

Sniper fire thundered against the Inn. He slammed the shutter. He counted four shots in quick succession, then the echoes of gunfire faded. He cracked the shutter and peered through. There was still no movement in the lengthening shadows at the perimeter of the clearing.

He closed the shutter. "Bastards."

"Are they attacking?" asked Allie.

He shook his head wearily. Through the adrenalin amping up his heart rate, he felt the full extent of his exhaustion sapping the last vestiges of his energy. He wanted nothing more than to slump to the floor. Despite the anesthetic, his knee ached dully, and his broken nose throbbed with each breath.

He fought back his fatigue. "No. Benoit's deploying mental disintegration tactics. Firing at us to keep us from resting. They're trying to break us down."

"We can't let that happen. When was the last time you rested?"

"I'm not sure."

"You look exhausted. You need to rest."

"If I'm not here to return fire, they might launch a surprise attack. What I need is more adrenalin."

"Damn it! You can't keep doping yourself up with adrenalin. It'll give you a heart attack, you idiot."

Shepherd knew she was right. He wasn't thinking clearly. But his problem was more than the fatigue that dulled his mind.

Learning that the Alzheimer's cure would be used by the French military to develop super soldiers had stunned him. It had opened a conflict between the reawakened soldier within him and the doting father he had become.

He would do anything in his power to help his little girl and the Alzheimer's cure might provide the breakthrough he sought. But now... His soldier side knew full well the gravity of what Lacoux had told them.

Creating cognitively-enhanced super soldiers would cause a paradigm shift in military affairs. It signaled a terrifying new beginning of genetic warfare. He dreaded what potential adversaries like Russia and China might do with the new technology.

He had a vision of a future where genetic "bombs" designed to cause defects in enemy combatants were used. A future where an army could attack its enemies by changing their physiology to make them dumber, slower, more afraid. A new world where terror groups could genetically assassinate political leaders by tailoring cancers specific to the target's DNA.

He saw the horror that could be created by the Alzheimer's cure, rather than only what it could mean for his daughter. It was a glimpse into hell. His military instincts told him it couldn't be allowed to be used for this purpose. That, if all else failed, they should destroy it.

But the father within him was aghast at the idea. To finally have something that could help Cassie, only to destroy it... He couldn't bear to think about it.

To save the cure for his daughter, he had to find a way to vanquish the mercenaries. But his confidence in his own military training and abilities had dissipated as he learned more about their capabilities. The discovery that Benoit was a bio-mod had demoralized him. Where was this man's weakness?

Shepherd wondered now if his decision to stay and defend had been a mistake. At the time, he'd thought they were confronting normal men, not a technologically advanced team led by a bio-mod. Would running have been the best option after all? He didn't know. What he did know was that he had no idea how to defeat them. And that terrified him.

Allie studied his face, and he realized she saw his anguish. Her green eyes filled with compassion and she slipped her arms around him and gave him a tight hug. He slumped against her, feeling her warmth, her softness.

Minutes passed. He didn't want to let her go.

"Hey." She caressed his forehead. "Is this because I called you an idiot?"

Despite her comforting presence, the darkness in his mind refused to lift. He didn't know how to tell her what he was feeling. "No. Just... I'm tired, Allie."

"I know."

"Benoit won't get tired. He won't stop. I'm not sure... I don't know..." He wondered what he could do. What he should do.

"Hey!" she said again. "We're going to get through this. I know that. I also know you need some rest." She eased away from him. "Come on. Let's find you somewhere to lie down for a while."

He didn't move. "Biologically modified. Jesus, Allie."

"What are you talking about? Biologically modified?" O'Connell interrupted. "What did Lacoux tell you?"

Allie explained.

O'Connell's pale blue eyes narrowed. "Benoit is a bio-mod?"

She looked surprised. "You know what they are?"

"An old colleague of mine from UCLA was doing some work in that field. Working with ampakines, like we are. We were exchanging notes.

"But he gave up. Said the side-effects were too detrimental. Severe headaches, insomnia, nausea and impaired, episodic memory. And the enhancement effects were negligible. His team concluded it was impossible.

"Now you're saying Lacoux's succeeded? If it's true, we're in deep shit. A fucking bio-mod? A goddamn mutated future-soldier? Wearing a nano-suit? How can we compete with that?" His pale eyes glittered with rage as he turned to Shepherd. "I told you we should've run! This is your fault. Damn you! What the hell do we do now?"

"I don't know."

"We put our goddamn trust in you. Now you say you don't fucking know?"

"Shepherd's kept us alive this long," Jan said. "We need to give him some time. You will think of something, sweetie."

Tired, tormented by his inner conflict, Shepherd found himself suddenly angry. He snapped, "Damn it, Jan! That's enough! Stop putting this on me!"

Jan began, "Sweetie—"

"Shut up, Jan. Please. Just shut the hell up."

He saw the hurt in his friend's eyes and hated himself. The rest stared at him with startled expressions. He couldn't face them anymore. Pushing away from Allie, he placed the Winchester on a table and hobbled toward the corridor.

"Don't you dare abandon us again!" O'Connell shouted.

He stumbled from the rec room.

* * *

SHEPHERD LAY ON the floor with his back against one of the benches in the scientists' laboratory. His shoulders were rigid with tension. His breathing was fast and shallow through his nose that felt swollen and misshapen.

For several minutes he just lay there with his eyes closed, trying to ignore the tumult in his mind by listening to the hum of equipment and the occasional shriek of wind through the jungle canopy. It was picking up, he noted absently. The storm couldn't be far off now.

"Shepherd!"

He opened his eyes. Allie was standing in the doorway. The concern on her face made him wonder how bad he appeared.

She sank down beside him and snaked her arm across his shoulders. Her attention was caught by the body of a mercenary sprawled on the floor in a pool of vomit. Her nose wrinkled at the pungent odor and she quickly averted her gaze.

She remained silent and he found her presence comforted him. His breathing slowed and deepened. His shoulders relaxed.

Eventually, she asked, "Are you okay?"

He stirred. "No."

"What is it? Your injuries? The adrenalin? Are you having a reaction to the medication you gave yourself?"

"No."

"Then what just happened out there?"

"I can't—"

"You can and you will. We need you. Your colleagues out there are confused, scared and worried that you've given up and abandoned them. Now tell me what's wrong."

"We may have to destroy the cure."

"Why?" Trepidation grew in her eyes as he explained why the Alzheimer's cure couldn't be allowed to be utilized by Toussen.

"No."

Shepherd was startled at the vehemence in her voice. "What?"

"I'll be damned if I'm going to destroy the cure. It means too much. The benefits it could provide to countless sufferers! What it could mean to Cassie. It's Alderton's legacy. If we don't get the cure out, it means Alderton, Marlowe and Klaus have died in vain. I won't allow that to happen."

"I know how you feel. But we may have to. We have to weigh the good it can do against its capacity for evil in the wrong hands. Toussen will use it to create biological monsters far more powerful than Benoit. An army of them. And it won't stop there.

"Perhaps we can find another cure with time. But if the bio-mod genie is let out of the bottle, it can't be put back."

"I don't accept that. There has to be another way."

"The only alternative is to somehow destroy Benoit and his mercenaries. But after what Lacoux told us, I don't know how to do that."

"Then you need to think! We can't destroy the cure. Not

now. Not after everything we've sacrificed."

"There is more at stake than your career!"

Allie flared. "Of course there is! You think I don't know that? I don't give a damn about my reputation and what developing the cure could mean for my career. I never have! What I do care about is the good it can do in the right hands. And I care about preserving Alderton's legacy. So we're going to have to think of a way to defeat this fucking Benoit."

"I don't know how to."

"Then we need to work together. Those are smart people out there. I'm willing to bet our collective intelligence is greater than that of one enhanced mutant. So let's start using it."

She stood and looked down at him. Her voice softened. "I can't begin to imagine how terrible it must be for you, having Cassie to worry about. But the best thing you can do for her right now is to stop feeling sorry for yourself and help us." She held out her hand. "Are you coming with me?"

Shepherd remained haunted, but he took her hand.

CHAPTER 33

BACK IN THE rec room, Shepherd walked straight up to Jan. "I'm sorry, Jannie."

"You're forgiven, sweetie," came the simple reply.

Allie gathered everyone together. "I know some of you want to run. You know who and what confronts us. But instead of running, the time has come for us to start working together."

O'Connell glared at Shepherd. "What about him? Why did he take off like that?"

"That's not important right now. He's back and he's staying," she said firmly. "What *is* important is what we do now. With Toussen wanting our cure for their future soldier program, you all need to understand the ramifications of it falling into their hands. Shepherd will explain it to you."

Shepherd detailed his fears of a new age of genetic warfare if the Alzheimer's cure was used by Toussen to develop super soldiers, of the impact it would have on global military affairs. He concluded by stating his belief that the Alzheimer's cure should be destroyed to prevent this from occurring.

A murmur of derision went around the group.

"You can't destroy it. That's our careers you're talking about!" Parker looked across at O'Connell for support.

"If it wasn't for you, we'd have been long gone before they arrived. Career?" O'Connell snorted. "If we ever make it out of here I'll make sure you get no fucking recognition for the cure."

Ignoring Parker's look of dismay he swung around to confront Allie. His face was flushed with rage and his pale eyes glinted like diamonds. "You and Shepherd are not destroying the cure. You'll have to climb over my dead body first."

"I agree with you," Allie said. "The Alzheimer's cure is Alderton's legacy and I don't want to destroy it either."

"I don't want it destroyed because of my daughter." Shepherd explained Cassie's condition. "But regardless of how I feel as a father, as a former soldier I know we can't allow it to fall into Toussen's hands. As much as it sickens me, I believe we have to destroy the cure."

"I'm sorry about your daughter," said O'Connell. "But you're not destroying our cure. No fucking way."

"I believe Shepherd is right," Jan said. "If the cure can be used to create super soldiers, we have to destroy it. So what if it'll establish our reputations? We need to think of the bigger picture."

"What the hell do you know?" O'Connell said. "You haven't spent years striving to achieve something like this. You're barely thirty years old. You'll be able to join another team, work on another project and start all over again. I can't."

"Our lives are on the line here!" Jan said. "Your reputation won't matter if you're dead!"

Allie interjected, her tone measured as she addressed O'Connell. "I know how you feel. I want to save the cure as much as you do. But I also understand Shepherd's concerns that it can't be allowed to fall into Benoit's hands.

"There has to be another way. It's up to us to find it. So we need to start working together. All of us." She held O'Connell's gaze until he nodded reluctantly.

"What do you propose?" he asked gruffly.

Allie turned to Shepherd. "First, you need support. Can

you retrieve the dead mercenaries' weapons and teach us how to use them? Once you've done that, you get some rest. No arguments."

"And their nano-suits?" O'Connell asked. "Why can't we get those and give these bastards some of their own medicine?"

A murmur went around the room. Shepherd saw their enthusiasm rise as they started doing what they were trained to do—analyze and solve problems. His own hope flared. "Good idea, but they're covered in batrachotoxin."

"I can wear a hazmat suit while I handle them," said O'Connell. "I can look at what we have in the bio lab to sterilize the nano-suits. The same ammonium mix that we use for the hazmat suits. Would that work?" he asked Mancini.

"Maybe," Mancini replied. "Probably."

"But who'll wear them?" Jan asked.

"I will," said Shepherd.

"So will I," said O'Connell.

Shepherd eyed him appraisingly. "Can you handle a gun?"

"I grew up in Bed-Stuy, asshole."

Shepherd smiled. "Then how long will it take to get them ready?"

O'Connell considered. "I'll need two hours."

"Great," Allie said. "That's a start. What else? Each of you is brilliant in your respective fields. We need to harness that intellect. What do we have that we can use to defend ourselves?"

"What are you looking for?" Mancini asked.

"The Inn is a highly specialized environment. We work with a lot of dangerous compounds. We need to turn that to our advantage."

"I can load more of the batrachotoxin into syringes."

"That's good," Allie said. "What else?"

Mancini's brow furrowed. "There's a pathogen I was working on. I might be able to engineer it into a form we can use to defend ourselves."

"How?" Jan scoffed. "Are you going to run up and inject it into them?"

"Syringes are useless against their body armor," Shepherd said.

"I think I can create a different delivery mechanism."

"What pathogen?" Allie asked.

"The batrachotoxin we extracted from the Melyridae beetle. It's more potent than that of the poison dart frog. O'Connell had us trying to develop new compounds from it."

O'Connell frowned. "We scrapped it because it was too dangerous."

"I can engineer it so the pathogen breaks down and becomes inert after a few hours."

"We?" Allie asked.

Mancini hesitated. Then he pointed at Jan. "The two of us were working on it."

"Okay," Allie said. "Can you make this viable, Mancini? We don't have much time."

"I believe so."

"We need it fast. Jan can help you."

"I'll be faster on my own."

"This is vital, Mancini. Are you sure?"

"Of course I am!" he insisted.

"Fine. Keep me informed," Allie said. Mancini hurried to the bio lab.

"I'll start sterilizing the nano-suits," said O'Connell.

"First we need to rebuild the barricade at the other

entrance," said Shepherd, "in case they use it in another surprise attack. You already know how to use a gun, so it'd save time if you worked on the barricade and the nano-suits while I train everyone else."

"First time you've made sense." O'Connell grabbed a khaki backpack from the pile against the wall and hustled away.

* * *

ALLIE HANDLED THE Herstal Minimi awkwardly. It was bulky and uncomfortable in her arms. Beside her, Parker looked just as uncomfortable as he handled the other Herstal Minimi.

Shepherd positioned her hands on the machine gun. "Tuck it in under your arm like this. It'll recoil, so be ready for its kick. Holding it in nice and tight will stop it bucking and help your aim.

"Keep your finger light on the trigger. Aim like this." He directed her gaze along the barrel. "And squeeze the trigger lightly. Fire in short bursts. It'll preserve our ammunition and keep the barrel from overheating and jamming. Do you all understand?"

They nodded.

Shepherd corrected Parker's grip on the machine gun. "Are you okay?"

Parker swallowed nervously. "I think so."

Shepherd clapped him on the shoulder. "Good man."

He took the Herstal Minimi from Allie and held it before Jan. "Your turn."

Jan's nose wrinkled with disgust, but he took the weapon and listened as Shepherd instructed him on how to use it.

A volley of heavy bullets smashed against the Inn. Shepherd seized the Winchester, cracked the shutter and scanned the clearing. It was empty. More shots followed, then the gunfire faded.

He closed the shutter. "It'll be dark soon. That's when the next attack will come."

Parker groaned. "We can't stop them."

"We hold the Inn and the cure. They must come to us, which means they have to cover that open expanse of clearing. That gives us the advantage. Trust me—we can hold them off.

"The worst thing we can do now is panic. When they start firing, you'll be scared. Don't give in to that fear. Control your breathing. Long, slow breaths. It'll help with your aim. Remember, short, controlled bursts. And keep listening to me. I'll tell you what to do. We'll get through this."

Seeing his exhaustion, Allie said firmly, "It's time for you to get some rest. We'll take turns to keep watch."

"I'll be in my room. Get me when night falls."

CHAPTER 34

THREE HOURS LATER, darkness had settled over the clearing like a heavy shroud. Shepherd peered through a shutter using the light-enhancing IDU he'd sterilized after retrieving it from Twisted Lip.

The clearing was tinged with an eerie gray-green, with the wall of jungle a rearing black mass beyond it. He saw no sign of movement from the mercenaries. Lightning scythed through the sky, whiting out the view through the IDU.

He eased away from the window and looked around the darkened rec room. Allie stood by the light switch, with Parker and Jan armed at the other window. He chanced another glance outside, wary of the sniper. The clearing remained empty.

Earlier, instead of finding rest in his room, the inactivity had allowed his mind to churn. It had filled with images of Cassie, waiting for him back home. She had trusted him to come home safely, and it looked like he would let her down.

Cassie had been only two years old when her mother died. She hadn't been able to comprehend that Claire wasn't coming back. For months after the accident, his little girl had waited by their front door, large gray eyes full of hope that her mom would return. It had broken his heart then and threatened to do so now.

His worry that she was in hospital tormented him. Had her condition worsened? Was it the seizures he so dreaded? And if her condition had indeed worsened, he had at his fingertips perhaps the only means of helping her, which his military side wanted to destroy.

He had to do something to help Cassie. The only solution

to his dilemma would be to somehow defeat the mercenaries. He knew he and the scientists couldn't hold them off forever. Benoit would proceed with caution, which perhaps gave them more time, but Lacoux was right—the outcome was inevitable. So what could they do?

If Benoit was a former elite Legionnaire, his military instincts would have been further heightened by the cognitive enhancing compound. They would be telling him his enemy was trapped, weak and surrounded. He could take his time and not risk losing any more men.

Perhaps then, their best recourse was to be as unpredictable as possible. The last thing Benoit would expect at the moment was an attack launched by the scientists. The problem with such a move would be how to get across the expanse of clearing without being seen.

He didn't have an answer for that, yet the more he thought about it, the more he became convinced that taking the attack to the mercenaries was the only move left that Benoit wouldn't expect.

But the memory of how his body had failed him in the laboratory nagged him. With his injuries, was he still capable of carrying out his own surprise assault against the mercenaries? He dismissed the thought with an effort; he had to be. The nano-suit would help. He just hoped O'Connell could get them ready in time.

He analyzed his strategy as he examined the clearing. How could he traverse the clearing without being detected? With the technology the mercenaries carried, it seemed impossible.

He started to fret. He was having difficulty breathing through his broken nose. His leg felt stiff and useless.

He forced himself to focus. Could he create a diversion?

211

But the more his mind worked, the stronger was his realization that Benoit had control.

More lightning ripped through the sky. He shifted away from the window, waited a few seconds and peered outside once more. He listened to the rumble of thunder, almost simultaneous now with the lightning.

Another flash of lightning forced him away from the window. When his eyes adjusted, he glanced outside. This time, the clearing was no longer empty. Dark shapes had emerged from the jungle and were sprinting toward the Inn.

Shepherd threw the Winchester to his shoulder, aimed for several pounding heartbeats as they drew within the rifle's range, then fired at the nearest mercenary.

His headshot missed, striking the man in the chest. He saw him sprawl to the ground, before rising back to his feet. There was a crack as the sniper returned fire, followed by a shower of sparks as a heavy-caliber bullet tore into the shutter. Shepherd slammed it closed. Another bullet clanged against the titanium. "Hit the lights!"

Allie flipped the switch. The rec room filled with glaring light and the floodlights burst into life outside.

Shepherd shoved the IDU away and jerked the shutter open. The mercenaries were fumbling with their own useless display units.

He fired, but his aim was off as his eyes adjusted. Before he could fire again, a sniper bullet smashed against the wall several feet away and he ducked. There was a long burst of gunfire from the other window. Parker. "Hold your fire and get down!"

A sniper bullet smashed through the shutter as Parker dropped to the ground. It cannoned into the far wall in a cloud of debris. Despite the floodlights, the sniper had found his range. He was good, Shepherd noted grimly. "Close the shutter!"

Parker didn't move.

Shepherd slithered across the floor as fast as his leg would allow. Keeping low, he wrenched the shutter closed. Another bullet clanged against it and whined away.

He crouched over the naturalist. "Are you hit?"

Parker lifted his head cautiously. His voice was hoarse with fear. "I'm okay. Jesus, that almost hit me."

"Keep down!" He waited for a lull in the sniper fire, then peered quickly through the shutter. The mercenaries had retreated.

"What's going on?" Allie said.

"It's over. For now." Shepherd flexed his leg, feeling the cartilage in his ruined knee grind against bone. He adjusted the heavy strapping. The stability it provided was keeping him upright, but the stiffening of the limb was limiting his mobility.

He wiped his sweating fingers on his pants, then reloaded the Winchester, using bullets stuffed in the pockets of his cargo pants. He checked to make sure no one had been hit by the sniper fire. They all looked shaky but intact.

Allie moved alongside. "What happened?"

"The floodlights turned them back, but we don't have much time." He tried to gather his thoughts through the dull throb of his broken nose. The mercenaries were reassessing now, but they would launch another assault. With the scientists' reserves of ammunition dwindling with each attack, he knew there was only so long they could defend themselves.

It was time to change the game. Be unpredictable. There was an ear-splitting crack of thunder. Maybe Mother Nature would help.

He retrieved Parker's machine gun.

"What are you doing?" Allie asked.

"When O'Connell gets the suits ready, I'm going out there."

She glared at him. "What on earth are you planning?"

"Allie, I need you to trust me. We don't have much time and I need to prepare."

As if to emphasize his point, there was a crack of gunfire and a pop. He limped to the window and eased the shutter open a fraction. Six floodlights, each thirty feet high, stood around the clearing. One of them was now dark. As Shepherd watched, there was another crack and a clang as another floodlight was hit. This time, the bullet missed its mark.

He closed the shutter. "They're shooting out the lights. I need you to take the Winchester and stand watch at the window until O'Connell gets back."

Allie seized his arm. "Not until you tell me what you're intending to do. You said you'd run your plans past me. So talk to me, damn you!"

There was another crack and faint pop. "I'm not playing Benoit's damned game anymore. I'm going to take the fight to him."

Her grip tightened. "What are you going to do?"

"I'm going to hit them from the jungle."

She looked incredulous. "I can't believe you'd consider such a risk in your state!"

"Right now, Benoit thinks they have us trapped. So we change our strategy. Do the unexpected. He knows they have us pinned down with overpowering force and numbers. That we can't leave the Inn without them seeing us. The last thing Benoit will anticipate is an attack by us on them."

"Why don't we give Mancini a chance? If he can weaponize the pathogen then perhaps we can use it against them."

"It's a big 'if' Allie. You know that creating such a pathogen under ordinary circumstances is a delicate process. Mancini is rushing—anything could go wrong. And even if he does weaponize it, he still has to come up with a way to deliver it without killing us in the process. I've thought this through. Believe me, this is our only course of action."

She was about to argue, then she sighed. "What makes you think you can get out of here without being seen?"

"The storm. It's the one thing Benoit hasn't been able to plan for. Their night vision displays will be useless when it hits."

"So will yours."

"Yes. But I know where they are and they won't know I'm coming."

Another crack. Another faint pop.

"Are you sure? Were you good? As a SEAL, I mean."

"Ranger," he corrected. "And yes. I was."

"What do the rest of us do?"

"You have the weapons. Keep a watch on the clearing. They'll be wary, so we have some time. But if they do launch another assault, keep firing for as long as you can, then get to the bio lab and barricade yourselves in. I'll come after you."

"Jesus," she said weakly.

"Trust me, Allie," he said softly.

Her green eyes were wide with worry, but she nodded.

Shepherd loaded a backpack with spare magazines he'd retrieved from the dead mercenaries. "I'll wait for O'Connell to get the suits ready. When the storm hits, I leave."

* * *

BENOIT WATCHED ROCHE shoot out the lights. Only one remained now. The schematics provided by Lacoux had revealed that the floodlights were powered via underground cables leading to generators kept inside the facility for protection against the weather. Rather than cut the power supply, Benoit had been forced to employ the more old-fashioned measure of gunfire.

As the floodlight swayed violently in the rising wind, he heard Roche curse, his finger paused on the trigger. Benoit fought back his impatience; Roche was the best shot they had and he was confident the sniper would get it done. But he had to do it quickly; the worsening conditions would soon make the task near impossible.

The wind seemed to be strengthening with every gust. Overhead, he heard it moan, the canopy rustling as it churned angrily. In the distance, he discerned a new sound, like a plane's engines whirring into life on an airport runway. His men had also heard it and got to their feet, staring skyward, uneasy expressions on their hard faces.

"What is that?" Halle yelled.

Benoit didn't answer. The sound was growing, the high-pitched whine reverberating in his ears. It was accompanied by a deep rhythm that rolled across the canopy of the jungle like bass drums played by angry gods.

The whine became a shriek. He crouched instinctively. With a blinding flash of lightning and crack of thunder that shook the heavy air, the storm hit.

The wind howled overhead, pressing the jungle canopy beneath its weight like a crushing hand. Heavy drops of rain blasted into the clearing. The deluge built until all that could be seen in the dim light was a shimmering gray curtain of water.

Forked lightning arced across the sky, accompanied by booming thunder that he felt in the pit of his stomach. Black pools of water sprung up all around them, glittering in the beam of his flashlight. The Inn disappeared behind the driving sheets of rain.

Benoit realized what this meant. His mind rapidly processed the capabilities of the man inside the facility who had so far eliminated four of his men. An adversary with instincts ingrained through military training and experience. One who would see the ferocity of the storm as an opportunity.

Halle shouted above the shriek of wind and rolling booms of thunder, "We need to find higher ground!"

Benoit disagreed. But rather than shout instructions he knew wouldn't be heard, he strode quickly amongst his men, readying them. "We'll attack in fifteen minutes. Front and rear. They'll have erected barricades, so we'll set charges and blow them up."

With the storm disrupting their communications, he sent one of his men to alert the mercenary stationed behind the Inn to prevent the scientists from fleeing. "Use enough C4 to destroy their defenses, but not enough to blow the facility up. You will form part of the assault team. Strike in fifteen minutes. Take prisoners where you can, but kill anyone who resists. Remember, Lacoux is inside. I want him alive!"

Halle followed close behind. "What are you doing? This area will be flooded! We need to find shelter!"

"No," Benoit shouted over the storm. "The soldier in there will use the storm to launch a surprise assault."

"In these conditions? Against a force as powerful as ours?"

He fought back his impatience. Why was Halle so slow?

Why couldn't he see what Benoit could? "It's what I would do."

Leaving the still skeptical Halle behind, Benoit ran to the edge of the jungle, checked his Herstal Minimi, sweeping away a brown cicada that was squatting near the trigger guard. The storm seemed to have stirred the insects up, and they were swarming around the mercenaries in frenzied clouds.

He wiped moths and black flies from his face, realizing as he did so that his headache was growing worse. The pain he felt at his temples seemed to be sprouting tentacles throughout his skull.

Ignoring the ache, he assessed the readiness of his men. They had scrambled rapidly into action, gathering at the edge of the jungle beside him. Despite his skepticism, Halle stood poised at his shoulder. The trackers remained behind, sheltering beneath the umbrella-like fronds of a large fern.

Rain cascaded into the clearing, the heavy drops exploding against the ground in a spray of mud and water. The wind tore at the rain, driving it sideways in a screeching gale of torn leaves and small branches. More lightning streaked above.

Benoit surveyed the terrain illuminated dimly in the glow of the lone floodlight, the heavy mud and spreading pools of water. It would slow his attack force but the curtain of rain would ensure his men remained invisible to the scientists. By the time they materialized out of the storm, it would be too late for them to defend themselves or launch their own attack.

Benoit raised his hand, ready to unleash his men in a final, devastating strike that would wipe out these scientists once and for all.

CHAPTER 35

SHEPHERD WATCHED IN awe as the storm rushed from the darkness with a wailing shriek. The jungle tossed and churned. Leaves and branches swirled into the air as if the rainforest was being savaged by a chainsaw.

Then the frightening vision was shut out by the rain, a solid gray sheet that swept across the clearing. The raindrops pounded the ground in volcanic bursts of mud and grass.

Jan and Parker were crouched at the far window, peering outside.

"Oh my God!" Parker shouted.

Jan's grip on his Herstal Minimi tightened, his smooth face tense.

Kneeling at the window beside Shepherd, Allie pressed the radio to her ear. "Mancini, have you made any progress?" She struggled to hear his response over the angry moan of the wind. "Mancini? I didn't catch that. Can you repeat?"

The radio hissed with interference. "…not completed. Need more time."

"Damn it, Mancini, we don't have it! Have you developed the pathogen?"

"Yes. Now need… delivery mechanism."

"I'm going to send Jan to help you."

There was a short, static-filled pause, then the interference cleared. "Okay," came the reluctant reply.

"Jannie! I need you to help Mancini!"

Jan handed Shepherd the Herstal Minimi and hurried away.

Shepherd gripped a weapon in each hand. He was anxious to leave while the storm provided cover. But he wanted the nano-suit for protection and for the support it would provide his knee. Where was O'Connell?

The roaring of the wind intensified to a deafening scream, there was a clap of thunder that shook the roof and a whump as the full force of the gale hammered the front walls. Rain drummed against the roof and cascaded around the Inn.

He decided he couldn't wait any longer. He hefted both machine guns, then decided he wanted his trusty rifle. He handed Allie one of the Herstal Minimis and took the Winchester. "I'm going to check on O'Connell. I need you to remain here to keep watch outside. Call me on the radio if you see anything."

* * *

HE HOBBLED AS fast as he could into the scientists' laboratory. "O'Connell, where are the suits? I need one now!"

O'Connell was dressed in a blue hazmat suit and standing before a tall rack that held the two nano-suits hanging upside-down beneath the protective hood of a biosafety cabinet. The specially designed rack was normally used to dry hazmat suits after disinfection by pressurizing them with warm air. The air exiting the suit removed the water vapor.

His voice was muffled. "They're not ready."

"What the hell are you doing with them?"

"I sterilized them by immersing them in a liquid solution containing quaternary ammonia and then wiped off the toxin. I dried them, then repeated the process twice. They're drying on the rack now. Then I'll test them for any residual toxin using wipe strips. Good enough? Oh, and I moved the bodies of the mercenaries into the supply room and reinforced the barricade at the rear entrance. What the hell have you done?"

Shepherd fought to control his impatience. They were

running out of time. He reached for the nearest suit. O'Connell shoved his hand away. "You want to get infected? Put a hazmat suit on or stay back."

"The ammonium must have sterilized them. I don't care if they're a bit wet!"

"After the first and second times I immersed them, I still found traces of the neurotoxin. Miniscule, but enough to kill you. This third clean should've eradicated all traces, but you need to wait until the tests come back negative."

"Damn it. How long?"

"Another five minutes. What are you intending to do with them?"

Shepherd outlined his plan to launch a surprise assault on the mercenaries.

"What do the rest of us do?"

"Allie will keep an eye out for the mercs. I want you to stay here and guard our rear."

"No problem. But I want one of the suits. And a gun. I'm not guarding your damn fort without a weapon."

"Fine." As he waited for the test results, his impatience mounting, his eye fell on the khaki backpack. O'Connell had placed it on the floor against a wall where it was out of the way as he rushed about preparing the nano-suits.

O'Connell saw the direction of his gaze. He positioned his bulky body between Shepherd and the pack. "Don't go anywhere near it. I'm not letting you or Allie destroy the cure."

Despite his anxiety, he felt a surge of exasperation. "Why do you think everyone is against you? Why are you so damned paranoid all the time? Allie talks highly of you. She says Alderton did as well."

"Alderton thought so highly of me that he promoted her above me."

"Allie told me it was a close call. She doesn't know what swayed Alderton in the end. But he must have discussed it with you."

"He gave me nothing but corporate bullshit. That the board was more comfortable with her appointment. The old bastard lied to me."

Shepherd's irritation faded as he saw the pain and bitterness in those pale eyes. "How did Alderton lie to you?"

O'Connell gave a harsh bark of laughter. "Okay. I'll tell you the sort of man John Alderton was. You know that before I joined Atione, I was a research team leader at Zarnife Pharmaceuticals in Paris?"

Shepherd nodded. He'd been given a brief background on each member of his new team when he had accepted his role.

"Well, it was my team that made the Tabazitone breakthrough."

Shepherd was impressed. Tabazitone had been shown to be effective in the treatment of prostate cancer because it worked by preventing the formation of microtubules which pull the chromosomes apart in dividing cells, such as cancer cells. It was a significant and highly profitable scientific achievement, one that resulted in a Biotechnology Heritage Award for the brilliant young English scientist, Louise Jones, who'd led its discovery. "That was wonderful work. I didn't know you were part of Louise's team."

"Louise Jones was on *my* team," he said bitterly. "She reported to me. I was the one who first recognized the potential of our project and fought for the funding to keep it going. Then we made the final breakthrough and everyone saw its promise.

"The problem was, I wasn't seen as marketable enough

to be the face behind it. Zarnife were struggling financially and wanted a big bump in their share price. They wanted someone younger, less rough around the edges. Someone who'd look good on camera, in the newspapers.

"So they promoted Louise Jones into my position. To keep me quiet, they concocted a sexual harassment claim against me—Louise fucking Jones again. It was utter bullshit. But they said if I complained, they'd sack me and leak details of the claim. I'd never work in the industry again."

Shepherd was appalled. "But how does Alderton fit in?"

"He heard the rumors that I was disgruntled and approached me. He knew I'd led the team, not Jones. He wanted to know what happened. When I told him, he offered me the job at Atione. Said he'd never screw me over like Zarnife did." His pale eyes gleamed in anger. "Well, the old bastard did. I was forty-five years old when I made the Tabazitone discovery. Thought that was my big break, the one that'd make my name. When they gave all the credit for it to Louise, I thought my chance had passed.

"Then, nearly five years later, we discover the Alzheimer's cure. And just when we do, what happens? John fucking Alderton promotes Allie Temple. Another bright, attractive, presentable young woman who'd look great talking to the world's media and potential investors."

"I'm sure that's not the reason he promoted Allie."

"Isn't it? Think about it. I have fifteen years more experience than her. It was my research team which made the breakthrough. Isn't it logical I would have been the one promoted?" The bitterness in his tone intensified. "But unlike Allie, I'm not polished enough, not enough of a fucking people person. Never mind that it's my bullying the people on my teams, pushing them hard, that gets all the results."

"Allie's brilliant and qualified for the role. She's also a team player. You're not. I'll bet that's why Alderton promoted her above you. She's the successor he wanted, the one who would carry on his legacy."

O'Connell studied him. "I should have known you'd stick up for your girlfriend. That's fine. I don't want your understanding. But now you know the truth, and it's a bitch, ain't it?

"I turn fifty next year. This was my last chance. I won't get another. So excuse me if I'm a little unsupportive of Allie's leadership. But as much as I detest her and don't think her worthy of her promotion, I know we're in deep shit out here. So I'll pitch in and do what I have to, which means carrying all of your sorry asses. Again." He turned away from Shepherd contemptuously and examined the wipe strips. "No result yet."

Before Shepherd could respond, a dull, concussive thud burst from the corridor leading to the rear of the Inn. O'Connell looked confused, but Shepherd knew what it meant. "They're attacking!"

He rushed to the door and peered around it. The corridor was strewn with debris. A large ragged hole had appeared in the barricade O'Connell had erected. Through it, he saw the heavy wooden door had been destroyed. The corridor's halogen lighting illuminated the sheeting gray rain. Two black-clad figures materialized, machine guns leveled.

He shot at the mercenaries with his Herstal Minimi. Their nano-suits repelled his withering salvo, but their visors were pushed up in the harsh light and he directed his aim at their exposed faces. Forced to take cover, they dove for the shelter of the storage room.

He ducked behind the heavy metal door to the scientists'

lab as the mercenaries returned fire, their bullets clanging against the steel and whining away. O'Connell crouched at his shoulder. Shepherd hurriedly handed him the Winchester and boxes of spare ammunition. O'Connell took them without comment, his pale eyes full of fight.

Allie's voice squawked from the radio. "Shepherd! I need help! Can you hear me?"

He didn't have time to respond. He fired a short controlled burst designed to preserve his ammunition and keep the mercenaries pinned down while he thought about what to do. They had attacked so fast. He'd thought he would have more time to launch his own surprise assault. Once again, Benoit had outsmarted him.

There was another burst of static from his radio. "Shepherd! They're attacking! I need help!"

"Answer her!" O'Connell roared as he fired down the corridor, reloaded smoothly and fired once more. The heavy magnum bullets smashed into the wall beside the storage room and the mercenaries backpedaled.

Shepherd used the pause to respond. "Allie! What's happening?"

"The mercenaries came to the door. They were carrying something in a backpack. I fired but couldn't drive them back—there was too much gunfire. But the shooting's stopped! I don't know why. I think they must've done something. What should I do?"

He realized what it meant and his fear swelled. "They've put charges on the door. Get back behind the bar. I'm coming to you!"

O'Connell fired the Winchester then heaved his bulk behind the door as bullets hammered into the wall near the entrance.

"Allie needs me," Shepherd said. "Keep the Winchester; it's more accurate. Aim for their faces. That's their only weak spot." He assessed this man. Could he rely on him to stand his ground?

"Go. I'll hold them back as long as I can."

As he hustled from the lab, he heard the blasts of the Winchester behind him, followed by a defiant shout, "Fuck you, assholes!"

He entered the rec room just as the door and the barricade behind it exploded. He threw himself behind the bar as debris screamed overhead, smashing against the walls and ceiling. Acrid smoke wafted through the air.

Allie and Parker were sprawled on the ground. "Are you okay?"

"Yes," they gasped.

Shepherd glanced over the bar and saw the hole torn through the barricade and the shattered door. Beyond were the dark forms of mercenaries as they charged the Inn. He couldn't repel the attack; they were too close. They were almost at the stairs leading to the doorway.

He waited until he saw the first of them framed in the hole, then fired a burst with the machine gun. The lead mercenary staggered but kept coming. "We can't hold them! We have to fall back!"

Allie ignored him, already on the radio. "Mancini! Damn you! Can you hear me?"

"...here, Allie. What's going on? There's gunfire all around us!"

"The mercenaries are attacking. We need the pathogen! Is it ready?"

A burst of static. "...don't have a delivery mechanism."

"Just get the damn thing ready. We're out of time!"

Bullets ripped through each shutter in a shower of sparks. The heavy-caliber ammunition whined above them, smashing against tables, chairs, into the roof and walls in a spray of wood splinters and metal fragments that gleamed like daggers and were just as deadly. A bullet snagged the strap of Parker's black backpack and it skidded across the floor.

"What are we going to do?" Parker yelled.

"We're going to barricade ourselves in the bio lab," said Allie, "then release the pathogen."

Shepherd realized she was right. There was no other option. "Go! I'll give you cover and hold them back as long as I can. Run!"

"Ben's still in the sick bay!"

"I'll get him." He fired another burst with the Herstal Minimi then crouched.

"What about Lacoux?" said Parker. "If we leave him in the meeting room, the pathogen will kill him."

"I have to help Mancini and Jan," said Allie. "That leaves only you to get him. I understand if you don't want to put yourself at risk for him. This is my decision, not yours. His death will be on me. But don't put yourself in danger. Not for Lacoux.

"Don't untie him. Drag his skinny ass in the damn chair if you have to. If you don't think there's time, leave him and get to the bio lab."

As she spoke, more bullets cracked against the wall. One of the halogen downlights exploded with a pop of shattering glass and a snaking coil of smoke joined the smoke drifting from the smoldering, eviscerated barricade.

An alarm sounded and the rec room was bathed in flashing red light as emergency bulbs burst into life. Water sprayed from nozzles spaced evenly between the bulbs.

"The fire alarm!" Allie shouted. "We'll be sealed off!"

"Go!" Shepherd yelled. "Leave your weapon!"

Allie left her Herstal Minimi on the ground and followed Parker as he bolted into the corridor.

The mercenaries barreled through the hole. Shepherd fired until the machine gun clicked uselessly, empty. He threw it aside and snatched up Allie's Herstal Minimi. He fired for as long he dared, wanting to preserve some ammunition, then before the mercenaries could respond he retreated into the corridor behind him.

CHAPTER 36

SHEPHERD HOBBLED BEHIND Allie, who tore along the corridor toward the laboratories. She only had seconds to act. The smoke had triggered the fire alarm, which in turn, had instigated the emergency containment response.

The greatest fears when planning the construction of this highly-specialized facility were the release of a bio-contaminant, and fire. The Inn had been designed to respond immediately to both. Every room was equipped with smoke detectors and specialized sensors to pick up on the presence of bio-forms.

The truly hazardous pathogens were kept in the bio lab, which was designed to bio-safety level four, the highest classification. A dangerous bio-contaminant release would most likely come from there.

The triggering of the emergency containment response resulted in oxygen automatically being pumped from the bio lab, suffocating any fire, and creating negative pressure that prevented any contaminant from escaping the room. The hatch to the lab was sealed immediately. The door to the scientists' laboratory took longer to seal; a full minute, to provide anyone inside time to escape.

Shepherd counted down inside his head. Allie had less than thirty seconds before the entrance was sealed. The bio lab would already be locked down. Her slim form raced along the corridor, its white walls glowing a macabre red under the flashing emergency lights, as if they were coated in blood.

Seconds later, she skidded to a halt beside the keypad outside the lab, entered the emergency override code, and the low-pitched alarm and flashing red light ceased. The spray from the overhead nozzles slowed to a drip.

She disappeared into the laboratory, heading for the bio lab.

Shepherd burst into the sickbay. Ben lay unconscious on the cot. He picked him up, hoisted him over his shoulder and limped along the corridor toward the bio lab. As he passed the meeting room, its door opened and Parker peered out furtively.

Shepherd shouted, "Forget Lacoux and get to the bio lab. The mercenaries are inside. Move!"

"I'll be right behind you!"

He hurried through the scientists' laboratory toward the bio lab. Beyond it, he saw O'Connell kneeling at the metal door and firing the Winchester into the corridor beyond. The man ducked back. "I can't hold them much longer!"

Shepherd hauled open the hatch to the bio lab. Inside, Allie was urgently speaking to Mancini, who was wearing a blue hazmat suit. Behind them stood Jan, also in a hazmat suit, hunched over several metal canisters on a bench.

Shepherd gently placed Ben on the floor and limped to the trio.

"We heard the fire alarm." Though Mancini's voice was muffled through the suit, he heard his panic.

"It's dealt with," said Allie. "I entered the emergency override. Do you have something we can use?"

Mancini seemed frozen in place. "There wasn't enough time."

"What are you talking about?" Shepherd demanded.

Mancini remained silent as if lost in his own fears.

"Jan? I need an update," said Allie.

His fingers were working delicately with several syringes

full of a clear liquid. "Mancini made the pathogen but couldn't produce a delivery mechanism for it. I'm working on it now."

"How long?"

"I need a few minutes."

"We don't have a few minutes!"

"I'm working as fast as I can. But I need more time. If Mancini had called for help earlier, I could've engineered something less primitive. In the meantime, I suggest you stand back until you have a suit on."

"What is this pathogen?" Shepherd asked. "Will it stop the mercenaries? Talk to me!"

The harshness of his voice jolted Mancini from his fear-driven stupor. "If we can deliver it effectively, then yes. But there's a problem."

"What is it?"

"It's a Hail Mary, scorched earth sort of thing."

Shepherd stared at him, dismayed. "What have you done?"

"I combined batrachotoxin with the influenza strain, which will spread it like wildfire."

"Oh my God," Allie said weakly.

"I told you it was a last resort," Mancini said. "It wouldn't be effective outside. Too easily dispersed, especially with this weather. But inside, in a contained environment, it'll be instantly fatal to the mercenaries."

"It could wipe out everyone inside the Inn!"

"Yes," Mancini said quickly, "But not anyone in the bio lab. This is a sealed environment. We can shelter safely here, while the mercenaries will be infected when they enter the inner core of the Inn. It would decimate them."

"And then what? As soon as we set foot outside the bio lab we'd be killed!"

"I bio-engineered it so it'll break down after a few hours, rendering it inert."

"Jesus, you've created a biological weapon!" Shepherd was stunned, then felt a flare of hope. It could work if they could unleash it upon the mercenaries without killing themselves in the process. "You weren't able to engineer a delivery mechanism in time?"

"No."

"Why didn't you tell me earlier?" Allie snapped. "Damn your arrogance. You should've asked for help. You've put everyone at risk!"

"No one could've put this together in the time I had," Mancini retorted defensively.

Shepherd forced himself to think. The staccato cracking of gunfire was interspersed with the heavier retorts from the Winchester. He heard O'Connell shout, "They're advancing! I can't hold them back!"

He tried hard to ignore his fear and the commotion around him, but he was acutely aware that unless Jan managed to work a miracle, they had the means to hold the mercenaries at bay, but no safe way to deliver it.

"Hurry, Jan," Allie urged. Then she turned to Shepherd. "We need to get suited up. I'll help you with Ben."

Shepherd hauled on a hazmat suit, as Allie did the same. Together, they suited up Ben. He noticed Allie's fingers trembled as she pulled at the heavy plastic material. Pale and sweating, breathing hard, she looked as anxious as he felt.

O'Connell hurtled into the bio lab clutching the rifle and his backpack. "I can't hold them back any longer! I pinned 'em down enough to make them cautious, but they keep coming. If we're going to release the pathogen, now is the time to do it!"

He dumped the rifle on a workbench, then carefully placed his backpack on the floor against the wall. He stood over it protectively as he hauled on a hazmat suit.

"Jan, we're out of time," said Allie.

"I'm almost finished. Is everybody inside?"

"Where's Parker?" said Allie.

"He was right behind me." Shepherd looked around hurriedly to ensure everyone was safely inside. Blue-clad figures milled about, hastily checking themselves and others for tears that could compromise the integrity of the hazmat suits, before clipping themselves into the yellow, filtered air-hoses hanging from the ceiling.

He tried to do a quick head count but found it difficult with all the movement. With the suits on, they all looked the same. But it looked like everyone was there.

He heard more gunfire. It sounded like they were almost in the scientists' lab. He realized that the longer there was no retaliatory fire, the more confident the mercenaries would become. They would be outside the bio lab in seconds.

"Now, Allie!" O'Connell roared.

"They're ready!" Jan shouted, clasping the two canisters.

Mancini examined them. "That's too crude! Aerosols? You can't release them from here! Not with this pathogen. Jesus!"

"With the hazmat suits on we can take the canisters outside and release the pathogen."

"But the suits might not be effective. Not against this!"

"Why can't we put it into glass vials and throw the damn things into the scientists' lab?" asked Shepherd.

"Because the glass might not break," Mancini replied. "And to do so, the hatch would need to be open, exposing us to possible contamination. Anyway, it's too late. If we unseal the canisters now we're dead."

Allie looked toward the open hatch. "But the suit might work?"

"Might! But anyone outside can't come back in. They'll be contaminated."

Allie grabbed the canisters and unclipped her air hose. Now she was relying on the powered air-purifying respirator in the suit; a considerably reduced level of protection.

Shepherd realized her intention. "No, Allie. Don't!"

She ran to the hatch.

"What the hell are you doing?" O'Connell's nasal voice rang out.

Allie's voice rasped with fear. "Just make damn sure the Alzheimer's cure gets developed!"

"No! God, no! Don't do it!" cried Shepherd.

She stepped outside and slammed the hatch closed.

O'Connell sealed it behind her. Shepherd shoved him aside, frantically trying to open it.

Through the window, he saw Allie fumbling to open the canisters with her gloved hands. Mercenaries loomed in each entrance to the scientists' laboratory. She ripped open the canisters and flung them at the intruders. Gunfire cracked.

"Allie!"

O'Connell and Mancini threw themselves on him. He stumbled forward, his head slamming sickeningly against the hatch. As his vision faded he saw Allie fall to the ground, disappearing behind a bench. Then Shepherd collapsed to the floor.

CHAPTER 37

BENOIT CROUCHED, FEELING the rain hammer against the back and shoulders of his nano-suit. The wind buffeted him from all sides as if trying to wrench him free of the thick layer of mud his knees had sunk into.

He had kept the majority of his squad back to provide cover as smaller advance teams attacked the facility from the front and rear. Both teams had now entered the facility and he'd ordered the men with him to cease firing.

More thunder rumbled overhead and the rain seemed heavier. Despite the warmth of the tropical deluge, he shivered. He had operated in foul weather before; as a Legionnaire, he had been trained to ignore it. But this...

He focused his attention on the radio embedded in his helmet. Despite the advanced nature of the bone convection technology, his ears were filled with bursts of static as lightning tore through the sky. But with the static he heard gunfire crackling through the radio and snatched voices.

A shout from Halle caught his attention. He glanced up as a figure sprinted through the rain toward the mercenaries and lurched to a halt. His men seized the sodden, mud-splattered individual and forced him to the ground while they checked him for weapons. He was shouting, his words inaudible through the tumult of the storm.

Benoit frowned. It had to be one of the scientists. But who? The man's face was disfigured, the muscles locked in spasm. He strode to the sprawled figure, grabbed his sodden hair and jerked his face up to examine it. The rain swept away the dirt, but the muscles of the middle and lower face had contracted, twisting and contorting the features beyond recognition.

The man screamed, "It's me—Lacoux!"

Astonished, he wondered what had happened to him. There was another shout and two more figures emerged from the storm. One was a mercenary, gripping another, much smaller, bedraggled man by the arm. The mercenary strode through the mud to Benoit, but before he could report, a scream reverberated through his radio.

He released Lacoux and tried to contact his men inside the facility. "Ferrand! Ardun! What's your status?" He listened intently for a response. The radio hissed. A voice grated, too faint to understand.

Another crackle of voices. Urgent. Someone was yelling. He heard more screaming. Benoit listened intently. His men or the scientists? The screams continued, but the gunfire had stopped. What was going on?

Lacoux seized Benoit's arm, shouting something. His words were ripped away by the tempest. Benoit leaned closer. "Get your men out of there! The scientists are going to release a toxin. Get your men out now!"

"Ferrand! Ardun! Fall back!"

Ferrand's voice rasped, distorted and faint, but full of fear. "We're fucking dying! Something in here…" His voice faded.

"Ferrand! Ardun! Fall back. Fall back now!"

There was another crackle, followed by a shriek that trailed to silence. Benoit's stomach tightened and for the first time during this trial, he felt fear. "Back to the jungle!"

The mercenaries put their heads down and ran through the raging wind and rain, leaving the place of death behind them.

CHAPTER 38

SHEPHERD SWAM SLOWLY to consciousness. He first became aware of a faint hum, then a vague murmur of voices. He lay there for a moment, listening.

His head was resting on something hard. It hurt. He attempted to shift his head and a searing pain jerked him fully awake.

He opened his eyes and a burning white light forced them closed again. He wondered where he was and how he had got there. He couldn't get his mind working; he felt dizzy and confused. His head was pounding and he realized he wanted to throw up.

He reached down to rub his stomach and encountered plastic. He opened his eyes and saw a white ceiling and the stark glow of fluorescent lights which still hurt his eyes.

Blinking, he rolled onto his side, intending to prop himself up on an elbow, but his head throbbed, the room spun and his stomach gave an oily lurch. He slumped back.

After a minute, the throb in his skull eased and his mind cleared. The mercenaries had attacked, the Inn had been overrun. He had retreated to the sickbay, gathered Ben and run for the bio lab. Then... Allie.

"No!" he struggled to sit up. He saw he was on a gleaming metal floor, encased in a blue suit.

He tried to get to his feet. His vision blurred and the room spun. He remained still, gathering himself.

As his vision cleared, he took in his surroundings. The bio lab was small and white-walled, about twenty square feet. Except for a tiny aperture in the hatch, it was windowless. Fluorescent lights hung in airtight boxes from the white ceiling, the harsh light reflecting off the stainless steel of a rectangular workbench in the center of the floor. Yellow hoses spiraled from the ceiling and were attached to figures in blue hazmat suits. A Class III maximum containment safety cabinet with gloves attached to the front and a built-in microscope lined a wall.

A huge, blue-suited figure loomed above him. Cerulean eyes peered anxiously at him through a hooded visor. "Sweetie?"

"Where's Allie? We can't leave her! What about the mercenaries? They're attacking! Help me up, Jan!"

"The attack is over. You need to rest for a minute."

"I can't rest. We have to help Allie. What happened to the mercenaries?"

"Allie released the pathogen. It stopped them."

"Allie's okay? Why didn't the emergency containment protocols kick in when the pathogen was released? Won't we suffocate in here?"

Jan's voice quavered with emotion. "Allie had already entered the emergency override code when the fire alarm was triggered. As long as it stays in place, we'll be fine."

Shepherd forced himself to think. "The pathogen worked? But Allie's suit protected her?"

But Jan's eyes flooded with tears and he turned away, too upset to talk.

"Jannie?" Shepherd frowned, struggling to remember. Everything had happened so fast. He remembered his fear as he realized her intention. A feeling of dread gripped his heart. His mind felt numb, as if to prevent him comprehending the dreadful reality of what had happened.

He climbed to his feet, fighting the wave of nausea that flooded over him. His head spun and he clung to a bench to support himself.

He breathed deeply to compose himself. The dizziness lessened and he found he was able to stand upright without toppling to the ground.

He shoved away from the bench and hobbled toward the hatch, moving from bench to bench, pausing at each to rest briefly. The suited figures watched him silently as he shuffled past, his boots scuffing against the floor. They looked as dazed as he felt. He reached the hatch and peered at the scientists' laboratory outside.

"Sweet Jesus," he whispered. He saw a large, bulky body on the floor. His heart hammered. He shifted position, scanning the lab, and saw three more black-clad figures sprawled on the ground. There were no other bodies.

He turned his attention to the mercenary closest to the bio lab. The man had managed to get a few steps inside the scientists' laboratory before collapsing. He was still clutching his weapon, his index finger curled around the trigger.

His pallid face was contorted, his eyes wide, staring and full of what looked like hemorrhagic blood. Dried blood caked his nose. His mouth gaped in an endless, silent scream. Through it had spewed a yellow mixture of saliva and vomit, which had pooled around his head. His torso was twisted, his arms and legs splayed at crazy angles, as if he had died in agony.

Shepherd searched for any signs of movement. Nothing. The Inn was still. Distantly, he heard the heavy drum of rain and felt the shudders as the Inn vibrated beneath the storm's assault. There was no sign of Allie.

"Allie!" He slammed his fist against the hatch. "Allie! Can you hear me?"

"I've been yelling for her, but there's been no response," said Jan.

"How long ago did she leave?"

"Ten minutes at least," said Mancini.

"Was she hurt? Did the mercenaries shoot her?"

"We don't know," said Jan. "She fell behind the bench over there. There's been no movement since. She doesn't have a radio."

"Parker didn't make it either," said Mancini.

"He was right behind me! I saw him."

"He never got here," Jan replied. He sounded drained.

O'Connell's voice was raw with fear and anger. "What do you propose we do now, Shepherd? Got any more of your bright ideas now we're trapped? Because they've worked fucking brilliantly so far."

Shepherd ignored him and pushed away from the hatch. He couldn't stand the sight of those bodies any longer. All he wanted was to be left alone with his own grief. He shuffled across to the workbench and slumped over it, numb, unable to comprehend that she was gone; that he'd lost her.

He grappled with his grief and remorse, trying to force it aside. It served no purpose. Not now. Cassie was waiting for him back home. He had to figure out what to do. But his mind could only focus on one thought—they were trapped in the bio lab. He had lost his only chance to launch a surprise attack on the mercenaries.

And with that last chance, he saw they had lost all hope. He could see no way of defeating the mercenaries now. There was no chance of escape. Allie was dead. The bile burned in the back of his throat; the bitter taste of defeat.

His mind turned to the cure. He remembered Allie's words about disposing of it; that instead, they would find another way. He realized there was no other way. They couldn't allow the mercenaries to get their hands on the cure. The time had come to destroy it.

CHAPTER 39

THE MERCENARIES SQUATTED in the few patches of ground not flooded. The storm ravaging the jungle canopy was starting to penetrate the lower story. Small waterfalls gushed down tree trunks and branches, cannoning off shovel-sized leaves and exploding against the jungle floor. Dark pools of water spread along the trail, absorbing the jungle litter.

The shock on the survivors' faces was illuminated in the glow of flashlights. Benoit's squad had been decimated; of the original thirteen, only five remained. Morale had been shattered. They had all heard the cries of their dying friends and instead of resolve in those usually hard eyes, Benoit could see fear.

He stood apart from the remnants of his squad. He had remained silent since reaching the shelter of the jungle. At first, he'd prowled furiously back and forth along the edge of the clearing. For the past few minutes he had stood motionless, his back turned to his men, staring out into the rain veiling the clearing, toward the facility.

He swiveled to study his men. They stirred expectantly as their leader strode toward them. Fear had drained all the fight from them and he knew they wanted nothing more than to go home.

He reached the huddle and halted. The hiss of air through his broken nose was audible even through the tumult of the storm. "Get up."

A murmur went around the group of squatting men.

"Get up!"

After a long pause filled with the booming of thunder, one by one, the mercenaries got to their feet.

Benoit raised his arm and pointed toward the storm-cloaked facility. "Our enemy is in there—so why were you squatting in the mud like terrified schoolgirls?"

They murmured to each other. Their words were lost in the wind, but the dissent on their faces was visible.

"We can't go back. Ardun and Ferrand's teams were fucking wiped out." Roche tapped his helmet. "We heard how they died, but we don't know what killed them. Whatever those bastards in there unleashed, we're not equipped for it."

Benoit took a step toward him. Roche flinched beneath the burning intensity of his gaze but held his ground. He halted a few inches before Roche, and the man's hand tightened on his FR-F2 rifle.

Benoit's own hand remained at his side. "I will not send you back in there, Alain, until we know what killed them." He held Roche's gaze, then he lifted his head to survey them all. "But we will find out what killed our boys. Lacoux, our scientist, escaped. He'll know what happened.

"We'll learn what those bastards have done and what we need to do to counter it. Then we'll wipe out these fucking scientists. We'll avenge the deaths of our boys. And we'll get what we came for. Do you understand me? No more of us will die. The only deaths now will be those of the scientists."

He looked around at all of them. "But in the meantime, we won't cower like dogs. We'll stand together like the proud soldiers of France we are." He jabbed his hand at the facility. "In there is a drug that our nation needs. I intend to take it. I have only one question for you—are you with me?"

More murmuring went around the group. Now Benoit saw pride in their eyes.

Roche raised his FR-F2. "You know we fucking are."

The rest of the group nodded.

Benoit gripped Roche's shoulder. "Be patient, Alain. Soon we'll be out of this jungle, comfortable and dry, drinking cognac over the corpses of those scientists." Benoit patted his backpack. "I brought a bottle for the occasion. The first sip will be yours." He held Roche's shoulder a moment longer, as he made eye contact with each man in turn.

He released his grip on Roche's shoulder and stepped back. "I'll talk to Lacoux and get the answers we need."

He strode toward Lacoux and the other scientist, who were sheltering on a patch of dry ground between the buttressed roots of a towering tree. He skirted the widening pools of black water, his ears filled with the shriek of the storm.

Then he sensed a presence behind him. He swung around.

Halle was following him. Looking disconcerted at Benoit's sudden reaction, he approached warily.

"What is it?" he demanded impatiently.

"We don't know what the scientists have unleashed in there. Whatever it is, it decimated our team in seconds. We aren't equipped to deal with such a threat. We should destroy the facility and wipe out whoever is left alive in there."

Benoit remained silent, his yellow eyes boring into Halle.

"It's time to abort the trial. You know we can't leave any witnesses. Let's blow the fuckers up and get the hell out of here."

His eyes narrowed. "So you've revealed your hand, Halle."

The man tensed. "We can't gain access without losing more men. The trial has failed. It's time to abort."

Benoit's face swelled with blood. His headache intensified and he clutched the side of his head. "I give the fucking orders."

Halle held his ground. "We've lost too many good men. It's time to bring the rest of them home."

Benoit's scream rose above the howl of the wind. "I don't give a fuck about the men. We aren't leaving!" He stepped menacingly toward Halle. "You were sent to observe. I'm in charge. I make the decisions.

"The trial hasn't failed. This is nothing more than a set-back that I'll overcome. Put in your fucking report how bad the intel was, the one *your* directorate provided. Soon you'll be able to include how I succeeded despite their incompetence. It isn't over until *I* fucking say so."

"You'll kill anyone you send in there. It's over!"

Benoit took another step. "You are weak. Stupid! I see things you aren't capable of seeing, you pathetic fool. You think you can tell me what to do? I'll crush you like an ant if you get in my way."

"But there's no way to get in! You can't risk any more men."

Benoit's anger vanished as abruptly as it had flared. He motioned toward the two scientists standing twenty feet away. "There's the answer to how we'll access the facility." He marched away toward the newcomers.

He closed on the scientists, who had their backs turned as they huddled from the deluge. They remained oblivious to his presence; the wail of the tempest combined with the grinding of the rainforest canopy, the rolling booms of thunder and drumming of rain made his movements inaudible even to his own ears. He halted before them—and sensed danger.

He threw himself to the ground, shielding his head in his arms. The bullet exploded against the tree before him. He rolled rapidly. He saw Halle standing ten feet away, eyes resolute, PAMAS G1 outstretched.

His move took Halle by surprise. But the man's reflexes were cat-like. He adjusted his aim and fired again. He kept moving, the bullet smashing against his back as he rolled in a blur of movement toward the two scientists.

Benoit's pistol was clutched in his hand as his legs drove him powerfully out of the mud to his feet. Halle lunged. His gun spat. The bullet hammered against Benoit's shoulder and ricocheted away. He staggered, regained his balance and seized the second scientist.

As Halle was about to fire, Benoit crouched and slung the scientist before him as a shield to protect his vulnerable head.

"Stop!" The man screamed, his terror so raw it made Halle hesitate just for a millisecond.

Benoit didn't hesitate. His arm darted past his captive with the speed of a striking cobra. He fired the PAMAS G1 once. The bullet struck Halle dead center in his forehead and he slumped to the ground like a broken marionette.

CHAPTER 40

SHEPHERD PROCRASTINATED FOR several long minutes, his desire to preserve the cure for Cassie preventing him from doing what had to be done. Finally, his head aching with the decision, he realized it was time to act.

He knew O'Connell and Mancini had gathered everything they could in relation to the cure. But he didn't know what else remained that the mercenaries could salvage for Toussen. He realized he needed to speak to O'Connell.

The scientist eyed him suspiciously through the visor of his hood. "What the hell do you want?"

"I need to know what you collected about the cure. Do you have samples?"

"Why does it matter? We're trapped in here!"

"Right now, the cure is the only thing that does matter."

O'Connell's pale eyes narrowed as he tried to figure out what he was up to. "Everything is in my backpack—all the samples and an iPad containing our experimentation and the formula for engineering it."

"Is there anything left that would allow Toussen to reconstruct it?"

"Not without the samples or the formula." His eyes widened in sudden realization. "You want to destroy it!"

"We have to. We can't let Benoit get his hands on it."

"I won't let you!"

"We have no choice. Now where is it?" He peered behind him and spied a backpack nestled on the floor against the wall.

He went to step past O'Connell when a large hand rammed his chest. "I said you're not going to destroy it!"

"What's going on?" said Mancini.

"We have to destroy everything related to the cure. Now."

O'Connell's bull head thrust forward aggressively. "It's your fault we stayed. We should've run when I wanted to. You got us into this mess. I'm done listening to you."

Shepherd's devastation at Allie's death, his worry for Cassie and his agonizing over the decision to destroy the cure morphed into anger. Further fueling it was his resentment that O'Connell had prevented him from leaving to help Allie.

His head ached from where it had struck the hatch, and through the pain permeated the realization that if he had been outside with her, he would also be dead.

O'Connell had most likely saved his life. But his rage had flared to the extent it was now irrational. Allie had died out there, alone, and the thought tormented him.

He shoved O'Connell's hand aside. "Get out of the way."

O'Connell didn't budge. "Fuck you."

His hand shot out, his gloved fingers groping for O'Connell's throat through the hazmat suit.

"Motherfucker!" He pounded Shepherd's hand aside and rammed his knee at his groin. Shepherd swiveled his hip to parry the blow and staggered as his injured knee buckled, but O'Connell had over-committed himself and he slung him off-balance.

Jan leaped forward and grappled Shepherd aside. "Enough!"

He fought briefly to free himself from Jan's bear-like grip, then heard a loud thump on the hatch. Through his rage, the thought registered that everyone outside was dead. So what had made that sound? He hesitated, his anger ebbing, replaced by confusion. He stopped struggling. "What was that?"

O'Connell's pale eyes remained full of fight and he hustled toward him.

There was another thump, louder this time, and O'Connell jerked to a halt. "What the hell?"

Jan released Shepherd and pointed toward the hatch. "Look!"

He limped to the window. A blue-suited figure was standing outside. Shepherd pressed against the glass. Allie's green eyes gazed back at him.

"Allie! Oh, thank Christ! I thought you were dead. What happened? Were you hurt?"

She pressed a hand against the window before tapping it against the side of her hood to indicate she couldn't hear him.

He gazed at her, unable to comprehend that she was standing before him. Her face was pallid and there were dark rings beneath her eyes. Her lips were compressed in a straight line. She looked terrified but she was alive.

Mancini darted to a workbench and returned with a radio. "There should be another in the lab outside." He pushed alongside Shepherd, held his radio to the window, pointed to it then gestured past her shoulder toward the workbenches.

Allie gave a clumsy nod, half her face disappearing as the bulky hood slipped forward. She stepped toward the nearest workspace. A minute later, she returned with a black, rectangular object.

Shepherd snatched the radio from Mancini. "Allie? Can you hear me?"

There was a hiss of static, then her voice crackled. "... can hear you."

"Are you okay?" Shepherd stopped, emotion welling into his throat. Now that he knew she was alive, he couldn't stand the thought of losing her again and was full of anxiety that she was alone and vulnerable, trapped on the other side of the hatch.

"I'm fine." She gave him a smile. "Are you okay? Your head looks dreadful."

Shepherd gingerly touched the pulpy egg on the side of his skull. His face felt tight with dried blood. His head still pounded and he suspected he had a mild concussion. "It looks worse than it is. What happened? We couldn't see you. We kept yelling."

"I couldn't hear you. I dove behind a workbench and was too scared to move. I thought the mercenaries would see me or the pathogen would penetrate the suit." Her gaze switched to Mancini. "Am I safe now? Would I be showing symptoms if the suit wasn't effective?"

Mancini took the radio from Shepherd. "I'm not sure. It dropped the mercenaries in seconds. The integrity of your suit seems to be holding for now. But if there's a weakness, a microscopic tear somewhere…"

O'Connell pushed alongside Mancini and Shepherd. "We can't let you back inside. You're contaminated."

Shepherd's anger returned. He went to shove O'Connell aside so he could get to the hatch controls. "We're letting her back in."

O'Connell held his ground. "If you let her in, we could all die!"

"He's right," Mancini said.

"We can't leave her out there!"

"I don't like it," said O'Connell, "but it's the right decision."

The radio crackled. "O'Connell is right. You can't let me inside."

He stared at her in anguish. But deep down, he knew she couldn't be allowed into the bio lab.

Allie studied Shepherd and O'Connell. Her tone was heavy with suspicion. "What were you two doing? Were you fighting?"

O'Connell seized the radio. "He wants to destroy the cure. I won't allow that to happen."

"I see." Her voice softened. "Shepherd, there is hope still. Now is not the time to destroy it. Later, maybe. But not now."

"Later?" snapped O'Connell. "No fucking way!"

"You said it yourself, O'Connell. Leadership is about making tough decisions. I don't want to destroy the cure any more than you do. But I believe Shepherd when he says the harm it could do in Toussen's hands outweighs the benefits it could provide."

O'Connell glared at her, but this time he didn't argue.

She switched her attention to Shepherd and Mancini. "Is everyone all right? Everything happened in such a rush. How is Ben?"

Shepherd grabbed the radio from O'Connell. He gestured to where a now conscious Ben was seated on the ground, his back against a workbench. His face looked pale and sick through the visor of the hazmat suit, but he was recovering. "Ben's fine," Shepherd said. There was no easy way to tell her. "But Parker didn't make it."

"No! What happened?"

"He went to get Lacoux and didn't make it back in time."

"Oh, dear God. I told him not to... oh, shit. Shit!" She looked at Mancini. "Is there a chance he could've survived?"

He took the radio. "No. He didn't have a hope."

"Even if he sealed himself somewhere?"

"Where?"

Allie racked her brains. "The MRI maybe?" The MRI was the largest piece of scientific equipment at the Inn, bisecting two small rooms adjacent to the naturalists' lab. It was designed to the highest bio-safety specifications, able to be sealed when analyzing infected animals.

"The odds of him making it there in time, climbing inside and sealing himself off are so remote they're almost non-existent," said Mancini.

Allie clenched her gloved fists in frustration. "Damn it! How long until the pathogen breaks down?"

"The original biological compound O'Connell and I worked on survived about two hours before it became inert."

"Then if he is alive, I need to find him before he suffocates in there."

"And do what?"

"I don't know. But what I do know is that I can't just sit around. I sent Parker to get Lacoux. I released that pathogen. I need to know what happened. If there's even the slightest chance he's still alive, I owe it to him to find him before it's too late."

Shepherd seized the radio from Mancini. "Allie, it's too dangerous to leave the lab. We need to work out how we're going to get the hell out of here."

"But the mercenaries are dead. I should be just as safe out there as I am in here."

"Benoit's smart. He wouldn't have sent a full team. He'll hold the rest back and try to figure out what we did. Eventually, he'll send in whoever is the most expendable on his team. I'm guessing it'll be one of the trackers."

"But I have some time." She pushed away from the hatch. "I'm going."

"Damn it, Allie. Wait here!"

The voice that crackled over the radio was firm. "I'm going to find Parker."

She stepped cautiously around the corpses, then into the corridor. She disappeared from sight.

Shepherd slammed the radio against his thigh. "Goddammit!" He seated himself on a workbench, where he probed his knee, cursing the restrictive hazmat suit.

"What are you doing?" Jan asked.

"I have to get out there and help her." His fingers found the strapping. It was crude, preventing him from flexing the leg. He tried to adjust it, wondering if he could loosen it without removing his suit.

"You can hardly walk. You're better off remaining here and helping us work out what we're going to do."

"I can't."

"You can and you will. You've asked us to trust you again and again, now it's your turn. Trust her."

Reluctantly, he stopped trying to loosen the bandage. He knew Jan was right.

"We need to start thinking this through," Mancini said. "We'll keep in touch with Allie, but we can't waste any more time."

Shepherd frowned. "We still have an hour or so."

Mancini looked uneasy. "I've thought about that further. The original compound took a couple of hours to break down. But with the engineering I did, the current pathogen could be more unstable."

"What are you telling us?" he snapped.

"That there may be less time than I thought."

CHAPTER 41

BENOIT STOOD BEFORE what was left of his mercenary squad. With Halle dead, only three men—Alain Roche, Marlon Gault and Henri Auger remained.

As their gazes shifted from Halle's corpse to himself, he saw the confusion in their eyes. Roche swiveled his FR-F2 away from Halle's crumpled body and toward his leader.

Benoit lowered his PAMAS G1 to his side; he needed these men. He had to convince them he was not their enemy. He held their suspicious stares, his mind racing faster than the wind assaulting the rainforest canopy above them. These were his men. Halle had been an intelligence officer, an outsider; he had to utilize that.

"Halle was a traitor. He sold his services to the Americans. He was going to steal the formula for them."

The doubt in their eyes lingered.

"AWR was worried about him. They saw this as a chance to draw him out and assigned him to our squad. They warned me to watch him and to kill him if necessary.

"Halle knew I was watching him. He saw this storm as an opportunity to kill me, then he would've told you I was the traitor."

Benoit took a step toward the three men. He had to roar to be heard above the shrieking wind. "You all served with me in the Legion. Do you believe I would betray France?"

Roche didn't move. His gaze bore into him. The FR-F2 held its position.

Benoit's own hand tightened on his pistol. The sniper rifle in Roche's grasp was not a weapon for close quarters. The Herstal Minimis gripped by Gault and Auger were another story, but he knew he would be able to kill all three men if necessary. He just hoped it wouldn't be.

Benoit intended to report back to AWR that poor intel had resulted in the losses his squad had suffered. That it was only his unique abilities that procured the formula AWR needed. With Halle dead, nobody would be able to contradict him. But his story would be strengthened if these men were alive to support it. If they backed his version of events, then maybe AWR would deem this trial a success and he would remain on the drug compound.

He felt a flash of desperation; he couldn't give his enhanced awareness up and revert back to being inferior.

Roche lowered the FR-F2. He spat at Halle's body and mouthed, 'Motherfucker.'

Auger and Gault hadn't moved. Gault eyed the mud-splattered scientists. "What about them?"

"They can tell us what those motherfuckers unleashed. They can get us inside and get us the formula."

The suspicion in Gault's dark eyes faded. He lowered his machine gun, followed by Auger.

Benoit relaxed, his fear of a rebellion subsiding, replaced by his anger at the loss of his men inside the facility. He strode toward the cowering scientists, grasping the side of his head as pain seared through his skull. As he towered over Lacoux, horror flared in the scientist's black eyes.

He was flanked by his mercenaries, all with weapons raised. "How did you escape?"

Lacoux motioned to the other scientist. "He freed me."

"Who is he?"

"Chase Parker—one of the naturalists."

"He said you wouldn't kill me!" Parker screamed, his eyes wide and frantic. A black backpack was slung over his shoulder.

Benoit seized it. "What's in this?"

"My work and some supplies," Parker replied, his voice trembling with fear.

"Do you have the cure?" He opened it and found an iPad, food and water.

Parker hesitated as if sensing his life could depend on his answer. "No."

Benoit turned to Lacoux for confirmation.

The man nodded. "He's only a naturalist. He wasn't part of the team that engineered the cure."

Benoit flung the backpack to the ground in disgust, then eyed Lacoux suspiciously. After Halle's betrayal, he trusted no one, not even this scientist who had once saved his life. "Why would he free you? Why betray his colleagues?"

The horror in Lacoux's eyes had been replaced by fear as if realizing he was talking for his survival. He spoke rapidly. "The weak fool came to save me from the pathogen the scientists released. I told him it won't stop you. That you will kill them all without mercy but you would let him live if he helped me escape.

"I also promised him recognition for the cure, which I knew he craved, and was going to be denied." His voice filled with contempt. "He was greedy enough to believe me."

Parker's face crumpled as he realized Lacoux's deception. "You bastard."

Benoit ignored him, still focused on Lacoux. "The pathogen they unleashed wiped out my men. How did you get out without being killed?"

"The scientists retreated to a bio lab, where they would be safe when they released the pathogen. They would have waited until the very last moment to release it, to give Parker a chance to reach them. That delay gave us time to run.

"When your men intercepted us, I told them what was going to happen, that they had to get out of there. One of them tried to contact you but couldn't get through. They assigned a man to escort us out and kept going after the scientists. They thought they could reach the scientists in time to stop them from releasing the pathogen."

Benoit looked to Auger, the mercenary who'd dragged Parker with him from the facility. Auger nodded his confirmation.

But his suspicions lingered. He stepped close enough for Lacoux, but not his men, to hear him growl, "Halle must have been sent by AWR to execute me if he thought their experiment was failing. He was their kill switch for this trial." He seized Lacoux's shoulders, studying the scientist's now terrified features, looking for a hint of betrayal in those black, glittering eyes. "Did you know? Were you behind it?"

Lacoux gasped. "No! It was never part of my plan. I thought he'd been included on the team because he knew you from before the experiment. He could provide the comparison they sought."

Benoit saw the surprise in his eyes. Maybe AWR had kept Lacoux in the dark about Halle's true role. Or maybe he was simply lying to save his life.

He wasn't convinced he could trust this man, but Lacoux could perhaps provide answers to the questions growing in his mind since Halle's attack. He released his grip on his shoulders. "Halle's reports for AWR mentioned side effects. That my eyes had yellowed. Why? What's causing it?"

"The yellowing is indicative of liver damage. But we can fix that. As soon as we get home, I can give you something to counter it."

"What about my headaches? They're getting worse."

"Nothing to be concerned about. An anticipated side effect that is treatable."

The wind's moan intensified, forcing Benoit to raise his voice. "When Halle attacked me, I sensed—rather than heard—the approaching danger. How is that possible?"

Lacoux's dark eyes narrowed thoughtfully. "The drug compound we gave you to elevate your intelligence must have enhanced the anterior cingulate cortex, or ACC, the area of your brain that acts as an early warning system."

"What does that mean?" He scowled in exasperation.

"After the Asian tsunami, scientists struggled to explain reports that primitive aboriginal tribesmen had somehow sensed the impending danger in time to join wild animals in a life-saving flight to higher ground. I drew on these reports during my own research into the existence of a sixth sense for danger, aware of the potential benefits to the Toussen future-soldier program.

"I identified that the ACC works at a subconscious level to help humans recognize and avoid high-risk situations by monitoring environmental cues and weighing possible consequences.

"The drug compound must have enhanced this region of your brain, which in turn alerted you to the threat posed by Halle."

But Benoit, studying him intently, saw again the flash of horror he'd seen in his eyes earlier. "What is it? What aren't you telling me?"

"It's nothing."

But Parker, standing nearby, was having none of it. "Tell him the truth, you lying bastard!"

Lacoux remained silent.

"What he's not telling you is that abnormalities in the ACC are closely associated with a host of serious mental problems including schizophrenia," screamed Parker. "He's turned you into a monster!"

Benoit seized Lacoux. "Is he right?"

The man struggled for composure. "No. You're fine. He's lying to you!"

"Or maybe it's you who's lying. Maybe you want me dead, just like Halle did." He shoved Lacoux away and raised his PAMAS G1 menacingly.

"Wait," Lacoux cried. "I'm the only one who can help you!"

"Really?" Benoit replied with contempt. "So far the intelligence you provided has helped kill most of my men. You've made me look foolish." He pointed his gun at the scientist's forehead.

"I'm the only one who can get you more of the drug!"

Benoit halted, his suspicion replaced by craving.

"You've lost many men. Halle is dead. AWR will deem the trial a failure. You'll be taken off the drug compound." He let his words sink in. "Unless I tell them that you won against overwhelming odds. That without my drug compound, you would never have obtained the formula for the cure."

Benoit felt himself burn with an insatiable hunger.

"Parker told me the pathogen will break down. When it does, we can get inside the facility. We can get you the cure. With Halle gone, only I can convince AWR that this trial was a success. Only I can create a more powerful version of the cognitive enhancement drug using the Alzheimer's cure. The effects on you will then be permanent. Can you imagine how that will feel?"

Benoit's eyes bored into him. He lowered his pistol. He

roared to be heard above the wind. "How will we know when the pathogen's broken down?"

Lacoux pointed to Parker. "We send in our guinea pig."

CHAPTER 42

SHEPHERD FELT HIS concern deepen as he studied Mancini. He had assumed they had some time to figure a way out of the bio lab before the pathogen broke down, allowing the mercenaries to enter. "How long are we talking about?"

Mancini's face was tense. "It could already have broken down."

"You said we had a couple of hours!"

"That was the original compound. This version was combined with the influenza virus to make it an airborne pathogen, designed to kill the mercenaries on contact. But I had no time to test it before we released it. Engineering it the way I did might have made it more unstable. It could've started breaking down within minutes of its release."

Shepherd felt his dismay flood through him. "So perhaps the only thing keeping the mercenaries at bay right now is their fear of the pathogen and their belief it's still active."

"We need to come up with a plan," said Jan.

He agreed. "We have to act fast now."

"And do what?" O'Connell snapped. "Have you forgotten the mercenaries are still outside? Even if we can leave the bio lab, we can't escape the Inn."

"Their fear should hold them back. We have some time before they launch another assault. We need to use it."

"How?" Ben asked.

Shepherd studied him for a moment, surprised by the kid's fortitude. He was pale but was recovering fast from his wound. "I'm not sure yet."

"There's another problem we have to consider," said Ben.

"We don't have time to waste listening to your bullshit," O'Connell snapped.

"Well, you need to."

"What is it, Ben?" Shepherd asked.

"This storm. It's getting worse. If we don't leave soon, the jungle will be impassable."

"Why?" He didn't care about a storm. All he could focus on was Allie and a way to defeat Benoit.

"These tropical storms are huge. They do a lot of damage to the rainforest. And this one is massive. These winds, the lightning, it'll soon be felling trees. Not to mention the flooding. We leave it too late and entering the jungle will be like playing Russian roulette with a fully loaded gun."

"A bit of rain won't hurt us," O'Connell said dismissively.

"You don't understand what these storms are capable of!"

"Let's just concentrate on getting out of here first, Ben," Shepherd replied. The longer Allie remained outside, the more his worry grew. "If the pathogen's broken down, the mercenaries can get inside. But we can also use the nano-suits and the weapons of their dead."

"We've tried holding them off and failed," said O'Connell. "That seems like delaying the fucking inevitable to me."

"I agree. So we still may need to destroy everything we have on the cure."

"I'm not going to let that happen!"

"You think I want to destroy it? It's the last damn thing I want to do! But this is about more than my desire to help Cassie or your goddamn career aspirations. Someone else will develop an Alzheimer's cure eventually. It just won't be us. But if you don't destroy it, we'll be responsible for all the harm it'll do in the wrong hands."

"Then you'd better figure out a way to defeat these mercenaries. Because we aren't destroying the cure."

Shepherd gritted his teeth in exasperation. "You aren't listening! I've told you I don't know how to defeat them. Not with the technology they possess, not with Benoit being a bio-mod."

"You understand their technology better than any of us. Allie said you were part of a team that traveled the world studying it. So use that knowledge. There has to be a weakness."

"I can't think of any."

"Try harder! What do you know? How do those nano-suits work? How do they repel bullets?"

Shepherd forced his worry for Allie aside. "They use shear-thickening fluid. It contains silica particles that harden upon impact."

"Is there a way to break it down? Is there anything inside the bio lab we can use?"

"I can make a more stable version of the pathogen," said Mancini.

O'Connell dismissed his idea. "We need to think of a way to attack them without killing ourselves in the process. Well?"

"When we tested the liquid, we found the only way to penetrate it was to force something through it slowly. Which doesn't help us."

"Can't we force through a syringe loaded with toxin?" said Ben.

Shepherd fought to control his impatience. "In theory, Ben, it could work. But in practice, do you think Benoit or one of his mercenaries would allow you to do that?

"Firstly, you wouldn't get close enough to do it before

he shot you. Then, if by chance you did get close enough, with that nano-suit on, he's strong enough to tear you limb from limb before you could complete the job. It's just not possible."

"We don't have any of the syringes loaded with neurotoxin left, anyway," said Mancini. "Do you want me to make some more?"

Shepherd patted his pocket, feeling the hard surface of the titanium canister against his thigh. "I still have one you gave me earlier. Besides, we don't have time." He couldn't resist his anxiety for Allie any longer. "We need to get Allie back here." He took the radio from Mancini. "Allie?" There was a burst of static.

The radio crackled to life. "Shepherd? Is that you?"

"Where are you? We need you back here."

"I checked the MRI, but it was empty. I'm now in the rec room." Her voice sounded tired and strained. "Parker isn't here."

"What?"

"I think we have a problem."

"Allie, what's going on?"

"Both Lacoux and Parker are missing. I can't find their bodies. But…" There was a splitting, tearing crack of thunder and a burst of static.

"Allie, can you repeat that?"

Another burst of static.

"…pack is gone. I need to check…"

"Allie, for chrissake. I need you back here!"

"Shit!" Her voice crackled. "Oh, shit. That son of a bitch!"

"What's going on?"

This time there was no static and her voice was clear. "When I checked the meeting room, I discovered that

Parker had untied Lacoux, even though I'd ordered him not to. I couldn't figure out why. Oh, my God."

"Allie!"

"Parker's backpack is gone. At first, I thought O'Connell had carried it to the bio lab. But then I remembered he took only the khaki backpack. Parker's is black. It's not here."

Another hiss of static. Her voice rasped over the radio. "I think that son of a bitch abandoned us. He must've left with Lacoux. The mercenaries! He can tell them when the pathogen will break down."

"Allie," Shepherd snapped. "Get back here!"

"I'm heading to you now. We have to get out of here."

They leaned toward the radio as her voice crackled, just a whisper now. "I can see movement. I think they're already here."

Then there was the sound of her breathing hard, as if running. "They're inside. They sent Parker in first and he's still alive. The pathogen has broken down!"

Shepherd filled with dread. "Allie, Get back to the bio lab!"

More heavy breathing, then a gasp. "Too far. Not going to make it in time."

CHAPTER 43

SHEPHERD STAGGERED TO the hatch and peered through, the radio crushed against his ear. "Allie, can you hear me?" He heard only static. He turned to Mancini. "The pathogen is no longer active. Get this hatch open!"

"If we open it, nothing will stop the mercenaries getting in," said O'Connell.

"They'll get in anyway."

"Then leave the weapons. You're not leaving us defenseless in here."

"Fine. I'll take one from a dead mercenary." He turned back to Mancini. "Hurry!"

Mancini pressed buttons on the instrument display. "I'm going as fast as I can. The air pressure in here is kept at a lower level than outside to prevent the escape of any toxins. It has to be equalized before I can unseal the hatch. It takes a few minutes."

"That bastard!" O'Connell said. "I can't believe Parker freed Lacoux and abandoned us."

Shepherd stripped off the hazmat suit. "Lacoux must've got to him. Told Parker he'd ensure his safety if he freed him."

"The traitorous prick."

"Just work on a way to get everyone out of here. I'm going to get Allie." He hobbled to a workbench, and leaning against it, tore at the bandage around his knee.

Mancini turned from the instrument display, his eyes widening as they took in Shepherd's faded khaki pants and navy shirt. "You shouldn't have removed the suit. If there are any active traces left of the pathogen you're a dead man."

Cameron K. Moore

He kept working at the strapping. He wanted enough bandaging to keep the unstable limb structurally supported while giving him the freedom to move. He would put up with the pain.

He stripped away another layer then stopped. It would have to do. "Mancini, get the damn hatch open!"

"Just a few more seconds."

Shepherd moved beside him. His knee felt more mobile, less like a tree stump. "Close the hatch behind me. Get everyone down behind one of the workbenches. I'll seal the entrance to the scientists' lab once I'm through. Got it?"

"Yes."

"What do you want us to do?" said Jan.

"Work on how to use the Inn against the mercenaries, Jannie. And stay down!"

Mancini hauled the heavy hatch open and Shepherd slipped out. He hobbled through the lab, pausing only to stoop and rip a Herstal Minimi from the body of one of the mercenaries. He checked its magazine was loaded and limped for the entrance.

He could move faster, but the joint was now less stable without the heavy strapping and he experienced the disconcerting sensation of his knee wobbling from side to side. He was aware that any sudden movement to his left or right could result in his knee collapsing beneath his weight. *So keep moving in a straight line.*

Reaching the entrance to the corridor he pressed himself against the wall. The glow of flashlights spilled through the doorway. He chanced a look outside the laboratory and saw the shadowy figures of the mercenaries making their way along the corridor, checking each room as they went.

He pressed back against the wall. They would reach him

in less than a minute. He lifted the radio. "Allie, I'm coming to get you. Where are you?" Again, he heard only static. He tried not to panic at her silence. "I'll find you."

He peered into the corridor once more. It was now clear but flashlights glowed from at least two of the rooms. They brightened as a pair of mercenaries emerged from Alderton's office. They advanced toward his hiding place, then disappeared into the next room along—Allie's office. The flashlight faded and the corridor darkened momentarily.

Shepherd rammed his fist against the manual override lever on the wall beside him and stepped into the corridor, hearing the door slam behind him and the clunk of bolts sliding into place. Immediately, the corridor was filled with red flashing lights as a series of bulbs in the ceiling burst into life, triggered by the manual override. The flashlight beams jerked around crazily as the surprised mercenaries looked for the source of the sudden light.

Their confusion gave him seconds, no more. Where was Allie? He hurried along the corridor, praying she was hiding in a room they hadn't yet searched. But which one?

Before him were the meeting room Lacoux had been held in, the sickbay and the naturalists' laboratory. He had time to choose only one before the mercenaries would be on him.

The glow of flashlights intensified as the mercenaries moved back toward the corridor. Shepherd looked around frantically. Where would she have gone? Choose. Now!

The radio crackled, the scratchy sound muted by the thunderous assault of the tropical storm. "…the naturalists' lab."

He stumbled as fast as he could, cursing his knee. He had several yards to cover. Multiple beams of light were playing around the corridor. Dark figures loomed in the doorways.

One emerged from Allie's office, turned away from him, looking up at the flashing lights. The mercenary began to swivel toward him.

He reached the naturalists' lab and tumbled inside.

The large, rectangular room was bathed in harsh red as though lit by the flickering blaze of a vast furnace. He blinked rapidly to adjust his eyes as he looked at the trestle tables standing in the center of the room and the heavy shelves lining the walls. The bared teeth of the mounted jaguar seemed coated in blood. "Allie!" he whispered. Where could she have hidden?

Through the gloom he saw a storage cabinet against the wall at the far end of the room, its doors closed. He took a step toward it.

A dark shape emerged from a narrow gap between the shelves and scuttled across the floor. A hand seized his arm. He jumped, his heart pounding, before recognizing the slim form. Allie. He embraced her fiercely, scarcely able to believe he was holding her in his arms once more. "Thank Christ you're all right."

She clung to him for a few moments before detaching herself. "They almost saw me. They must be outside."

"We have to get out of here." He heard the thumping of heavy boots. His mind raced. How many mercenaries were there? How cautious would they be? Where could he and Allie hide? Even if they somehow managed to penetrate the mercenaries' line and escape into the jungle, the bloodcurdling howl of the storm made the rainforest seem every bit as dangerous as the Inn itself. There was no safe place for them to go.

The footsteps neared the entrance to the lab. With a sick feeling in his gut, he realized they were trapped. He turned toward the doorway, leveling his Herstal Minimi.

"In here!" Allie seized his arm and dragged him deeper into the laboratory. Blinking in the gloom, he saw another door.

The footsteps stopped outside the lab. A flashlight probed the room. A figure stood silhouetted behind it, large and menacing, the distinctive outline of a Herstal Minimi etched against the light. In the corridor, Shepherd saw more figures move past, heading for the scientists' laboratory.

Allie and Shepherd stepped into the next room. He was disorientated, then recognized the gaping maw of the MRI machine jutting through a large perspex window. The scientists used the MRI to diagnose the results of testing performed on animals.

It was contained in two interconnected rooms. The first room was for the technicians, who operated the scanning equipment. It was a small space, dominated by a fifty-inch display hanging from the ceiling, and was pristine, not having been used since the techs had been sent home with the naturalists. But it was sealed from the MRI lab beyond. They had nowhere else to go.

Allie hissed in his ear. "I saw them head down the corridor. The others are trapped!"

"I triggered the manual override. The sealed door to the scientists' lab will hold the bastards for a while. They don't have the code to the keypad. And they won't risk using explosives so close to the bio lab, where the cure is contained. Not until they have what they want."

But Shepherd was acutely aware that he and Allie were also trapped.

She threw open the round hatch of the MRI machine and clambered inside. He thrust his shoulders in behind her and forced his way into the machine, feeling a sharp pain from his knee.

He groped behind him and pulled the hatch closed. It swung back open with a creak. *Shit.* Finding no way to lock it, he looked ahead for Allie. The circular tube of the massive MRI was almost three feet wide and eight long and she was already at the far end.

She fumbled with something and cursed. The darkness was broken only by the intermittent red light spilling in from the tech room and the flashlight beam that was brightening as the mercenary closed.

He heard a soft thump, a click, and with a squeal, the hatch at the far end of the machine opened. Allie lowered herself into the room beyond. Shepherd pushed his bulk forward, grabbed the lip of the machine and hauled himself out.

He slammed the clear perspex hatch shut behind him. Through it, he saw the distorted face of the mercenary illuminated at the far end of the MRI. The figure climbed into the machine and scrambled toward them. He looked for a way to lock the hatch and found nothing. "Allie! How does it lock?"

With a heavy clunk, the machine burst into life. The inner tube glowed with harsh white light. Machinery whirred. There was a click and the hatch snapped into place. He stepped back in surprise.

"I switched it on!" Allie was standing at the far wall, her fingers splayed against a console with flickering lights. "It only locks when it's operating."

Shepherd hobbled to the door that led to the corridor outside. He opened it a crack and saw three tall figures in black nano-suits ten feet away. Their backs were to him. One of them held Parker, whose short, plump body looked helpless alongside the powerful frame of the mercenary.

Lacoux stood beside them. All were facing the sealed door to the scientists' lab. As he watched, the sound emanating from the MRI caught their attention and all looked around. He closed the door quickly and stepped away. They were trapped.

"Shepherd!" Allie pointed at the MRI.

The mercenary had halted, looking around the interior of the machine with a confused expression. His confusion turned to surprise as the Herstal Minimi was jerked out of his grasp, fixing itself to the inner wall of the MRI as three Tesla of magnetic force tore at the steel receiver of the firearm. He wrenched it free and scrambled backward until he reached the far hatch and kicked. It remained shut.

There was fear on the mercenary's face now as he fought to control his machine gun while scrabbling at the hatch with his heels. Shepherd saw he was trying to point the barrel of the wildly bucking weapon at it. Then his attention was caught by a small, dark, baseball-shaped object attached to the flank of the mercenary's nano-suit. "Oh, shit. Turn it off! Now!"

"Why?"

"He's carrying a grenade!"

CHAPTER 44

ALLIE HASTILY PRESSED the off button. "This will take a few seconds. It has to power down."

"Get out of here!"

His gaze fell on a small door set into the wall. He heaved it open, grunting with effort; it was heavy, solid steel. They crawled into a tiny room with steel walls blemished by dark stains. Reaching back, he hauled the door toward him.

There was an ear-shattering thump and he saw the searing radiance of a fireball through the narrowing crack before the door slammed shut, leaving them in darkness. He fell on top of Allie and the room shuddered as though the Inn was being ripped apart.

He crouched low over Allie's body as the explosion rumbled around them. There was a concussive jolt as the shockwave hammered the steel door. The walls of their tiny room shook and the floor lurched, nearly throwing him off balance. Fearful that their bolt hole was about to collapse around them, he hugged her to him, trying to shield her body with his own.

They huddled together on the ground until the roar of the explosion and the shaking of the room ceased after what felt like an eternity, but had been only a few seconds.

"What happened?" Allie yelled.

"The grenade exploded." As he spoke he heard the distant wail of an alarm.

She struggled to her haunches. "That's the fire alarm."

He opened the heavy steel door a fraction. A wave of heat burst in, bringing with it the acrid odor of burning plastic, metal and human flesh. The room outside was a mess of twisted, molten pieces of machinery. The MRI had disintegrated, torn by the explosion into scattered fragments.

The wall separating the technicians' lab from the room housing the MRI had collapsed, with shattered pieces of glass gleaming as they melted in the orange flames raging throughout the room.

Blood stained the remnants of the MRI. A blackened leg jutted from beneath a chunk of plastic. A tangle of entrails sizzled like fat sausages as they cooked on the burning floor. On the far side of the room lay the scorched husk of the mercenary's upper torso. A mist of water sprayed from a sprinkler fixed stubbornly to the scorched roof that now looked in danger of collapsing.

Choking smoke burned Shepherd's throat and stung his eyes. Coughing, the tears streaming down his face, he slammed the door closed.

He felt around until he found Allie's hand and squeezed. "Are you all right?"

"My ears hurt," she said, breathing heavily.

His own ears rang with a high-pitched hum but they didn't feel like they had ruptured. Allie's voice sounded tinny and distant but at least he could still hear her. The steel walls of their bolt hole had shielded them from the worst of the shockwave. Images of the torn body of the mercenary filled his mind and he offered up a silent prayer, grateful they were still alive.

He felt around in the darkness. Inches above his head his fingers brushed against steel. Reaching past her, he found he could touch metallic walls all around them. The air in the confined space was hot and dry. It was like being trapped in an oven. Beads of perspiration broke out on his forehead and he gasped for air until he realized he could still breathe, that the cramped box wasn't airtight. He took a few deep, calming breaths. "Where are we?"

"The incinerator room," she wheezed.

The incinerator was where tested animals were disposed of. Quarantine requirements specified they could not be released alive and their bodies couldn't be exposed to the pristine rainforest for fear of contamination. So they were euthanized and incinerated, their ashes flushed into the waste containment system below.

He felt her shake against him. She uttered a strangled, choking sound and his concern flared. "Allie? Are you all right?"

She coughed.

"Allie! What is it?"

"Claustrophobia."

Shepherd's mind flashed back to her hesitation at entering the cramped bio lab while they were searching the scientists' laboratory for any clues as to Jouvet's murderer. He remembered her pale and sweating in the bio lab before they released the pathogen. At the time he thought it had been anxiety, now he realized it was something worse.

He wrapped his arms around her and held her against him. He went to rub her forehead and found perspex instead. "Take the suit off."

Over her ragged breathing, he heard the rustle of the suit as she removed it. He held her tight against him and stroked her forehead. After a minute she relaxed. Her breathing steadied. "Keep your eyes closed. You'll be fine, Allie. There's plenty of air in here. Breathe deeply, nice and slow."

She pulled away from him. "Oh, shit!"

"You're okay."

"Not me! The others! In the bio lab."

"The mercenaries can't get to them for a little while."

"You don't understand. When the fire alarm is triggered, air is automatically pumped from the bio lab to starve any flames of oxygen and create negative pressure to prevent any contaminant from escaping the room. They'll suffocate. We have to get them out."

Shepherd tried to remain calm. "How?"

"The emergency override."

"Where is it?"

"It's in the…" her voice trailed away.

"Allie?"

"It's in the scientists' lab."

"Can't they get to it from the bio lab?"

Her voice was muffled against his chest. "The bio lab seals automatically if there's a fire. If they're inside, they won't be able to get out."

"They locked themselves in to protect them from the mercs. Isn't there another override switch inside the bio lab?"

Her trembling hands clawed at him in anguish. "No."

"The door to the scientists' lab is sealed. I triggered it when I came out after you." His mind reeled. "The mercenaries are already at the sealed entrance. Christ! Isn't there another way to get them out?"

"No!"

Shepherd gripped her as the dreadful realization sank in. "How long? When will their oxygen run out?"

"It takes twelve minutes."

His mind filled with images of their colleagues trapped in the bio lab as the oxygen was pumped out. He imagined Jan's smooth, tanned skin slowly turning a bluish-gray, the cerulean eyes bulging from their sockets, then the last strangled gasp for air before his friend collapsed to the ground. He forced himself to think. "The hazmat suits. They'll have air."

"The oxygen flow to the suits is cut off automatically when the fire alarm is triggered, to ensure all the air is pumped out."

Jannie…

Twelve minutes.

CHAPTER 45

BENOIT PICKED HIMSELF up from the ground where the force of the explosion had thrown him. Gault got to his feet beside him. He looked stunned, but was otherwise unhurt, despite the smoldering debris littering the floor.

He realized their nano-suits had protected them from the worst of the explosion. Down the corridor a shaken Roche stood at the hatch, holding the terrified scientist, Parker. A shocked-looking Lacoux was standing beside them. Red lights still flashed, but now they were accompanied by an undulating alarm that reverberated in his ears.

He struggled to comprehend what had just happened. He and Gault were about to open a door to investigate a strange sound beyond it when a shockwave had blasted them backward. The door now hung at a crazy angle. A section of the wall beside it had collapsed. Through the opening, he saw roaring flames and the outline of twisted machinery. He stepped forward but the heat of the fire against his unprotected face forced him back.

He accessed the RIF. "Auger? Respond!" But even as he did so, his racing mind had already concluded that Auger must be dead. No one inside the room could have survived that blast. Not even the nano-suit would have saved him.

The hissing silence over the RIF confirmed his fear. The bone convection technology was sensitive enough for him to hear Roche, at the far end of the corridor, mumble, "Fuck."

Benoit's anger surged. What had caused the explosion? Had Auger encountered someone? Based on information provided by Parker, Lacoux had estimated the pathogen would break down sooner rather than later and had urged

277

Benoit to send Parker in as a guinea pig.

The mercenaries had surged along the corridor to trap the scientists before they too had realized the pathogen had broken down. Benoit had directed Auger to clear one final room that Parker informed them was the naturalists' lab. But it had been a cursory measure; they expected all the scientists to have retreated to what Parker called the bio lab. Now Benoit wasn't so sure.

He instructed Roche to stay put, then together with Gault, rapidly backtracked to the naturalists' lab where they had last seen Auger. They found an entrance into another, smaller room then were forced to halt, their path blocked by fire.

He saw twisted, smoldering machinery. He stared into the flames, struggling to control his anger, which burned with the intensity of the fire. He had lost another man.

Without knowing what or who had been in this mangled room with Auger, Benoit could only conclude that the grenade the mercenary was carrying had exploded. But why? Auger had been an intelligent, efficient soldier. He ruled out carelessness. A trap by the scientists? Maybe.

Benoit vowed they would pay. He turned on his heel. Wary of more traps, he and Gault rechecked the rest of the facility, then he instructed Gault to hunt for an extinguisher to put out the fire; he didn't want the place to burn down before it yielded what he wanted. Alone, he returned to the sealed hatch where Roche, Lacoux and Parker waited.

He studied Lacoux anxiously. This man was vital to him getting more of the drug compound; he wanted him safe. "You weren't injured by the explosion?"

Lacoux shook his head. "No, my friend."

Satisfied, his concern faded, leaving only rage. He seized

Parker. "You told me the scientists would all be trapped in the bio lab. So what the fuck caused that explosion?"

Parker's mouth worked, but no sound came out. His eyes rolled. With his white, sweating face, he looked like he was about to pass out with fear. "I don't know!"

Benoit seized the scientist's plump throat. His headache intensified until it seemed to pulsate in time with the fire alarm echoing through the facility. He fought the urge to crush the larynx beneath his fingers. "Where are the fucking scientists?"

His face turning red, Parker couldn't talk. Instead, he pointed with a shaky finger at the perspex window in the closed door behind him.

"Don't kill him," Lacoux said. "We may need him."

Benoit released him and Parker slumped to his knees, gasping for air. Stooping, Benoit peered through the window and saw what appeared to be a laboratory full of workbenches and scientific equipment.

At the far end, he saw another, heavier hatch with a digital display glowing through the gloom. In the center of the hatch was another window through which he saw movement. A panicked face pressed against the perspex. More figures milled about. Fists pounded against the window.

Benoit hauled Parker to his feet. "What's going on in there?"

Parker peered through the window, then stepped back, a horrified expression on his face. "No!"

"Tell me!"

"The fire alarm! When it's triggered all the air is pumped from the bio lab. They'll suffocate. We have to get them out!"

Benoit digested that, his anger subsiding. "How long do they have?"

"Minutes. Help them!"

"Can they escape?"

"No. The hatch to the bio lab is sealed. They can't get out."

Benoit relaxed. There was no rush now. He didn't want to risk losing any more men by sending them to open the hatch; the soldier—who Parker had informed them was called Shepherd—was most likely armed and had proven too dangerous.

No, he could let the facility take care of these scientists who had caused him so much trouble. He didn't need them; Lacoux could show him what he needed for the formula.

"We wait here," he told Roche. He shoved Parker toward the keypad on the wall. "Use him to try to open this door."

"I don't know the code," Parker rasped, ugly bruises sprouting on his throat.

"Then we'll break it down when the scientists are dead."

He peered through the hatch and decided that after the scientists were dead and he had the formula, he would get Parker to explain the workings behind the pumping of oxygen from the bio lab. It would look good in his report to AWR.

CHAPTER 46

SHEPHERD SLAMMED HIS palm against the steel side of the incinerator in frustration. He wanted to do something to help his friends. Anything. But what?

Allie clung to him and he felt her tears soaking his shirt. "What are we going to do?" Her voice was muffled against his chest. "Jannie, Ben, Mancini—they're dying in there!"

He held her tightly. He didn't know what they could do.

"I'm suffocating," she moaned. "I need air."

"There are still flames outside, Allie."

"I don't care." Her breathing was labored.

"Wait here." He released her and edged across to the heavy door. He pulled down on the handle and cautiously opened the door a fraction. Heat and orange light from the flames spilled in.

He opened the door wider and looked out. The mercenary's leg had been almost completely consumed by the fire; all that remained was charred bone. Part of the roof had caved in, blocking their exit. *Shit*. Now what?

The raging fireball had subsided, the flames ebbing as the sprinkler took control. A layer of water covered the floor. As he watched, it flowed over the doorway, past his feet and into the incinerator room.

He saw no flashlights or any movement, either in the MRI room or the tech room beyond the collapsed wall. The flames had kept the mercenaries at bay, for now at least. Not that it helped them.

He heard a cough and turned back. "Allie?"

"I'm fine," she managed to say.

Illuminated by the flames, she looked like a pale, waxen

statue. He took a step toward her. An orange flicker caught his attention and he looked down. The flames were reflecting off the water as it slid across the floor like a river of molten lava. He frowned. What was nagging at him?

Then he realized the water level inside the incinerator room wasn't rising. "What's happening to all the water?"

He studied the ground, able to see it for the first time in the radiant light cast by the fire. "What's that?" He pointed at a darker shadow in the center of the floor and knelt, probing it with his hands. "Allie?"

"It's the drainage system. It's where we flush the incinerated remains of lab animals."

"Where does it go?"

"To the sewer."

Shepherd tried to remember the layout of the facility. "Does it connect to any of the other rooms?"

"Yes, to the labs. It's how we clean spillages."

"Can we get into it?"

"I don't know."

The metal grate was approximately three square feet of crisscrossing iron bars, each bar a half-inch thick. It looked damned heavy. It also looked like it hadn't been moved in years; the repeated flushings of water had rusted it into place.

He tried to force his fingers into the square holes but they were chunky and it was a tight fit. Allie pushed him aside and tried. She got her fingers through but lacked the strength to shift the grate.

Shepherd tried shoving the barrel of his Herstal Minimi through the metal bars, but the barrel proved too wide.

Aware they were running out of time, he thrust his fingers into the grate once more. This time he managed to squeeze them through to the middle joint of each finger before they jammed. He still couldn't curl his fingers around the iron bar enough to get a grip.

He gritted his teeth against the pain and forced his fingers deeper. He felt the tearing as the flesh peeled back. His blood had a lubricating effect and he was able to drive his fingers in another inch, curled them, and this time had a firm hold. Taking all the weight with his arms, shoulders and back, he heaved. The grate didn't budge. "Move, you son of a bitch!" He hauled the grate with all his strength.

It shifted.

He heaved again. With a rasp of metal on metal, the grate popped up. He levered it aside, then winced as he pulled his fingers free. They were a pulpy, bloody mess.

He shoved his head and shoulders inside the gap and looked around. About two feet below, the drain opened into a metal duct. He pushed himself further in. The duct was narrow, roughly two and a half feet wide, and he looked into complete darkness.

He had no idea how far it went, or worse, what it might contain. The air was stale and fetid, with the rancid odor of sewage. It was like shoving his head into the gaping maw of a carnivore.

"I'm going to follow it. See if it'll bring me under the labs. Wait here."

Allie eyed the dark cavity, her face pale and tight with fear. "I'll go first."

"Jesus, Allie. What about your claustrophobia?"

"I'll manage." She pushed him aside. "I'm smaller. I'll be able to move faster. And I don't want to be behind you if you get stuck." She gave him a quick smile that faded as fast as it had appeared. She took a deep breath. "Make sure you follow me, okay? It'll help."

He went to protest, then realized she was right. "I'll be right behind you."

She peered into the blackness of the gaping hole. She closed her eyes, her chest heaving, fighting to control herself. Then she looked at him, gave a stiff nod, and slithered into the duct.

Shepherd waited a few seconds then followed. He found himself in complete darkness. He had struggled to get his shoulders into the tunnel leading from the cavity and had been forced to do an awkward half-somersault that resulted in him lying on his back. But he was inside.

He took a moment, assessing his surroundings. He was lying on a hard metal surface with no give. He suspected the duct cut through the solid concrete foundation supporting the Inn.

He pushed up with his hands, finding the top of the duct inches above his nose. His left shoulder pressed hard against metal, with a gap of only a couple of inches between his right shoulder and the duct.

The air was warm and humid and he blinked as sweat trickled into his eyes. The smell of sewage intensified, leaving an ugly taste in the back of his throat. He felt around until he found the Herstal Minimi and placed it on his legs with the barrel facing away from him.

"Shepherd! Are you there?" Allie croaked. She wheezed for air.

"I'm right here, Allie." He reached over his head, found her waggling feet and squeezed them.

"Just don't leave me here."

"I'll be right at your heels."

"Okay." She took some deep breaths. "I can't see a damn thing."

"We'll be fine."

He drew his good leg up as far as he could before his knee jammed against the ceiling, then thrust himself backward. His left shoulder squealed against metal, but he moved a couple of inches. He felt the friction burn through his thin cotton shirt as he scraped the duct. Continuing the snake-like movements, ignoring the pain from his bad knee, he followed the steady thump of Allie's legs.

"Are you behind me?"

He reached out, but couldn't find her ankle. She was slithering along at a faster pace than he could manage. "I'm here."

"I can't feel you!"

"I'm right behind you." He forced his leg to pump faster.

"Oh, God. Talk to me!"

"I'm here."

"Tell me something, anything. Distract me. Your knee. I saw the scar. What happened?"

This was a topic he usually didn't talk about; it brought up too many dark memories. But he found his desire to comfort her outweighed his old demons. Allie was confronting her worst nightmare; he could do the same.

He felt his head bump against her feet. He wrapped his hands around her ankles, giving them a squeeze. "I'm right here, Allie. Deep breaths. You're fine."

He swallowed, tasting the bile in his throat. "I was wounded in Afghanistan. An IED. We were escorting a convoy of captured militants back to base for interrogation. One of the trucks hit a mine on the side of the road. We lost some men. I was lucky; just caught some shrapnel in the knee. I was sent to Germany for rehab, but it was too damaged. I was out of the Rangers."

"Oh." She sucked in a deep breath with a keening whine.

"So that's when you trained to be a medic?"

"I'd been with the Rangers for five years. Most of it with the same platoon. After the training, then deployment, they were my brothers. My family. I couldn't accept I was no longer a part of it."

He gave her ankles another squeeze. "They helped me get into college. I went on to medical school. When I finished, I rejoined the military as a medic and was embedded with the Rangers again for a while, but my knee couldn't handle the scrambling, the carrying of wounded men. It flared up.

"That was it. This time I was out for good. I was lost and felt bitter about it for a long time. Then I met Claire. She gave my life meaning again. We had Cassie. I went into private industry, then was approached by the USAMRMC. Things were good…" His voice trailed away.

"What happened?"

"A car accident." As Shepherd stared into the darkness, a hollow, empty feeling that he hadn't experienced in years returned to the pit of his stomach.

"Tell me."

"Claire shouldn't have been driving. My knee had been playing up. I could hardly walk."

"Couldn't you have had a reconstruction or something?"

"I had one after the initial injury, but I was left with ongoing problems. It needed a tidy-up, but it was a busy time. Cassie was two and running around. I was busy with work. Claire was trying to juggle work with being a mom. Too much was going on. I kept putting it off." He caught his breath. The memories flooding back were old but just as vivid and every bit as painful.

"Claire was driving Cassie to a playdate. They were hit by a drunk driver."

"I'm sorry."

"So was I. And angry, bitter, guilty. For a long time, I blamed myself. I drank for months afterward to help me deal with it. Then my dad stepped in. Told me it was time I manned up and took care of my little girl. He was right. So I got sober. Haven't drunk since."

Allie's feet thudded against the duct and she moved ahead. Wriggling his shoulders, he followed, his hands eventually catching up to her legs.

"After blaming myself, my knee and the war that injured it, the drunk driver, I realized I couldn't live with all that hate and bitterness. It was destroying me. It was hurting Cassie. And with the diagnosis of her CDD, it took all our mental strength to cope with the new challenge. So together, Cassie and I moved on."

They edged along in silence. He estimated a few minutes at least had passed. How much time did they have left?

"I see something. Light!"

Shepherd followed the banging of her feet as fast as he could. Now he saw the glint of light on the stainless steel metal of the duct.

"There's another grate! Overhead!"

He heard her grunt, heard the sound of banging.

"I can't shift it! Oh, Christ! We're running out of time!"

"Move, Allie!"

"I can't go any further," she gasped. "There's a hole just in front of me. The duct must drop into the containment tank."

Light fell across his face and he looked up. Above his nose was a grate of solid iron bars. Through it, he saw a ceiling bathed in flashing red light. An alarm droned. He shoved the metal framework. It didn't budge.

"Quick!" Allie shouted.

Shepherd thumped the iron grid, ignoring the pain in his damaged fingers, but it didn't shift. He pulled the Herstal Minimi up over his eyes and jammed its muzzle into the corner of the grate. The air burst through his lips as he strained.

He felt movement. He shoved harder, feeling the tendons in his forearms and wrists stretch to snapping point. Then with a metallic groan, it scraped free.

Shepherd shoved it out of the way, grabbed an edge and hauled himself up. It was a tight squeeze. He almost jammed. But he kicked his feet against the duct below, wriggled free and found himself on a white floor, looking up at workbenches. He was inside the scientists' laboratory. A fine mist of water from the overhead sprinklers sprayed him. He scrambled to his feet, almost slipping in the water covering the floor. "Allie!"

"I'm here!" Her face appeared and he pulled her up alongside him.

Over the undulating screech of the fire alarm, Shepherd heard the desperate pounding of fists against hard plastic. He hobbled toward the hatch leading to the bio lab. White faces stared at him. They had taken their hazmat suits off.

"Hang on!" He seized the handle, trying to throw it open. It didn't move. He threw himself at it, using all his weight, Allie joining him. There was a burst of static and Shepherd realized the radio was still stuffed deep in his pocket.

He pulled it out. "It's sealed," Mancini's voice crackled. "It's automated. The only way to open it is to enter the override code!"

On the wall beside the hatch the keypad. Allie started to punch in the code when they heard a loud thud on the door that opened into the corridor. They turned. In the door was a tiny window of thick perspex through which they saw a face staring at them in surprise. The yellow eyes and broken nose were immediately recognizable—Benoit.

Allie withdrew her hand from the keypad. "Oh, no."

Entering the override code would open the hatch to the bio lab but also unseal the door to the scientists' laboratory, the last barrier between themselves and the mercenaries in the corridor.

CHAPTER 47

ALLIE'S HAND HOVERED over the keypad. "What do we do?"

The scientists peered through the window in the bio lab hatch. Jan's cerulean eyes were wide with alarm, his face flushed as he gasped for air. His gaze implored Shepherd to help.

He felt sick. Despite the mercenary leader outside, he knew he had to open the hatch. He couldn't allow Jannie, or any of them, to die in there.

O'Connell's fists pounded at the window. Behind him, Shepherd saw Ben clutch his throat as he struggled to breathe.

Mancini's voice rasped over the radio. "We're running out of air!"

"I can't leave them to die," Allie whispered, preparing to punch the code into the keypad. "I can't."

"I know." He tightened his grip on the Herstal Minimi.

The yellow eyes staring at them through the window were now full of curiosity. It was as though Benoit was watching an interesting experiment unfold before him, and he was waiting to see what they would do.

He observed Shepherd look frantically from the bio lab containing the scientists to the door holding the mercenaries at bay. The strange eyes filled with comprehension of their dilemma. 'Open the door,' he mouthed slowly so Shepherd understood him.

He glimpsed another mercenary, standing poised, his machine gun leveled at the door in anticipation of it opening.

Benoit raised a large finger and pointed at the keypad. 'Open it,' he mouthed once again.

Allie stepped back from the keypad. "Oh, God, what do we do? He'll kill all of us."

Shepherd's nausea intensified. He couldn't allow Jan to die. But Benoit would kill them all anyway. Once the mercenaries were through, how long could he hold them off? And even then, they would be trapped.

The wail of the fire alarm filled his head, distracting him. He tried to ignore the incessant sound that reminded him they were almost out of time. There had to be an alternative…

He felt the yellow eyes of the mercenary watching him. They gleamed hungrily, full of confidence in the outcome.

He turned to the bio lab. The red digital display on the hatch showed an oxygen level of thirty-four percent. At thirty percent, everyone in the bio lab would be unconscious.

O'Connell motioned feverishly.

Shepherd raised the radio.

Breathing hard, his lips blue, O'Connell said, "I have an idea."

* * *

SHEPHERD SHOVED THE heavy workbench into place. He stood back, assessing the crude barricade he and Allie had built against the laboratory door from work benches, metal cabinets and the larger pieces of equipment.

Would it give them enough time? It would have to do. Through the small window in the bio lab hatch, he saw O'Connell issuing instructions. His gestures were slow and uncoordinated. Then he doubled over and crumpled to the floor.

"The barricade's ready. Get the hatch open. Now!" He waited, ready to support the barricade against the mercenaries, while she ran to the keypad. The door rattled and juddered as a heavy body driven by the powerful nano-suit slammed repeatedly into it.

The mercenary pulled back and for a moment he saw Parker, his face full of terror as Benoit dragged him to the window. Parker was saying something and repeatedly shaking his head. Shepherd guessed the mercenary leader was demanding to know what the scientists were up to.

The yellow eyes reappeared. The curiosity in them had disappeared, replaced by burning rage.

Shepherd flipped him the finger. He wanted this man as angry as possible; an angered man was careless.

"It's opening," Allie shouted.

With a clank and a hiss, the locks slid back and the door unsealed. The red lights stopped flashing and the alarm faded. The sprinklers died to a trickle. The door rammed against the barrier. The workbench screeched across the floor. The door shook as bodies thudded against it. The barricade shuddered but held.

Allie struggled with the handle on the hatch. "Help!"

He seized the handle and together they forced it open. He stood back to allow air to flood into the bio lab. Jan's huddled form lay on its side, facing away from him. Ben and O'Connell lay on their backs, grasping their chests. Their eyes were closed, their mouths gaped in blue, oxygen-starved faces.

"No!" Shepherd shouted. Then he saw movement at his feet.

Mancini was on his knees beside the hatch. "Thank Christ," he gasped, breathing deeply.

Gunfire cracked deafeningly behind them. Shepherd knew the barricade wouldn't last more than a few minutes. He stooped through the open hatch and pushed into the bio lab, Allie following.

Ben stirred and groaned. Shepherd limped past him and crouched over Jan. He gripped his friend's shoulder and rolled him toward him. His eyes were closed, his lips blue.

"Jannie!" Shepherd shouted desperately.

He gasped, his great chest heaving in huge, shuddering breaths. The blue tinge to his face turned a healthier red. He opened his eyes, breathing deeply for several seconds before attempting to stand, his movements still uncoordinated and jerky as his body recovered.

Shepherd helped him to his feet.

"Thank you," Jan wheezed.

"You look terrible, Jannie."

The cerulean eyes glared at him. "Pot calling kettle, sweetie!"

He smiled in relief.

There was another burst of gunfire and Shepherd heard the squeal as the heavy workbench and machinery were forced back, inch by inch. "We have to move!"

The scraping of the barricade was abruptly cut off as O'Connell shoved the hatch closed. He made some rapid adjustments on the instrument display, then jammed a chair against it. He hustled over, his face shining with sweat. "That's it. I've sealed the hatch to the bio lab. Let's get out of here!"

Ben gestured urgently at them with his good arm. "Get over here," he wheezed. He and Mancini were staring into a square hole in the middle of the bio lab floor. A metal plate had been thrown to one side.

"The drain unsealed when Allie entered the override code. We can use it to escape."

"But we can't get back into the MRI room from here," Shepherd said, "so where are we going to go?"

O'Connell's voice grated in his dry throat. "The bio lab has a separate sewage system."

"But we won't fit down there," Allie stared in dismay into the square cavity.

Shepherd leaned past her. At the bottom, he saw a small, round tunnel disappear into blackness. Unlike the duct leading from the incinerator room, the pipe was only a few inches across.

O'Connell shook his head impatiently. "Not the pipes. The emergency containment tank!" He ripped open a small, square plastic shield on the wall, revealing a button, which he slammed.

A soft bell chimed and the metal floor at the base of the square cavity opened to reveal a dark, round tunnel.

Shepherd stared into the chasm. "How far down are we talking about?"

"About ten feet. No more." O'Connell replied.

"Won't Parker or Lacoux know about this? We could be ambushed!"

"Parker was only a naturalist; he was hardly ever in the bio lab. And that motherfucker Lacoux hasn't worked here long enough to see this in operation. He could have provided the mercenaries with the layout of the Inn at the functional level, but he would know nothing about what's below us."

Shepherd hesitated, uneasy at the idea of accepting a plan he hadn't been involved in preparing. He listened to another burst of gunfire and remembered Allie urging him to be more inclusive; to trust them and use them as a resource. "Okay. I'll go first. Then Jannie. Then send Allie. Jan and I will be at the bottom ready to catch you."

Her eyes were round pools of fear as she gazed into the

pit and he saw her hands shaking. "You'll be fine. We'll be with you every step of the way." He squeezed her hands. "Okay?"

She didn't answer, her gaze fixed on the aperture.

Shepherd saw the Winchester lying on a workbench. Realizing they were dead anyway if O'Connell's plan failed, he threw his Herstal Minimi on the bench and picked up the rifle. He wasn't about to leave his trusty Winchester behind.

O'Connell lumbered to a workbench and returned with a flashlight. He handed it to Shepherd. "Move!"

CHAPTER 48

BENOIT WATCHED THROUGH a gap in the barricade as the hatch to the bio lab swung closed. He stepped away from the door, feeling his frustration boil within him.

He had been taken by surprise at the sudden appearance of the man he guessed to be the soldier and a woman in the scientists' laboratory. Then he watched with clinical interest as they struggled with the dilemma confronting them.

Seeing the soldier steel himself for a final stand, Benoit and Roche had readied in anticipation of the door being unsealed as the duo tried to save their friends. The man and woman built a barricade before fleeing like rats into the bio lab. Trapped rats, he'd thought. But where had they come from? Was there another way out after all?

Benoit directed Roche to keep working at the barricade. He accessed the RIF to contact Gault, ordering him to return to assist Roche. Then he grabbed Parker. "Where did those two scientists come from?"

"I don't know!"

Benoit shook him. "Think!"

"The drainage system. Maybe they used that."

His anger soared at this unexpected development. He shook harder. Parker's head lashed back and forth.

"We may need him," Lacoux said.

Benoit shook Parker once more but was careful to control the power in his arm. Lacoux was right; he didn't want to break this man's neck. Not yet. "Can they use it to escape from the bio lab?"

"I don't know! I'm a naturalist. I don't use the bio lab."

"But I use it," said Lacoux. "It's a contained environment

and the drain inside is small. They can't get into it."

Benoit's anger subsided as he realized that the scientists were trapped. He thought how best to use this. He reached a solution, one that would spare his men any risk of confronting the dangerous soldier trapped in there. "Can you operate the system that controls the airflow into the room?"

Lacoux smiled as he realized his intention. "Of course." A look of pride passed across his face. "That's very clever."

Benoit turned to Roche. "Break down the barricade, but then wait."

"What about the scientists?"

"They're trapped. We'll suffocate them."

Roche and Gault heaved their bulk at the door. With the screech of metal, it opened another couple of inches.

Finally satisfied that the facility was under their control, Benoit's mind turned to his report to AWR. How could he explain the losses his team had suffered?

"When are you due to report in?" Lacoux asked.

He felt a pulse of gratification that he'd kept this man alive. Lacoux understood him. He was on his side and with him, maybe the disaster that was this operational trial could still be turned around.

He glanced at the watch strapped to his wrist. In contrast to his sophisticated nano-suit, it was a simple, black, durable Timex that he'd worn for years. "Every twelve hours. My status report is now two hours overdue."

"Is that part of the operation at least functioning as we'd planned?"

Their planning had required Benoit's status updates to be reported back to the mercenaries' launch. Gilles Durand, a fellow mercenary and skilled mariner who had piloted their boat along the treacherous river systems from Manaus, had remained with the launch to guard it, but also to maintain contact with Toussen via the craft's satellite. Durand would relay the updates to Toussen.

Benoit informed Lacoux how the TIS had failed underneath the jungle canopy, making communication with the launch impossible.

"No one expected any trouble from a bunch of scientists. Durand will put the delay down to a communications failure due to weather conditions. But the longer he goes without hearing from you, the more alarmed he will become," said Lacoux. "We planned that if he suspected your team had run into difficulty, his next step would be to report this back to AWR and ask for instructions. This is precisely what we don't want."

"So what do we do?"

"We have to control the message filtering back to AWR. To do so, you have to get in contact with Durand. Now."

The launch was too far away for the RIF to function. Benoit pulled the TIS from the pouch on his suit to send a message to him. He tapped the screen, but it remained stubbornly blank.

Lacoux frowned. "There's too much interference inside the facility with the HEPA filters overhead and the steel reinforced roof. You need to get outside into the clearing. Even with the storm, it's your best chance."

"I'm not leaving until those fucking scientists are dead."

"Getting in contact with Durand is more important than the scientists now. They're trapped. I can take care of them. They'll be dead very soon and then I can lead the search for more of the formula, as we originally planned. You're not needed here. Go, my friend."

Benoit turned his attention to Roche and saw his two

men almost had the door open. This would be over in minutes. Lacoux was right.

He pulled Roche aside. "Look after Lacoux. I don't want anything to happen to him. Keep the other scientist alive until we have everything we need. Then kill him."

He strode outside into the deluge.

CHAPTER 49

SHEPHERD LOWERED HIMSELF into the cavity, positioned himself carefully with his elbows until he was centered over the hole beneath him, and dropped.

His stomach swooped; he was enveloped in darkness. He felt his shoulders buffeting the side of a tunnel, then with one last bump, he plummeted into a wider space.

Falling back on his parachute training, he just had time to tuck his knees into his chest before he crashed against a hard metal floor. But his bandaged knee wouldn't fold completely, jutting out awkwardly as he slammed into the ground.

He rolled to the side away from the damaged limb, breaking his fall. But as he hobbled back to the tunnel, the pain in his knee intensified and his limp was more pronounced.

He flicked on the flashlight. "Your turn, Jannie! Tuck your knees in."

Jan landed and rolled to his feet like a cat.

"Show off," Shepherd mumbled, feeling the ache in his leg.

"Just one of my many attractions, sweetie."

"Next!"

One by one they came through, Shepherd and Jan catching each neatly. The last to land was O'Connell, who kept them waiting a few heart-pounding moments.

"What took you so damn long?" Shepherd said, getting slowly to his feet. O'Connell had cannoned into him and Jan, sending them scattering like ninepins.

O'Connell brandished his backpack. "I told you I wasn't going to destroy the cure or let those motherfuckers get their hands on it."

300

"We're not out of here yet," he reminded him. The mercenaries would have smashed past his barricade by now. Then there was only the sealed bio lab hatch to keep them out. But once they were through that... He hoped O'Connell's plan was going to work.

He shone the flashlight around, taking in the gleaming metal walls. The tank was huge—about fifteen feet long, eight wide. It stank of ammonia, with the air toxic enough to sting his eyes and nasal cavity.

He found he could stand easily, with several feet of clearance above his head. "Where are we?"

"Emergency containment tank. It was built for the bio lab. If we have a release of any chemicals or infected fluids, we can hit the emergency containment button and direct it here. Then it can be treated and sterilized and pumped into barrels for transport back to the States. They get picked up every season."

Attached to the end of the tank was a metal ladder climbing to a large, smooth, circular hatch in the roof. "How do we open it?"

"We can't," O'Connell said. "It can only be opened from the outside."

"What?"

He pointed down to a circular valve ringed by hydraulic machinery. It was about eighteen inches across. "We use the pump valve instead."

"We can't fit through there!"

"No, not all of us. But one of us can." He pointed at Allie, who was crouched at the back of the small group, her face deathly pale, arms folded across her knees, breathing deeply. "The barrels have already been collected for this season. The valve ends in the containment vault. From there,

Allie can get outside, then get to the access tunnel to the hatch above us."

"Shit!"

"What's wrong?" he asked. "Allie can do it. She's small enough."

"She's claustrophobic," Shepherd replied.

"Fuck me."

Shepherd stared at the valve in dismay.

O'Connell's nasal voice filled with urgency. "Do you understand what's happening? The bio lab is filling up with oxygen as we speak. I've set the controls to maximize the oxygen levels. When the mercenaries open the hatch, the metal chair I wedged against it is going to scrape across the floor and produce a spark, which in that oxygen-rich environment, will blow this place to kingdom come. I figure we have a few minutes. Maybe less. So, we need to get the fuck out of here. Now."

The men glanced at Allie, who straightened and joined them. "What's wrong?" She listened in silence, her eyes widening as Shepherd explained.

O'Connell wiped sweat off his face. "Christ, Allie. I didn't know you were claustrophobic. But you're the only one who'll fit. You have to do it. There's no other way."

He knelt, peeling the rubber seal from the valve. A black aperture gaped like the orifice of some hideous creature and looked about as inviting. Water trickled from it.

"Why is there water?" Shepherd tried to keep the unease from his voice.

"The storm. Must be some flooding outside, forcing its way in. I'm sure it's fine," he added for Allie's benefit. He explained what needed to be done once she was outside. "Got it?"

"I think so. Let's get this over with."

Shepherd reluctantly handed her the flashlight, then seized her in a tight embrace. "Be careful." She wrapped her arms around him fiercely and, standing on her tiptoes, crushed her lips against his before turning away.

She knelt before the dark hole and looked back at them. "See you on the other side." Terrified but resolute, she slid her shoulders into the hole.

CHAPTER 50

BENOIT FORCED HIS way through the driving rain, the two trackers alongside him. He had found them sheltering in the jungle fringe, beneath a large fern, where he had instructed them to remain before the final assault on the facility.

The lure of money had kept them from fleeing despite the setbacks the squad had encountered. But from the fear and trepidation in their eyes, he knew they were close to abandoning the operation. He wondered if they were more frightened of the storm's fury or his own.

He dismissed the thought; it didn't matter. What did matter was that he still needed them. With the storm threatening to flood the region, he might need their skill to get back to the launch in the morning. So he had grinned reassuringly as he informed them the assault had been successful, that they could shelter from the storm in the facility.

When the doubt in their eyes failed to subside, he had pulled the bottle of cognac from his backpack, promising they would share it with the mercenaries once they were inside. That had convinced them.

He herded them along the track toward the Inn. The following day, once they were safely at the launch, he would kill them; they would have served their purpose.

He wondered at his lack of empathy. Once, he would have kept his word and delivered on his promise of money. He realized the change was a result of the drug compound Lacoux had given him and gave silent thanks to the scientist for freeing him from the burden of caring.

None of them mattered. Not these trackers who would soon die, his lost men or Halle, whom he had murdered.

Only inferior beings mourned the loss of minions who had served their purpose. All that mattered was completing the operation and receiving more of the drug compound he craved.

By now, Roche would have control of the facility. The scientists should be dead, Lacoux would be free to retrieve the formula they needed. Then he would ensure he received more of the drug compound. The only possible problem Benoit foresaw was his failure to contact Durand at the launch.

The TIS had been no match for the power of this storm; all his efforts to send a message to Durand had failed. But the possibility of communication failures in this hostile environment had been factored in during the planning of the operation. AWR wouldn't be alarmed yet. They would wait ninety-six hours before mobilizing the backup force that had remained in Manaus.

But the longer it took for Benoit to make contact, the more it would reflect badly in the final report. He was fully aware that although effectiveness (retrieving the formula) was the key success indicator for this trial, process efficiency (number of team fatalities and the speed of the operation) would be factored into an assessment of AWR's future soldier's performance.

He was certain that the setbacks they had encountered, the losses his squad had suffered, were not his fault. He had been given poor intelligence. But he was also aware that getting out fast with the formula, destroying all evidence of what had taken place, while providing a logical explanation for the fatalities could persuade AWR of the operation's success. If not for his enhancements and superior performance, the operation would have failed. With Lacoux's influence, he remained confident that the trial would be seen as enough of a success to continue with the program. He would receive more of the drug and it would be even more powerful after Lacoux had utilized the Alzheimer's cure.

A savage gust of wind almost lifted him off the ground and he fought to keep his balance. They were halfway across the clearing. The Inn was just visible in the dim light cast by the sole remaining floodlight, which juddered in the tempest.

He squinted to see through the rain, continually wiping water from his eyes. It mingled with the mucus that streamed from his broken nose in the humidity. The nano-suit stabilized him, steadying his legs as the storm tore into him as though trying to sweep him from the clearing. The smell of ozone was heavy in the air as jagged forks of lightning ripped through the sky.

Benoit shivered as a sudden chill of foreboding gripped him. He didn't understand why but he sensed danger and wanted to get to the Inn as quickly as possible. He dragged his foot from the dirt, feeling the nano-suit fight the suction of the thick mud. There was a crack of thunder, a flash and the stunned mercenary landed on his back.

He scrambled to his feet and froze, staring in disbelief. The facility had transformed into a blazing fireball that mushroomed into the night sky. It had been the shockwave of the explosion that had flattened him.

Debris rained around him. Burning wood and twisted metal speared into the mud. He staggered as a chunk of molten plastic barreled against his flank before being deflected by his liquid armor.

He threw himself back to the ground. He registered movement and saw one of the trackers jerking and quivering on his back, his face red pulp from which jutted a dagger of metal.

He waited until it was safe, then got slowly to his feet. The facility was gone. In its place was a shattered ruin from which flames flickered and smoke billowed. His ears ringing, he struggled to make sense of what had happened.

As he watched, the flames raged against the assault of the torrential rain, before slowly ebbing. He took a step forward, trembling with the fury that engulfed him as the full extent of the disaster sank in. No one could have survived that inferno. His men were dead, Lacoux with them. The formula was destroyed. The utter failure of this trial meant he would receive no more of the drug compound.

Benoit skirted the burning debris, surveying the ruin, wondering if there was anything he could salvage. The smoldering wreckage mocked him. His rage grew. Pain seared through his brain like a bolt of electricity and he gripped the sides of his head in agony. Then from the corner of his eye, he saw movement.

He swiveled, his boots sticking in the mud. Barely visible through the rain, shadows flitted across the clearing. Wiping the dirt and water from his eyes, he stared hard and realized what he was seeing—a series of figures scuttling toward the jungle. Three of the figures were large and bulky; any one of them could have been Roche or Gault, but they lacked the distinctive, ant-like outline of the nano-suits.

They had to be scientists. His anguish and fury centered, finding a focus that helped alleviate the pain in his skull. He would make these scientists pay for what they had done. Accompanying his desire for revenge was a tiny flicker of hope. If the scientists had somehow orchestrated the explosion to escape, then maybe they carried the formula.

Perhaps the operation wasn't a total failure after all.

Benoit checked he had his weapons—his Herstal Minimi, his PAMAS G1. His Camillus combat knife remained sheathed in its pouch on the right leg of his suit; his revenge would arrive swiftly, but be delivered slowly, painfully.

He hauled the surviving tracker from the mud. "Move!" Fighting the rain and wind, he plunged into the jungle, the nano-suit driving his legs like pistons as he set off in pursuit of the scientists.

CHAPTER 51

"Stop!" Shepherd screamed to be heard over the shriek of the wind, the booms of thunder that vibrated the heavy, humid air and the remorseless pounding of torrential rain against the rainforest canopy.

He had driven them on for almost twenty minutes, he estimated. They had followed Ben along the scantest of paths before joining the main access trail. Despite the flooding, they should have put some distance between themselves and what was left of the Inn.

Looking at the bedraggled, mud-soaked figures trailing behind him, he realized that, like himself, they were exhausted and could use a short break.

He glanced around uneasily. The intensity of the tropical storm assaulted his senses. Thunder cracked against his eardrums. Flashes of lightning pierced the darkness through gaps torn in the canopy, searing his eyes. Rain tumbled with the dull roar of cascading waterfalls, glimmering a silvery-gray when illuminated by the beam of the flashlight.

He was soaked to the skin and coated in thick mud from trudging through knee-deep pools of murky water and silt. Worst of all were the downward bursts of wind that occasionally ripped through the widening gaps in the canopy and carried with them swirling leaves and small, jagged branches that scythed out of the darkness, forcing them to duck.

One by one, the rest of them gathered around him, gripping their knees and breathing heavily.

"Five minutes, no longer." He took the flashlight from Ben, who had led the way. With only the one flashlight, visibility had been poor, so Shepherd had ordered them to walk with a hand on the shoulder of the person in front.

He shone the light across each of their faces to make sure all were there. The narrow ray of light cast by the flashlight looked fragile as the inky blackness pressed in around them like a living entity that swallowed light.

But it illuminated the clouds of mosquitoes, black flies, moths and clawed beetles which had been stirred into a frenzy by the storm. The insects swarmed over them, leaving bites and scratches on exposed flesh.

Like himself, they all appeared bedraggled, mud-splattered and exhausted. "Is anyone hurt?" They all shook their heads, to his relief.

After Allie had freed them, they had been only halfway across the clearing when the Inn had disintegrated. Given the magnitude of the explosion, he could scarcely believe nobody had been hit by flying debris.

He picked out O'Connell with the flashlight. "That was some plan."

The scientist's pale eyes glinted with satisfaction. "Blew the fuckers to hell."

"Are you sure they're all dead?" Mancini said.

Shepherd felt Allie's arm snake around his waist. He drew her even closer, reveling in the feel of her against him, her softness and warmth. "They're dead. All of them. Allie and I saw Benoit just outside the scientists' lab. If he was inside, the rest of his men would've been with him."

Relief washed over him with the realization that he wouldn't have to confront Benoit. He knew he couldn't have defeated such an enemy. He was no longer the man he'd been as a Ranger.

And even if he had been, he knew the biologically modified Benoit would have been too strong, too well-armed and too clever for him. An image of an army of bio-mods filled his mind and with it came a feeling of dread.

Allie felt his body tense. "What is it?"

"Just glad they didn't get their hands on the Alzheimer's cure." He saw the backpack slung over O'Connell's shoulder and was grateful he had prevented him from destroying it.

The darkness that had filled his mind ever since he'd realized they might have to destroy the Alzheimer's cure finally cleared. He contemplated the potential benefits it represented and his thoughts turned to Cassie. What had happened to his daughter?

Again, Allie read his mind. She reached up and pulled his head toward hers. Her lips touched his ear. "She'll be fine." Her hand caressed his chest. "I'd like to meet her."

He felt his heart pound. The thought of dating again after so long filled him with a terror equal to that of the mercenaries. He summoned up his courage. "I'd like that. A lot."

"This is great. I'm happy for you both," said O'Connell. "But how the fuck are we going to get home?"

Shepherd forced his mind to focus. "The mercenaries will have arrived by boat. We're going to take it."

"Won't it be guarded?" Jan asked.

He unslung the Winchester and patted it. "Benoit will only have left a small team to guard it. One man, maybe two at most. Their comms will be down, as ours are. They won't know what's happened here.

"We're a bunch of scientists, not a serious threat. They certainly won't be expecting an attack. If Ben gets me close enough without being seen, I can take them out with the Winchester."

He might no longer be a Ranger, but he still trusted his

marksmanship. His hand tightened around Allie's waist. He would get them all on that boat. Then, he hoped, he would never have to draw on his old skills again. He was a father and a scientist now, not a soldier. And that suited him just fine.

Reluctantly, he removed his arm from Allie and read-justed the bandage around his knee. The increased mobility was making it easier to move, but the joint was unstable and he had taken a few tumbles along the way. The anesthetic had worn off and, with each stride, he had felt pain jolt from his swollen knee to the pit of his stomach. But the pain was nothing compared with the thought of getting home. He straightened, eager to get moving.

"I need more time," said Mancini.

Shepherd considered, before deciding a few extra min-utes couldn't hurt. "Another five minutes. No more."

"No," Ben said. "We should get moving now."

Taken aback at the forcefulness of his outburst, Shepherd studied him. Once again he'd been surprised at his fortitude; Ben had refused to allow his shoulder wound to slow him down as he'd led the way through the jungle. The arduous journey along the treacherous trails had hurt him, however; the yellow glow cast by Shepherd's flashlight revealed the pain in his eyes as he looked around at the jungle, along with the apprehension on his mud-splattered face. "We have to hurry!"

"Why?" O'Connell said. "The mercenaries are dead. I need a break."

"This isn't just any storm. I think it's a *derecho*. A powerful windstorm, accompanied by a band of thunderstorms. A *derecho* packs winds of more than a hundred miles an hour and they can be enhanced by downburst clusters embedded inside storms like the one over us now. These wind gusts can exceed two hundred miles an hour. It'll hit this region like a bomb."

"What makes you think this is a *derecho*?" Allie asked.

"Marlowe was worried when the storm band was first picked up on the radar. He explained it to me; he was concerned the storms would develop into a *derecho*. Now we're out here in it, I think he was right."

"Oh, for fuck's sake," said O'Connell. "Grow some balls, you little punk, and stop panicking. We'll be fine."

"I know a hell of a lot more about this rainforest than you ever will," Ben retorted.

"Ben's right," Allie said. "We should listen to him and get moving. Now." She gave O'Connell a warning glance and he glowered at the younger man but remained quiet.

In the moments of silence that followed, Shepherd realized no argument remained amongst the group now as to who was their leader.

"Okay, Ben, you take the lead," she said.

* * *

BENOIT FORGED HIS way along the tiny path, following the tracker. He could discern no sign that the scientists had traveled this way, but the man in front of him never faltered.

The grinding jungle clawed and dragged at him, scraping across his nano-suit. The tiny-framed tracker slipped past each obstacle while he smashed his way through the clinging branches and snaking vines.

Through his night-vision IDU, he saw a disorienting pattern of gray and black. He pushed it aside, relying instead upon his flashlight. With the tracker being prodded along by the muzzle of Benoit's PAMAS G1, they pushed on through the gnashing green hell.

Thirty minutes of this was enough to subdue his anger.

Soon, it was replaced with fear. The jungle had a malevolence that set his teeth on edge. The storm had transformed it into a ravaging beast, full of hidden dangers.

He heard crashing and booming noises in the distance, reminding him of the endless power of the thundering surf on the shores of the Skeleton Coast in Namibia. He fought against his fear, wondering where the tracker was taking him.

They stumbled out of the jungle and onto the wide expanse of a path. He recognized the access trail. Branches were strewn along its length as if the rainforest had been savaged by an ax.

The tracker scurried around, his nose close to the ground, moving leaves and branches carefully aside. He studied torn vegetation on the side of the trail before kneeling alongside a series of impressions in the mud that, now he saw them, Benoit realized could be footprints.

The tracker pointed. "That way."

The scientists were heading toward the river. Toward the mercenaries' launch. He was confident he could follow them on this trail, but even so, he decided he would keep the tracker with him, just in case.

But they would have to move fast. If the man became a liability, he would shoot him. He aimed his PAMAS G1 at him and he froze. "Keep up or die."

A fresh burst of pain lanced through his skull, bringing with it his anger and desire for revenge. Feeling the reassuring power of the nano-suit, he plunged through the mud after the scientists.

CHAPTER 52

HIS KNEE THROBBING, Shepherd checked his watch to find how long they had been traveling. They had skirted the tiger traps he'd set, now black pools from which jagged stakes jutted. He had noted with chagrin that they had failed to snare any of the mercenaries.

Ben lurched to a halt, causing Shepherd to thud into him, almost sending him sprawling.

"What's wrong?" he said. Behind him, he felt repeated jolts as everyone collided with the person in front of them.

"What the hell are you doing up there?" shouted O'Connell.

"Don't move! Stay still!"

Looking over Ben's shoulder, Shepherd saw a brown and gold dappled creature crouched low on the trail, its ears pressed back against its heavy head. Its bared teeth glinted yellow in the flashlight. A primordial fear from deep within his belly flared. "Jesus!"

"It's a jaguar. We've climbed a small hill and this area is relatively drier than the surrounding jungle. It must be sheltering from the floods."

Allie moved alongside Shepherd. Everyone else crowded close behind them. "What do we do, Ben?" she asked.

"Shoot the fucker!" said O'Connell.

Ben shouted over the howl of the wind, "Stay calm. Just don't move. It's scared. Of the storm and us. Any movement will trigger an attack. If we stay still, it'll leave."

"You'd better be right," said O'Connell.

Ben held up his good arm for silence. He didn't move, his gaze fixed on the jaguar.

The cat's ears flickered around, as if examining the threat posed by each crash of heavy branches, each rumble of thunder that boomed overhead. Its long, thick tail flicked from side to side.

Shepherd wondered if he could unsling and aim the Winchester in time. But the cat didn't move. Neither did Ben. His calmness gave Shepherd some comfort. Maybe the kid was right.

The cat flattened itself to the ground, its ears pressed back, and with a snarl, it charged.

"Fuck!" cried O'Connell.

The cat shot past them and down the trail. Ben swung around, his flashlight picking up the speeding jaguar and the sinister, ant-like shape that materialized out of the darkness.

Shepherd's stomach filled with thick, oily fear as the flashlight picked out the broken nose and the glare of yellow eyes. The mercenary pounded along the trail, clutching a flashlight in one hand, a pistol in the other.

He saw them and without breaking stride, he raised the pistol. The jaguar streaked like a tracer bullet, low across the ground toward the rapidly approaching threat. Now Benoit saw the danger and dropped to one knee, leveled his pistol and fired.

The cat fell, its forehead striped with blood where the bullet had creased it, rolled to its feet and spun to face Benoit. It crouched low, circling the mercenary as it readied to charge once more.

Before Shepherd could unsling his Winchester, the tearing crack of slowly splitting wood cut through the air.

"Run!" Ben screamed.

They sprinted along the trail away from the mercenary, who fired once more at the jaguar. The cat took off and disappeared into the jungle. Looking over his shoulder, Shepherd saw Benoit rise to his feet and look in their direction. There was no outrunning him. "Get off the trail. Hide in the jungle!"

Before they could respond, the cracking sound from the jungle intensified, culminating in an immense retort that burst from its depths like cannon fire. With a whoosh, the air seemed to be forced through it, followed by crashing. Then a final thud shook the ground beneath them like an earthquake.

"Everyone down!" Ben threw himself flat on the ground. Jan, Shepherd, Allie and Mancini followed suit.

"We need to run!" O'Connell lumbered along the trail, then lurched to a halt as a whirring drone reverberated through the rainforest.

Shepherd saw Benoit's tracker behind him, gazing up into the darkness with terrified eyes.

"Get down!" Ben screamed at O'Connell.

He hesitated, then dropped flat on his stomach as, with a roar like fighter jets, a cloud of debris tore from the rainforest. Lianas, branches, earth and leaves roiled above them.

Benoit threw himself to the ground as if sensing the threat screaming toward him from the dark jungle. The tracker went to follow suit but his reaction time was slower. Small trees javelined over the trail. A huge branch punched through the tracker's torso, snatched him from the ground and speared him through the air, his limbs flailing. He disappeared into the night.

Despite his fear, Shepherd was awed, realizing a massive tree had toppled beneath the weight of the wind's assault. As it dropped, the network of smaller trees connected by intertwined vines and lianas had been hurled through the rainforest as if from a slingshot.

Gradually, the torrent of jungle refuse thinned. The whirring drone died until all that was left was a cloud of leaves fluttering to the ground.

Shepherd scrambled to his feet. "Run!" He jerked the Winchester from his shoulder and flicked off the safety lock.

Benoit leaped to his feet, raising his gun. Shepherd didn't have the time to take the careful aim a headshot would require, given the murky light cast by Ben's flashlight. Instead, he went for a body shot, hoping it would throw off the man's aim and buy them some time to flee.

The magnum bullet struck dead center in the chest. Benoit staggered backward.

Shepherd grabbed Allie and shoved her off the trail, the others following. As he dove into the jungle, he saw the mercenary regain his balance and sprint toward them, the leg muscles of his nano-suit bulging and writhing like serpents. With his yellow eyes gleaming, he looked alien. Insect-like. Indomitable.

At that moment, he lost his last remnants of hope.

The rainforest closed around them. Sharp branches clawed at them, tangled lianas wrapped around their legs, slowing their progress. Shepherd and O'Connell took the lead, using their combined bulk to bulldoze a path for the others.

Behind them, Ben clutched the flashlight, using it to probe their way ahead, pointing out any gaps in the dense foliage that would allow them to forge away from their pursuer.

Benoit was close. Even above the maelstrom, Shepherd heard the sharp splitting of branches, the cracking as boughs were snapped. The nano-suit was allowing the powerfully-built mercenary to smash his way through the jungle. He was now only feet behind them and closing fast.

As Shepherd looked over his shoulder he saw the glow from the mercenary's flashlight through tiny gaps in the vegetation. The broken branches they left as they fought their way through the jungle acted as signposts for him to follow.

He realized they couldn't outrun him. He stepped aside and allowed the others to run past him. He raised the Winchester, waited until he saw a flash of light, then fired.

He heard more crashing and fired again. The Winchester had a four-round capacity. He'd fired three shots. There was no time to reload. Preserving his last bullet, he tore along behind the others.

As he ran, his mind raced through their options. The bio-mod was relentless. He had no weaknesses. Shepherd's mind was dulled with fear and a growing feeling of resignation. *Think!* Yet more than ever, he found himself feeling like a helpless father, rather than the trained soldier he'd once been.

He was a scientist. The man behind him was a mutant—an enhanced killing machine.

As panic threatened to overwhelm him, his desperate mind sifted through what he knew about the technology Benoit possessed. The only weakness he knew of was his exposed head. His last remaining bullet could suffice.

But visibility was poor and aiming the cumbersome rifle in the dense jungle would be difficult. He needed a clearing, somewhere to ambush him. But first, they would have to put some distance between them.

Ignoring the pain in his knee, he pushed past the

struggling Mancini, who was being helped along by Jan and Allie. He shouldered Ben aside and fell into step beside O'Connell. "We have to go faster!"

The man's large, round head swiveled toward him. His face was dripping with sweat and blood from numerous scratches. "Can't fucking go faster."

Shepherd peered ahead, but he couldn't see any sign of a clearing in the murky light.

His hopes of an ambush faded and his desperation grew. Glancing across, he saw the backpack still slung over O'Connell's shoulder. The cure. He felt a hollowness in his heart as he realized they couldn't let Benoit get his hands on it.

They had been so close to escaping. He had almost convinced himself they would get out of here, that Cassie would receive treatment with the cure. If only there was another way, that Benoit had another weakness to exploit. But all Shepherd had was the rifle. His only weapon.

Then he felt the weight of a hard titanium container against his thigh and realized that it wasn't.

He remembered Ben's words back at the bio lab, how they had scoffed at him. But perhaps the kid had been right after all. And with that realization, a tiny ray of hope flickered to life. The last remnants of the soldier within him discounted the idea; it was too risky. Suicide. But as a desperate father, he knew it was all he had.

He shouted to O'Connell, "Keep going! Find somewhere to hide." He pointed at the backpack. "Destroy it if Benoit finds you."

"What are you doing?" said Allie.

Shepherd shoved her toward O'Connell, who seized her by the arm and dragged her roughly along with him.

He lurched to a halt. He turned, aiming the Winchester as best he could with one arm. With his other hand, he hauled the slender metal canister from his pocket, opened it and withdrew the syringe containing the batrachotoxin Mancini had given him.

Remembering what its twin had done to the mercenary back in the scientists' laboratory, he carefully flicked the rubber stopper from its needle, closed his fist around it and waited.

Only seconds later he heard the smashing of branches, saw flashes of light that grew closer. Then Benoit burst through the vegetation, his black suit gleaming beneath patches of dirt.

Shepherd saw the fiery glow of his yellow eyes in the murky light cast by the mercenary's flashlight. Those eyes flickered in surprise as they took in his adversary.

He fired. Benoit ducked to one side. The magnum bullet smashed into his shoulder. The heavy bullet slowed his charge, but he was too close for Shepherd to reload.

Benoit smashed the weapon from his hand and directed the PAMAS G1 at his skull. Rather than run, Shepherd darted beneath the mercenary's raised arm, using Benoit's towering height to his own advantage.

Benoit reacted with lightning reflexes, swiveling to aim. Shepherd charged behind him. He leaped onto Benoit's back, wrapped his legs around his thick torso and one arm around his throat. The mercenary's flashlight fell to the ground, illuminating them in a yellow glow.

Benoit lowered his chin to protect his windpipe. Shepherd squeezed with all his strength. The mercenary wheeled about, clawing at him with one hand. He twisted his arm over his shoulder, swinging the pistol toward

Shepherd, who kicked it from his hand.

Benoit charged across the heavy ground, trying to flip him over his shoulder. He clung, horrified by the man's strength. It felt like he was riding a wildly bucking bull. His head whiplashed back and forth. His grip started slipping. He couldn't hold on for much longer.

He stabbed the syringe at the mercenary's exposed face, but Benoit must have seen the glimmer of the needle, deflected the strike and flung himself backward to the ground.

The impact drove the air from Shepherd's lungs. No longer able to reach the man's face, he placed the tip of the needle against his flank, feeling the hard protective shell of his nano-suit.

His instincts screamed at him to ram the needle through the nano-suit with all of his remaining strength. But he stayed his hand. As he was crushed into the thick mud by Benoit's weight, he put aside his soldier's instincts to fight and put his faith in his scientific training.

He pushed the needle slowly. Rather than use excessive force, he allowed the sharpness of the tip to do the work. Nothing happened. His despair soared. Then he felt the needle move. The tip penetrated the outer shell. But his strength was fading. His lungs were screaming for oxygen.

Benoit rolled powerfully. Shepherd fought to hold the needle in place. He was sucked free of the mud. He clung to the mercenary like a limpet, working at the needle. If he broke free of his grasp, he knew he would be torn apart.

Benoit slammed him back against the dirt. Shepherd absorbed the impact with his body and held the syringe in place. He felt his face go under.

The needle edged inwards. But it was too slow. He

felt light-headed and knew he was losing consciousness. Distantly, he heard Benoit's roar of triumph as he crushed Shepherd beneath him, drowning him in the mud.

Then he heard another shout. "Motherfucker!" The weight crushing him eased as Benoit was struck from the side. He rose from the mud, Shepherd clinging to him, the PAMAS G1 lying on the ground.

He saw the bulky form of O'Connell charge forward. Benoit smashed him aside with a swinging arm and he crumpled.

Another shape loomed. Jan. Benoit swung to face him. Jan seized his arm and hung on grimly as he was flung violently about.

Shepherd felt the needle penetrate deeper. Another millimeter.

Benoit shrugged Jan aside. Ignoring the clinging Shepherd as a dog would an irritating flee, he strode toward the pistol. He seized it and swung it toward Jan, who cowered.

Shepherd bucked his weight around, trying to throw the mercenary off-balance. Jan went to run but the gun leveled toward him.

Benoit jerked spasmodically. Shepherd lost his grip and fell to the ground. He looked up and saw the syringe embedded in the mercenary's flank. His yellow eyes glared and he convulsed. Frothy spittle spewed from his mouth.

Benoit gasped, his hands clutched his chest, then he collapsed to the ground. Violent muscle contractions shook his entire body. His limbs flailed and thudded into the dirt.

Slowly the convulsions lessened until only his legs were kicking against the ground. Then finally, the twitching of his giant body stopped. The mercenary lay still.

CHAPTER 53

ALLIE RUSHED FROM the darkness. "Shepherd!" She knelt over him. Ben hovered behind her.

With Allie's support, he staggered to his feet. He hobbled to the prostrate figure of Benoit and saw the strange yellow eyes staring sightlessly up into the darkness.

He shook with adrenalin, relief flooding through him. Then he saw O'Connell lying motionless in the mud. He was dead, his neck broken by Benoit's savage blow. His pale eyes gazed upward. In death, his blunt features had lost their fierce intensity and he looked almost peaceful.

Allie knelt beside him. "Oh, no."

Shepherd closed O'Connell's eyes, his heart heavy as he did so. The man had been a bully, but he had also been a fighter. He silently thanked him for attacking Benoit when he had, knowing it had saved his own life.

Then he retrieved the backpack lying on the ground, checked the contents, found the samples still intact and exhaled with relief.

Allie looked at Benoit's corpse and shuddered. "What happened? How did you kill him?"

Shepherd explained, "It was Ben who gave me the idea. He found the way. But I thought I was gone until O'Connell attacked. He gave me the time I needed to get the syringe into Benoit."

Allie's voice filled with sadness. "He was such a bastard, but he sacrificed himself to save the Alzheimer's cure. If we get out of here, I'll make sure it's named after him. He deserves that, at least."

"If we're going to get out of here, we'll have to hurry," said Ben.

Mancini tore his gaze away from the fallen mercenary and gazed around at the rainforest. "We're lost."

"Ben, can you get us back to the main trail?" said Allie.

He pointed at the broken branches and torn leaves and lianas left in Benoit's wake as he'd pursued them. "Looks like he left a big trail for us to follow. I'll get us back."

Shepherd flexed his knee and stifled a groan. The fight with Benoit had worsened it to the point where even the heavy strapping failed to support it. He tried putting his weight on it, but the joint almost immediately gave way.

Allie hurried to support him. "What are we going to do? You can't walk on that!"

"Then I'll drag myself to the damn river. My little girl needs me."

He tried another step, but with the same result. With a sinking heart, Shepherd knew she was right. For a moment he despaired, then his gaze settled on the black-clad Benoit. "I think I know something that will help."

Ten minutes later, he pulled the nano-suit up over his shoulders.

Rather than any form of zip, the suit had parted down the back, the polymer strands slowly yielding like sticky glue, as Shepherd wrenched it from the corpse. He reasoned that unlike the aerosols, the syringe had delivered all of its deadly load into Benoit's flesh. But he still scrubbed it inside and out with leaves and dirt and offered up a prayer as he pulled it on.

As Allie tugged at the back of the suit to bring it together, those strands re-raveled and the suit sealed itself to his body. He took a step, and felt the nano-muscles writhe and flex, conforming to the contours of his frame. It was like being massaged, but with an underlying sense of unfathomable power.

He took another step, bracing himself for his knee to give way. He felt a sharp pain in the joint but, as his leg wobbled, the nano-muscles flexed, stabilizing him.

A confidence swept through him that he hadn't felt since his days as a Ranger.

"How does it feel?" Allie asked. "Can you walk?"

Shepherd responded with a broad grin. "It's remarkable. I feel like a teenager again. My old team at WMRD are going to drool when they see this."

"We have to go," said Ben.

Shepherd retrieved Benoit's PAMAS G1, Herstal Minimi, SPECTRA helmet and accompanying IDU. He checked that both guns were loaded. He would rather have had his trusty Winchester, but the rifle would be a dead giveaway for what he intended. The pistol and machine gun would have to do.

He grabbed O'Connell's backpack containing the cure and slung it across his shoulder. "Get us to the river, Ben."

EPILOGUE

SHEPHERD HURRIED INTO his daughter's hospital room.

A phone call with his father as soon as he'd arrived in Manaus had prepared him but the sight of her propped up in bed with her forearm encased in a pink cast stopped him in his tracks.

She lay on her side staring out the window, but her tousled blond head whirled as he entered. "Daddy!"

In two long strides, Shepherd was at her side and she was wrapped in his arms.

He held her tightly, thankful all she had suffered was a broken forearm. It was a bad break and given her condition, the doctors had opted to keep her in hospital for monitoring.

But it could have been far worse.

"Daddy! You're smushing me. Careful of my arm."

"Sorry, munchkin." He eased his grip and studied her. With her blond curls and petite frame, she was the picture of her mom. Her only resemblance to her dad was her large gray eyes.

"Are you all right, munchkin?"

Her eyes shone. "I climbed all the way to the top of the tree!"

He tried to hide his smile. How she could climb the giant oak tree in her grandfather's yard with reduced control of her limbs was beyond him. She had been on her way down when she'd slipped.

His mom and dad had been waiting outside her room when Shepherd and Allie had arrived after a mad dash from JFK airport. His mom had immediately taken in his battered appearance and hobbling gait and fixed him with a stare he knew so well; he'd have questions to answer when she got him alone.

Her shrewd gaze had then swept over Allie, who had an arm wrapped around his waist to support him. She gave an approving nod before glaring at her husband. "Cassie and your father were playing hide and seek while I was marking exam papers." His mom was a teacher at a local school.

"I never thought she'd climb the damned tree," his father mumbled.

Shepherd had chuckled, guessing at the trouble his dad had been in and knowing it wasn't entirely his fault. Despite her condition slowing her reflexes, Cassie had been itching to take on the challenge of climbing her grandfather's towering oak tree. Shepherd and his mom hadn't allowed it. She must have bided her time for him to be away and his mom busy before seizing her opportunity.

She had her mom's determination. "Cass, I told you not to climb it."

"Yes daddy," she intoned. "I promise I won't do it again." Her eyes told another story.

He hugged her. Her head snuggled against his shoulder, then lifted as Allie walked into the room, clutching an enormous fluffy toy dog.

"Is that for me?" Cassie said breathlessly.

"It sure is, honey." Allie placed it in her arms.

His daughter disappeared into the soft fur with a delighted squeal.

Allie caressed his shoulder. 'She's gorgeous,' she mouthed.

He smiled. He took her hand in his, wondering if he looked as tired as she did. The freckles stood out on her face, her paleness accentuating the dark circles beneath her eyes.

Only hours earlier they had touched down in JFK airport

after a long flight from Manaus, which they had reached at the end of a treacherous trip along the Madre de Dios in the mercenaries' craft.

Stealing the launch had been straightforward. Armed with mercenary weaponry, wearing the nano-suit with the helmet visor down to mask his face, he looked like one of the mercenaries and had been able to approach close enough to eliminate the lone, unsuspecting sentinel on board with a single shot through the visor from the PAMAS G1. It was a cold-blooded killing that had sat heavy in the pit of his belly during the long journey to Manaus and subsequent flight to New York.

Before they had all separated, Jan had given him and Allie huge hugs then had gone home to his boyfriend, Erik.

Ben had ignored the private car sent by his father, jumping instead into a cab to take him to the family's Upper Eastside mansion, which he intended to move out of as soon as he was financially able. He no longer wanted to live off his father's money, he had declared to them all. It was time he became his own man. A full-time position at Atione would help, he'd added, with a hopeful smile at Allie.

Shepherd squeezed her hand gently, realizing they were being watched. Cassie peeked over the stuffed animal, studying her. "Are you a friend of daddy's?"

She nodded. "Yes, honey."

"Allie might come and visit us next week," Shepherd added. "Then we might all stay and Nonna and Poppa's holiday house at the Jersey Shore. Does that sound okay, munchkin?"

Cassie gave a wary nod, before throwing her arms around him. "I missed you."

"I missed you too, Cass."

Allie slipped away. Several minutes later Shepherd joined her outside Cassie's room. His parents retreated to a discreet distance.

"I have to go to Atione. Mancini and I will hand over all our research on the Alzheimer's cure. Then I need to get in touch with the families of Alderton, Klaus, Marlowe, Parker and O'Connell. So many died." Her eyes clouded with grief and she buried her face against his chest.

Shepherd wrapped his arms around her tightly. "I'm staying here with Cassie until she's discharged. Then I need to hand over the nano-suits to my contacts in WMRD. After that, I'm taking Cass to my parents' holiday home. Will you still join us?"

His heart pounded like an awkward teenager's. They had discussed this on the plane, but he wondered if she still felt the same now they were actually home.

She reached up and kissed him. "I'm taking a month's leave as soon as I've finished contacting the families of those we lost. I would love to spend it with you and Cassie."

He released her reluctantly. "Then we'll see you soon."

He watched her leave, knowing that "soon" couldn't come fast enough, then hurried back to his daughter.

* * *

A WEEK LATER, Shepherd was in Fort Detrick. "Early Christmas present for you." He gave the sealed package containing the two nano-suits to Samuel Alvarez, his former colleague from WMRD.

Sam grinned, turning the package over in his hands. The engineer's dark eyes gleamed as he studied it. "I've been waiting to get my hands on these ever since you called me. You were cagey on the phone, my friend, but now you're here, tell me everything about them."

His eyes narrowed into the look of concern Shepherd remembered from their time working together as he detailed what the suits were capable of, and the future soldier program run by Toussen.

Sam grimaced. "WMRD's been disbanded. The cost of maintaining it was thought to be too high. But don't worry, I still have friends in the White House who'll deal with those bastards at Toussen."

"Good." Shepherd was relieved his part in neutralizing this threat was complete.

"You heading straight home? I have some urgent phone calls to make now, given everything you've told me, but maybe later we could catch up on old times?"

Shepherd shook his head. Cassie was with his parents at their holiday home on the Jersey Shore. He and Allie would be joining them as soon as he returned home. He was anxious to get there and for Cassie to get to know the new woman in his life.

But he had one more thing to do first. "Can't. Been summoned by Brandt."

"Brandt? Jesus. You know we call her the Golden Assassin?" He took in Shepherd's raised eyebrows. "For the brutal way she's sliced through bureaucratic red tape since she arrived here and… well, you'll see. Good luck."

An hour later, Shepherd sat facing Dr. Olivia Brandt across a desk. Honey-blond hair cascaded to her shoulders framing the most piercing blue eyes he had ever seen. They radiated authority, combining with intense intelligence to reinforce the impression that this was a person to be reckoned with.

And Shepherd knew she undoubtedly was, as the new head of the U.S. Army Research Laboratories.

Her office reeked of power. A picture of the president hung behind her desk, accompanied by the American flag. The brown walls were adorned by photos of Brandt shaking hands with various military dignitaries, of being awarded the Bronze Star Medal which itself was framed on the wall.

His gaze fell from her piercing eyes to her neatly organized desk, where he saw his personnel file from his time at WMRD. He braced himself for a barrage of questions about the events at the Inn.

Instead, the fierceness of her gaze softened slightly. "How is your daughter, Lieutenant Shepherd?"

He was thrown by the personal nature of the question. "I'm no longer a lieutenant. Call me Shepherd. Cassie is fine. She had a fall and broke her forearm, but is back home from hospital."

"There was no regression with her Heller's disease?"

He frowned, wondering how she knew about Cassie's condition. How far did her reach extend? "No. Her condition remains stable."

"But there is hope with the Alzheimer's cure that your girlfriend, Dr. Temple, is leading the research on at Atione?"

His frown deepened. How did she know about his and Allie's burgeoning relationship? "Yes. The initial test results are encouraging. Dr. Temple will try to get Cassie included on the human trial when it gets to that phase."

"How are the other survivors? Ben Burg, Jan Hlasek, David Mancini?"

"Dr. Temple has included all of them on her team."

"And your knee?" Her gaze shifted to the crutches resting against his chair.

"I have reconstructive surgery scheduled for next week."

"Excellent. Now." Her perfectly manicured fingers

opened his personnel file. "I read through your file, Lieutenant."

"Shepherd." Irritation crept into his voice.

"It's impressive."

He shifted impatiently. He wanted to be home with Cassie and Allie. "Dr. Brandt, I thought I was brought here to brief you about the Toussen future soldier program. If so, let's get on with it, please."

Though her voice remained low, her predatory gaze intensified. "I didn't bring you back here for a briefing, Lieutenant. I brought you back to put you in charge of your old team, which is being reactivated."

He stood. "Then this is a waste of time."

Her tone hardened. "Sit down. Hear me out, please."

He remained standing. "I'm listening."

"Your news on the future soldier program and the nano-suits have caused quite a stir, Lieutenant. The JASONs are preparing a paper on the implications of this new technology, and the future threat we face, given the new world they envisaged is now upon us.

"The Senate Intelligence Committee is demanding to know how we at ARL dropped the ball. As a result, a new team is being assembled to respond to these threats—a team armed with both the technical knowledge and the military muscle to anticipate and understand the threat, then eliminate it.

"It goes without saying that any knowledge as to the existence of the team, to be codenamed Trident, will be denied. This will be a highly specialized team, and you are one of only a few with the unique combination of science and military training required to lead it."

She gave him a smile, one made wolfish by small, pointed

canine teeth. "I too am one of the few. But my role will be to protect your existence, to manage the relationship back to the Intelligence Committee and the White House, and to deal with the inevitable pressures that will be brought to bear. Results will be expected. The JASONs, with all their influence, will be watching. Which is why I want you to lead the team."

"Then I'm sorry, but I'm not leaving my daughter again." With the help of his crutches, he turned and hobbled toward the door.

Over his shoulder, he heard her voice. No longer soft, it scythed like a sword through the tension now filling her office. "I have made it a lifetime's habit of getting what I want, Lieutenant Shepherd, by whatever means necessary. Take time out to be with your family. Recuperate from your surgery. Then we will talk again."

CPSIA information can be obtained
at www.ICGtesting.com
Printed in the USA
LVHW081119051122
732438LV00016B/919

9 781925 764789